Emperor Mollusk VERSUS the SINISTER BRAIN

By A. Lee Martinez

Gil's All Fright Diner
In the Company of Ogres
A Nameless Witch
The Automatic Detective
Too Many Curses
Monster
Divine Misfortune
Chasing the Moon
Emperor Mollusk Versus the Sinister Brain

Emperor Mollusk VERSUS the SINISTER BRAIN

A. LEE MARTINEZ

www.orbitbooks.net

Orbit
Hachette Book Group
237 Park Avenue, New York, NY 10017
www.HachetteBookGroup.com

First Edition: March 2012

Orbit is an imprint of Hachette Book Group, Inc. The Orbit name and logo are trademarks of Little, Brown Book Group Limited.

Library of Congress Cataloging-in-Publication Data
Martinez, A. Lee.
Emperor mollusk versus the sinister brain / A. Lee Martinez. — 1st ed.
p. cm.
ISBN 978-0-316-09352-1
I. Title.
PS3613.A78638E47 2012
813'.6—dc23 2011033214

10 9 8 7 6 5 4 3 2 1

RRD-C

Printed in the United States of America

To all the usual folks: Mom, Sally, Nik, Russell, the DFWWW, my agent, my editor, Orbit Books, the people who buy the books, Optimus Prime, and the rest. You're still just as important as you ever were and this is a lot easier because of you.

To Atomic Robo, for keeping my love of comic books alive and well.

And to Victor Von Doom.

Emperor Mollusk VERSUS the SINISTER BRAIN

There's no sound in space, but my saucer cannons simulated a shriek with every blast. A swoosh followed every barrel roll. And when my autogunner scored a hit, a sophisticated program supplied the appropriate level of response, ranging from a simple ping to a full-fledged explosion. I could have programmed it to provide an explosion every time, but that would've cheapened the experience.

The atmosphere burst with color as the cannons belched their staccato rhythm. My ship blasted the enemy fighters to scrap, but an impressive fleet stood between my target and me. The shields were holding, but I had only a few moments before I was disabled.

I'd gone over my exo options before mission. Neptunons might have been the smartest race in the galaxy, but outside of our exoskeletons, we couldn't do much more than flop around. We could drag ourselves across the floor, a means of mobility both embarrassing and ineffective. Our brains had grown too fast, and we just hadn't possessed the patience to wait around for nature to bestow what we could give ourselves. Over the centuries, we'd only grown smarter and squishier.

The obvious choice for an exo on this mission would've been a big, burly combative model. But I'd opted for stealth, taking a modified Ninja-3 prototype. It stood barely five feet tall and space limitations meant it didn't pack much weaponry. But I wasn't planning on fighting every soldier on the station. It sounded like a laugh, but time was a factor. Terra was a little over six minutes from total subjugation.

I slipped into my exo, loaded myself into the launch tube, and prepared to fire.

"It was a pleasure serving with you, sir," said the craft's computer.

"Likewise."

I ejected, rocketing through space in a jet-black torpedo that was practically invisible in the darkness of space. A stray plasma blast could've gotten lucky and struck the torpedo. If it didn't destroy me outright, it would knock the torpedo off course, either sending me spinning into the void of space or plummeting to Terra. But I'd done the math and decided to take my chances.

The torpedo breached the station's hull. I kicked open the torpedo's door and exited. There were no guards. Only a couple of technicians gasping for air. The artificial gravity held them in place, but the decompression had taken all the oxygen.

A security team stormed the room. I vaulted over their heads before they got off a shot. A few punches from my exo's four arms knocked them all senseless before they could even realize I was behind them. The Ninja-3 had several built-in blades, but I tried not to kill people just for annoying me.

I took a second to grab the emergency oxygen masks off the wall and toss them to the technicians.

Then I was on my way. My exo's camouflage feature allowed me to avoid guards. I slipped through the security net without much trouble, though it took a few minutes. By the time I reached the device, I was running short on time.

The immense orb hovered in a containment field. Hundreds of lights, purely ornamental, blinked across its surface. Its ultrasonic hum filled the chamber. Only a Neptunon could hear the sound without having their brain melt.

I blasted the device. It shattered into a thousand little pieces. There was nothing inside. Just a ceramic mock-up of a doomsday weapon.

A door opened, and a Neptunon in a hulking exoskeleton marched into the chamber. He banged his hands together. Their metallic clapping echoed.

"You didn't think it would be that easy, did you?" he asked.

All Neptunons look alike. We even have trouble telling each other apart. It wasn't surprising that this one looked like me, but the resemblance went deeper.

The clone had been a mistake. I don't often make mistakes, but I own up to them when they happen.

"A decoy," I said.

Emperor Mollusk, Mark Two, laughed maniacally. Had I really sounded like that? The clone carried a set of memories minus a few years of experience and the personality to match. Looking at yourself, at who you used to be, wasn't pretty.

"You should see the look on your face," he said. "How does it feel to be outwitted?"

"Someone was going to do it eventually," I replied. "At least I can take some small comfort that I outmaneuvered myself."

"Yes, if anyone could do it..." He raised an eye ridge in a pompous, self-satisfied manner. We don't have eyebrows.

"The fleet, the personnel, the space station," I said. "This must have cost you a small fortune."

"Ah, but it was necessary, wasn't it? I knew that only one being in this system had the knowledge and ability to pose any significant risk to my plan. I couldn't hide an operation like this without something to distract you. So I devised a small game for your amusement. Little clues leading to a fun diversion then a full-blown operation that was every bit as involved and complex as the real thing. But at the heart of it... nothing."

I said, "Meanwhile, you build your weapon somewhere else, somewhere unimportant, somewhere unnoticed. It was exactly what I would've done."

"And now nothing can stop me. In three minutes, Terra shall be mine."

"You don't want it."

He chuckled, but one look at my face told him I was serious. Neptunons might not have the most expressive features, but we get by.

"Having billions of dominated souls chant your name in unison can be great for the self-esteem. Although, really, self-esteem was never our problem, was it?" I asked.

Mark Two studied me skeptically. He suspected a trap, trying to figure out my angle. There was no angle. Just a lesson learned.

"Once you're crowned Warlord of Terra, you'll see that it's a lot more responsibility than I... we... planned."

He scanned for any sign of deception. I had never been a very good liar. Strange, considering my hobby as a world conqueror, but it was a conscious choice. Being a skilled liar might have made the job easier, but telling the truth, with the occasional lie by omission, increased the difficulty level.

"Let me tell you how everything will go if you succeed," I said. "You'll become ruler of this world. You'll hold it in your hands like a beautiful blue pearl. That'll be enough at first. Just to have it.

"But then you'll start tinkering. Oh, you'll have the best of intentions. You'll fix those little pestering problems the Terrans themselves never could. Hunger. War. Poverty. Those will be easy, a long weekend.

"After that, you'll struggle against the relentless urges that drive you. You'll realize, intellectually, that there's little left to do. But you won't be able to help yourself. Terra will become your own personal science project until your inevitable nature nearly destroys the world. Several times.

"Now, providing you manage to prevent this, you'll learn some restraint. But it'll always be there. That insistent desire, that nagging need. You'll never be able to suppress it. Not completely. And you'll find yourself wondering if tomorrow is the day you destroy it, most probably by accident."

Mark Two said, "I'll learn from your mistakes."

"Or you'll just make slightly different variations of the same ones. Regardless, the Terrans have been through enough under one warlord. They don't need another."

A klaxon blared, signaling the final countdown. I pushed a

button on my exo, and the station blast shields lowered. Mark Two frowned, realizing that I'd hacked his systems.

Mark Two shook off his confusion and resumed his laughter. "I don't know what happened to you in the time since you were me, but it doesn't matter. Terra will be mine, and there's not a thing you can—"

"I already stopped it. You didn't think you could hide your operation in Minneapolis from me, did you?"

He smiled. "No, that was merely another decoy."

"Of course, it was," I replied. "As were your machinations in Lisbon, St. Petersburg, and Busan."

His smile dropped.

"I'll admit you almost had me with Melbourne," I said. "But the decoy in Geneva was sloppy work, if I may be so bold as to offer some criticism."

He wasn't angered. He was curious. He was me, after all. And I was rarely frustrated by my failures. I preferred using them as learning opportunities.

I pressed another button. I kept the gravity and lights on for convenience, but everything else in the station went dead. The countdown ended. The doomsday device, the *real* device hidden aboard this station, wound down.

Mark Two glared. "How did you—"

"I'm you, remember. Just you with a few more years' experience. Everything you've done, I've already thought of. Every contingency plan, every possibility, I already did five years ago before you were even hatched from your tank."

He hid his incredulity behind a scowl, but I sensed it. If the situation were reversed, I'd have been the same. I hadn't been one hundred percent certain that I would foil his plans.

But I was a humbler guy now than I was when I had been him.

His mottled flesh darkened with rage. I could see where he was coming from. I'd failed before, but I'd never been outwitted. But I'd never had to face off against myself. Now it'd all gone freshwater for Mark Two, as the old Neptunon saying went.

His hulking exoskeleton lumbered forward. "You may have stopped me this time, but you won't be around to stop me the next."

He threw a clumsy punch that would've pulverized the Ninja-3 if I hadn't sidestepped the blow. He followed that with a haymaker that I danced under. I glided behind him and used a microfilament blade to slice open the hydraulics behind the exo's right knee. It wobbled but didn't fall.

He hadn't even bothered to change the specs. Perhaps he wasn't a perfect clone after all.

Mark Two teetered on his damaged leg as he struggled to line me up in his sights, but it was a simple thing for me to scamper up his back. I stabbed a few vital systems along the way. The last thing I hit was the stabilizer. His powerful exo tumbled over, ten tons of scrap metal.

A hatch opened, and he ejected in a smaller exo. The clear, fluid-filled dome that held his head bubbled with his frustration. I'd never lost my temper like that, but then again, I'd never been foiled so effortlessly. Or maybe the cloning process had simply been incapable of re-creating every bit of my pragmatic genius. He must've known his backup was no match for my Ninja, but in his anger, he didn't care. I dodged the blasts he sent my way and dismantled his exo with three efficient cuts. It clattered to the floor in pieces.

He flopped around, glaring daggers. Neptunons could survive out of water for extended periods, but it wasn't comfortable.

"You can't stop me," he gurgled. "I'll be back."

"No, you won't."

I activated the station's self-destruct countdown. Just a little something I'd slipped into his blueprints when he wasn't looking.

"So that's it?" he asked. "You're just going to leave me here to die?"

"I'm afraid so. No hard feelings."

Mark Two undulated in a shrug. "No, I suppose not. I'd do the same to you if the situation were reversed."

"I guess I haven't changed so much after all," I replied.

We shared a laugh.

"Just tell me something. It would've worked, right?"

"It would have worked," I said.

He grinned. "That's something at least."

"Yeah, it's something."

I made my escape without incident, boarding my automated rendezvous craft, and watched the station explode from a safe distance.

It was quite beautiful.

Then I pondered the small world below, oblivious to its own fragility.

I no longer held my official title of Warlord, but the Terra Sapiens, the most plentiful inhabitants of the planet, still worshipped me as a de facto god. Though they no longer made a big show of it.

In the first few years of my reign, I'd managed to solve a few of their problems.

I'd ended their wars by introducing aggression suppressants to the water supply. It didn't make them any less disagreeable, but it kept them from rioting over the outcome of sporting events and shooting each other over imaginary lines drawn on maps.

I'd solved their energy crisis with the discovery of the molluskotrenic energy field. Its boundless energy production now supplied endless amounts of power to the people of Terra. More power, every day. I hadn't figured a safe way to switch it off yet, and the vast abundance of the energy was beamed harmlessly into space. There was still too much, and if the engine I'd built to harness it ever suffered catastrophic failure it might very well destroy the engine. Or possibly blow a hole the size of Pluto in this world.

I had a contingency plan should that happen, an alarm that would alert me when it was time to leave the planet. In the meantime, I did my part. I kept every light in the house on and never turned off the TV.

I'd repelled the invasion of the Saturnites. Without me, the Terrans would've been digging their planet hollow for their Saturnite masters. The mole people of the Undersphere Empire would've fought back, and the whole thing could've been a disaster with the Terra Sapiens caught in between.

I'd sent the Saturnites scurrying off to their homeworld in such a hurry they hadn't stopped to pick up all their soldiers, and a few thousand warriors were left on the planet. Fighting was all Saturnites knew, and you'd think rock-skinned warriors on a planet of mammals would have an easy time of it. But those aggression suppressants had been top-notch. Terrans didn't fight wars anymore, and Saturnite soldiers were under standing orders to not cause any trouble.

Some had become police officers. Others were bodyguards. Some had taken to petty crime and leg breaking. But most of them, not truly being hostile and finding themselves stranded on an alien world, had taken up manual labor.

The Saturnite bagboy crushed my eggs.

"Oops."

The cashier rolled her eyes. This probably happened quite often. "Cragg, what did Mr. Mooney tell you about being careful?"

Cragg frowned. "It was an accident."

"I'm so sorry, Lord Mollusk," said the cashier. Try as I might, I couldn't break them from calling me *Lord.* "We'll get you new eggs."

"It's not necessary," I replied.

"Oh, but we insist."

"Really, it's fine. After I put them through the nutrient extractor, it won't matter."

The extractor, necessary for me to digest Terran foodstuffs, turned everything into a colorful paste. I usually dumped all my groceries into the extractor as soon as I got home and shoved the paste into the cupboard. But the cashier insisted. I was a hero of Terra, and the inhabitants liked me. They didn't have any other choice.

All the other employees were busy at the moment, and rather than send clumsy Cragg after the eggs, the cashier decided to fetch them herself. This left me alone with him. He glared with murderous resentment but didn't say a word.

The cashier returned with my eggs. She put them in a bag herself, loaded the bag carefully into my cart, and smiled. "Thank you, Lord Mollusk. Come again."

Cragg trailed behind me, pushing the shopping cart through the parking lot to my saucer. It was a compact model, but it still took up two spaces. I helped him throw the groceries into the storage compartment. He squeezed the bags a little too tight. I heard glass breaking and my bread was no doubt mutilated.

When I handed him a couple of bucks for his trouble, he growled, "You think you're better than me?"

My first instinct was to say yes, I did, but I couldn't kick a Saturnite when he was down.

"Hero." He spat a few pebbles onto the concrete.

I could understand his frustration. We were both conquerors. The biggest difference between us was that I'd succeeded while he had failed. But history is written by the winners. Especially winners with access to global mind-control devices.

"If you don't want the money—"

He snatched away the cash, glowered at it. My picture looking up at him from the bills probably didn't help heal the wounds.

"Have a nice day," I said.

"Screw you." He stomped away.

I climbed into my saucer and rocketed over the city. I didn't get very far before a Venusian scout craft appeared like a cigar-shaped bird of prey. Its shadow fell over my ship.

An all-too-familiar gray-scaled Venusian commander appeared in my monitor.

"Hello, Zala," I said.

She snarled. If I'd been the sensitive type, I might have wondered why so few people smiled when talking to me.

"Emperor Mollusk, you are hereby ordered to land immediately."

"Do we really have to do this now?" I asked. "I have a... thing... I have to get to."

"Your... thing... will have to wait." She leaned in close to the screen. "Don't make me shoot you down."

A cursory scan of the Venusian craft informed me that I could disable it with the push of a few buttons, but I was bored enough to see what Zala wanted from me. As if I didn't know already.

The Venusians had had it in for me since I'd tried to conquer their planet after falling short on Neptune. I hadn't really come close to subjugating Venus. Only claimed a couple of continents for a few weeks. No good reason they shouldn't have been over that by now.

But there was that time I'd fed their Beloved and Immortal Queen to sand scrakts. After that, I was guaranteed a place among their most wanted. I still felt bad about it. I hadn't even done it on purpose, but so far, a sincere "Whoops, sorry about that" hadn't done much to ease the tension.

I found a street big enough for both my saucer and the scout craft. The Venusians crushed a Toyota with their landing gear. The Terrans might've panicked at the sight, but my appearance meant everything was under control so they just carried on with their business. A cop started redirecting traffic.

"Thank you, Officer."

The officer smiled. "My pleasure, Lord Mollusk."

A Venusian battleguard squad descended from their ship. Battleguards clank. It was all the armor.

This was just my everyday, walkin' around exo, but it had some upgrades. A steel-blue paint job with metallic detailing. A few feet taller to allow me to see the world from a Terran's point of view. It wasn't as combat ready as the Ninja-3, but it had a few extra gadgets to give even a fearless Venusian battleguard pause.

Venusians were a reptilian species. They came in many colors. They sported tufts of feathers along their spines, and biochemical flashes glinted in their eyes. The effect could range from sparkles to burning glares. They were also the only sentient species in the system that still had tails.

Zala, the tall, lanky commander, stood at the front of the battleguard. Her scales were a bluish shade of gray. The few feathers visible on the back of her neck were red with flecks of orange and purple. Her eyes barely glowed. Normally, they'd glitter with righteous rage at the mere sight of me.

She pointed her scimitar at me. The sharp edge could slice through titanium provided she got a good swing behind it. "Fugitive Mollusk, I have been ordered to place you under protective custody. Please come with me immediately for your own safety."

This was surprising. I liked being surprised. It happened so rarely.

"Can you repeat that?" I asked.

Zala sighed. She was having trouble with the words, so foreign to her.

"Don't make me say it again."

I grinned. "Oh, one more time. Just to be sure I heard you correctly."

"Protective custody," she replied softly. "For your own safety."

"My own what?"

She snarled. I smiled.

"Correct me if I'm wrong," I said, "but aren't you more interested in, and I believe this is your most commonly used phrase, *bringing me to justice*?"

"You aren't going to make this easy on me, are you?"

"Why should I?"

Zala sheathed her scimitar.

"You will be called to count for your crimes, Mollusk. But it has come to our attention that your life is in great danger, and

I have sworn to see you placed on trial before the High Court. And the only thing that could prevent my keeping that sacred oath is my death. Or your own. And I cannot allow that."

"I'm flattered you still care," I said. "Even after all these years."

Her eyes sparkled. "Venus never forgets."

"I have an amnesia ray you could borrow if it will put this nonsense behind us. Not that I mind these impromptu visits. They do brighten my day."

"I will not be mocked, Mollusk."

"Who's mocking?" I replied. "I was beginning to feel neglected. Of all my enemies, you've always been my favorite. I enjoy your indefatigable passion. Most everyone else would be discouraged after the string of failures you've experienced. But not you. You always come back, ready for a fresh lesson in futility. It's inspiring in a way."

She scowled. One day, I'd push her too far, but it was just another experiment I couldn't resist. A study on the limits of the Venusian honor, so perfectly embodied in Zala, the most perfect of their perfect warriors. I comforted myself that my death would most likely be efficient and painless when I found that limit.

But today was not that day.

Zala said, "Whether you like it or not, you are under my protection now. Are you going to cooperate? Or will I be required to incapacitate you?"

"If you could incapacitate me, I'd be sitting in a Venusian prison right now."

She sneered.

"Thanks for your concern," I said, "but I don't really need your protection."

"You don't understand, Mollusk. People want you dead."

"I heard you the first time. Should I be surprised? I've made a few enemies. Now, if you'll excuse me..."

Zala gestured, and her battleguard stepped forward.

"Seize him!"

I held up my hand, and the guards hesitated.

"I don't know if Zala gave you the story of the last battle-guard that attempted any reckless seizing, but you might want to reconsider this."

She glared. "He's bluffing. We will drag him to Venus, to a hero's welcome."

"I wasn't aware you gave scorched skeletons parades on Venus."

"If he had anything dangerous, he'd have already used it."

"I resent that. I'm trying to not vaporize people just for being annoying."

"If you're really interested in penance," said Zala, "then you should have no problem surrendering yourself to us."

"I never said anything about penance. I just said I'm keeping my vaporization tally down."

"Have you no conscience?" she demanded. "Do you feel no remorse for your crimes?"

"Define *remorse*."

She snarled. Her left eye flashed. I'd said the wrong thing. I did that sometimes. I blamed it on my upbringing. For all our technological and scientific achievements, Neptune education didn't cover conversational skills. Especially with the less advanced species that shared our system.

"Seize him or may the Eleventh God strike you down as the cowards you are!"

That got them moving. Venusians took their gods very seriously. Probably because, unlike so many other divinities, they intervened quite visibly in mortal affairs, and nothing set them off more than a show of cowardice. Given a choice between vaporization and explosive decapitation (the Eleventh God's smite of choice), they did what they had to do.

They drew their rifles. They had to put down their swords and shields first. The primitive weapons clattered to the pavement. They attempted to blast me, but their weapons clicked and spit puffs of smoke from the barrels as they pulled the triggers.

"Focus pulse," I said. "It disables sophisticated electronics by draining their power source. Effective, though its range is limited to a few hundred feet. And it's easy to counter with some basic shielding. You really should consider updating your weapons technology."

"We'll cut you out of that tin suit if need be," said Zala.

Her guard drew their scimitars and charged at me. The skill of the dreaded Venusian swordmasters was the stuff of legend. Deservedly so. When facing off against their grandmaster, I'd only survived by developing an exo with six swords, and even then, I'd had to cheat to win. Although it was only cheating if you lost.

The Venusians had disagreed, but I'd won, so it was irrelevant what they thought.

Before they could bring their blades to bear, my saucer unleashed a magnetic field neutralizer. The armored battleguard rocketed up in the air, up and away until they were tiny dots floating above our heads.

I excluded Zala from the effect.

"You're a coward," she said.

My brain didn't burst out of my skull. You might think that my colorful history with Venus would've angered its gods. They were a brutal, unforgiving lot, but they limited their wrath to Venusians. I'd had dinner with six of the eleven divinities once, and if you could get past the ritual blood drinking, they were a fairly likable and jovial group.

"Mollusk, if you willingly board my ship, I swear to you, by the Unspoken Name of the Forgotten Thirteenth God of Most Hallowed Venus, that no harm shall come to you and that I will not take you anywhere against your will."

She lowered her blade and pointed it at my feet. She bowed. It wasn't much of a bow, barely a nod of her head. But it was a gesture that spoke volumes of her commitment. It must've wounded her warrior's pride terribly, though the only trace of reluctance was in a slight paling along her neck and a wilt in her feathers.

Venusians didn't make vows to their gods casually, and the Thirteenth God was reserved only for the most unbreakable of oaths.

"Okay, you've got my attention."

I lowered her battleguard slowly to the pavement. A residual magnetic charge caused them to stick together.

"Talk to me. But in my saucer. Your minions can catch up."

Zala boarded my saucer, and we took off. I trusted the battleguard would know where to find us once the charge wore off.

"So what's the problem?" I asked.

"Haven't you heard a word I've said? There are assassins coming to get you."

"And haven't you heard? Assassins are a fairly common occurrence in my life. You'll have to give me more than that."

"Even the Celebrants of Oblivion?"

"Hmmm. That is serious."

She studied my face. When we chose, Neptunons could do inscrutable better than anyone with the possible exception of the Sol Collective. But, outside of clouds of sentient helium, we were the top of the list.

"You don't believe me?" she asked.

"No, but I'm intrigued. If you don't mind me asking, just how did you find out about this assassination order?"

"Venusian intelligence is the most efficient in the system."

"And how did they find out?" I asked.

"That information is issued on a need-to-know basis."

"They didn't tell you, did they?"

"I don't need to know the details. I have my orders."

"So they could be making it all up," I replied, "for all either of us knows."

Zala said, "For what purpose?"

"I don't know. Just considering all the possibilities."

"I am a decorated veteran of the Imperial Protectorate. They wouldn't dispatch me unless the situation was of the highest priority."

"Uh-hmm."

"What is that supposed to mean?"

"Oh, nothing."

Zala had been third in command of the Protectorate not so long ago. Then I'd conquered half of Venus on her watch, and she'd been demoted to a field agent in the aftermath. To be sure, she was a high-ranking agent, but a demotion was still a demotion. And, whether she ever admitted it or not, part of her obsession with capturing me was to redeem an otherwise spotless career. As a symbol, Zala was useful to her queen, but perhaps they no longer trusted her with anything important.

We landed on the roof of my townhouse and took the lift down to my loft. The lights snapped on, and she scanned the post-modern furniture that came with the place. I had a few pieces of art. Some Neptunon seascapes to remind me of home. The original *Mona Lisa* that Leonardo da Vinci had hidden away for fear that Terra would never be ready for the secrets of faster-than-light travel encoded in its brush strokes. The miniaturized Tower of Pisa, which refused to stand straight even at only eight inches tall. The skull of the Loch Ness Monster, unfortunate victim of a Scottish chupacabra outbreak. Edison's spirit radio; it didn't contact ghosts but the one-dimensional entities of another plane, though the entities liked to screw around and he could be forgiven the mistake.

"Souvenirs," I said.

Zala studied a huge painting, dominating a wall. I was the subject, standing in my most regal exo, looking majestic with an atom clutched in one hand and Terra in the other.

"I didn't ask them to paint that," I said. "They did it on their own."

Zala shook her head, took in the rest of the room.

"You live here?"

"Whenever I'm on the continent. I have a few dozen other homes scattered across the globe. But this is my primary home."

"I thought it would be..."

"...wetter?"

"Well, yes."

I could've explained to her that once Neptunons matured, we spent most our time plugged into exos. While it might be nice to get out and stretch every twelve hours, it also made us feel a bit vulnerable. Given that we were little more than highly developed brains in spongy bodies, we didn't like exposing ourselves to the capricious whims of a dangerous universe with only cartilage and a camouflage reflex to protect us.

We didn't talk about it, but there was a definite inferiority complex running through Neptunon society. It was why we didn't mingle with the rest of the system and why the homeworld was locked away behind an impenetrable force field. It was that unspoken paranoia that ran through the heart of every Neptunon, leading us to develop the greatest technology. The irony was that, aside from our wonders of science, there was nothing particularly valuable on the homeworld. Nothing worth invading over.

But those wonders of science...they were a hell of a prize.

This wasn't lost on my people, who continued, without any sense of irony, to advance science in fantastic and inconceivable ways to deter our envious neighbors while only making ourselves a more desirable target, fueling our science-tastic furor to remind everyone that we were the smartest beings around, even as it fueled our paranoia.

I kept this to myself. I might not have much love for Neptune, but I was as loyal as the next exiled supervillian so I saw no reason to share it with a Venusian agent.

"I keep a tank in the bedroom," I said.

"Don't you have a security system?" asked Zala.

Two dozen legs skittered quietly behind her. Her finely honed reflexes kicked in, and she spun around with her gun already in her hand. The giant centipede hissed and clicked its mandibles. She blasted it, point-blank, but it only scorched the creature's armor. It lunged and, with one snip of its scissor-like jaws, clipped the weapon in half. The centipede knocked her to the floor and used its immense bulk to pin her there. Like any good Venusian warrior, Zala planned on going down fighting, and she wrestled and punched at the monster.

I emitted an ultrasonic signal. The beast climbed off her and scampered to my side.

"Good girl, Snarg." I patted her between the antennae, and she squeaked.

Zala stood. "By the hidden moon, what is that?"

"My pet ultrapede."

"I wouldn't expect you to have a pet."

"Snarg was a gift of the ambassador of the Undersphere. She's the fiercest ultrapede ever bred for the royal family. How could I turn down a gift like that?"

Snarg narrowed her seven milky white eyes as I scratched her palps.

"She was already formidable. I just modified her a bit, added a few beneficial mutations and cybernetic upgrades, and voilà, the perfect security system."

"I would expect something more high tech from you."

"Yes, you would. And that's why I don't have anything like that. Security networks can be hacked. Technology can be circumvented. Snarg is more reliable and surprising. She's also sweet as can be."

The ultrapede crawled away and curled up on the couch.

"You shouldn't let it on the furniture," said Zala.

"Who could say no to that face?"

Snarg shrieked contentedly.

"I would still think you'd have a more elaborate system." She picked up the two pieces of her broken gun.

"Don't really need it. The Terrans love me."

"But you must have experimental technology here that could be dangerous in the wrong hands."

"Oh, I have a few things lying around, but nothing that could do much damage anymore. I have a secure storage facility elsewhere where I keep the more amusing research. But I haven't been there in years."

I could tell she doubted me.

"I'm not conquering anymore," I said. "I keep telling you. I gave that up."

"You can't change who you are, Mollusk. You see the universe as your own personal plaything, other lives as tools to your own twisted ambitions."

"I see the universe as a grand mystery," I replied.

"One that you can exploit as you see fit," she said.

"I prefer to think of it as experimentation for the greater good."

She spit out a harsh laugh. "Define *the greater good*, Mollusk."

"I can't. That's one of the mysteries I'm working on."

I projected an equation on a viewscreen on the wall.

"I thought I had a passable proof for a few hours. Then I found I dropped a seven, and the results became meaningless. But I'm optimistic enough in my own brilliance to think I can still crack the problem."

"You can't honestly view morality as an experimental process."

"Why should it be any different than anything else? At least I'm honest enough to admit that I haven't found the answer yet instead of arbitrarily declaring X is dishonorable while Y is not."

She studied the lines of numbers and symbols. "Tell me, Emperor. Where do all your crimes fit in this?"

I highlighted a portion. "It's this variable right here."

"I would expect it to be bigger," she said with a smirk.

"I did too. But then it turned out that I was overestimating the value by several powers."

She read the frown on my face.

"And that displeases you?" she asked.

"Considering the effect I've had on the system, the fact that it's such a minor factor only proves I'm missing something vital. Or maybe not. Perhaps the equation is right, and I'm just too dissatisfied with the answer to admit it."

I dumped the groceries, bags and all, into the extractor. It hummed to life.

"Well...?" asked Zala.

"What?"

"What's the answer your equation has given you?"

"I thought you said morality couldn't be proven through experimentation."

"It can't," she said. "Whatever answer you reach will surely be a reflection of your own twisted perceptions."

"Hoping for a glimpse into the inner workings of my mind?" I said. "I'm surprised you care."

"Indulge me, Mollusk. Indulge yourself. If there's one thing

I know about you, it's that you do enjoy any chance to showcase your much-commented-upon intellect."

"It is very satisfying," I admitted.

"You want to tell me." She leaned against the counter with a condescending smile. "Don't act as if you showed me that equation by accident."

Most of the time, Zala was easily manipulated and stubbornly predictable. But she also had her flashes of insight. Those two qualities put her on the short list of enemies I counted myself lucky to have made.

"Meaningless," I said. "That's the answer."

"Yes, but what do you think it means?"

"You don't understand," I replied. "Meaninglessness is its meaning. It doesn't matter how I manipulate the numbers. Whether I multiply compassion or square cruelty, even if I allow myself to remove the specter of fallibility and double the predestination quotient, even assuming that intelligent life is not just inevitable but an end goal for the universe itself, it always adds up the same."

I pushed a button and faded the equation from the screen.

"It's a zero-sum game. None of it matters."

Zala said, "It's a convenient form of nihilism, Emperor. One that lets you avoid any guilt for your crimes."

"Being convenient doesn't make it wrong," I said. "And even if the numbers proved otherwise, I'm not interested in atonement. Not as you might define it."

"Still trying to convince me you're out to better yourself?"

"I'm just accumulating data," I said. "Everything else is only flotsam on the tide."

The extractor spit out two buckets of goop. The white stuff

was inedible by-product. Snarg slipped off the couch, and undulated excitedly. She waited until I gave her the okay to dive into it.

I opened my helmet dome, dipped a tentacle in the second bucket of multicolored goo, and took a taste.

"I'd offer you some," I said, "but it'd rot your digestive track."

"Thanks anyway." Zala scowled. "Is the machine always that loud?"

A vibration ran through the building. It wasn't the extractor. The rumble threatened to shake the townhouse off its foundation.

"Hmmm." I lowered my dome. "I guess Venusian intelligence was onto something after all, Zala."

The south wall disintegrated and a squad of jetpack assassins flew into the room.

The assassins pointed strange rifles in our direction and fired. Zala ran in one direction. I ran in another, giving the killers more targets to worry about, dividing their attention. My focus pulse failed to disable their weaponry. Supertechnology was a constant arms race. Today's death ray was tomorrow's marshmallow toaster.

Several razor-sharp discs sliced through my exo. My left arm locked up, and my left leg malfunctioned, slowing my run. I lost track of Zala and Snarg, but I trusted they could take care of themselves. I wouldn't do anyone much good without a hardware upgrade.

Half of the assassins pursued me. Their guns whirred as they spit out their barrage of discs. The damaged exo's evasive maneuvers protocols were functional enough to avoid having one slice through my brain. One did get awfully close, punching through my dome and grazing my cheek. The dome shattered, spilling salt water. I didn't let it distract me.

I jumped into the lift at the end of the hall. A shot cut my arm off. It fell to the floor with a clatter. The other arm was no good. The leg made dodging all but impossible. Several more rounds cut through the exo. My severed left leg spurted fluid. Dozens more pierced the torso. The exo did its job though. It kept bobbing and weaving to avoid making my vulnerable head an easy target. Its anticipation worked beautifully and, even with all the damage, was able to thwart any killshots.

Snarg skittered up behind the assassin and neatly beheaded him with one snip of her pincers. She screeched, warbled, and made a tremendous distraction of herself, just as she was trained to do. It bought me the time needed for the lift to zip down to the subvault.

Dozens of exoskeletons lined the small room. I didn't have time to be picky. I managed a few steps on my faulty legs before they gave out. I punched several buttons and remotely activated the Gunslinger unit. It clomped over, bent down, and scooped me up in its hands. The process took longer than I would've liked, but it wouldn't do to be squished by my own exoskeleton.

The exo dropped me into the pilot's seat. The dome sealed. There wasn't any water in the storage tank to make the ride more comfortable, but I had other concerns. An explosion destroyed the lift and when the smoke cleared the assassins were moments away from skewering me.

I took cover behind a hulking exo. Its armor was just thick enough to provide some protection.

"Surrender, Mollusk," said an assassin. "We've got you cornered."

"I was about to say the same thing."

I activated every exoskeleton in the room. They closed in on the enemy. The commandoes fired wildly, and they disabled a few of them. But not all. And the assassins' screams of terror ended abruptly as the various models sliced, pummeled, and blasted them.

I grabbed a jetpack attachment off the wall, snapped it into place. Sensor readings indicated that Snarg and Zala were still alive. Three unauthorized life-forms remained. I was more concerned with the attack vehicle hovering outside my home. I flew up the shaft, all the way to the roof, and surveyed the hovercraft.

The crescent profile, the low hum of its engines, and the gleaming silver and gold chassis all marked it as Atlantese in design. I'd never had any conflict with Atlantis, but I'd gotten my hands on schematics of their warcraft, studied their weaknesses. Just as a precaution.

A rumbler mounted on its nose had knocked the hole in my wall, but as an antipersonnel weapon, it wasn't much of a threat. The pilot tried to discourage me with a few hundred rounds of heavy artillery. I flew upward, and the shells exploded around me. A blast from me took out the main gun. He tried the rumbler. It sent spasms through the building. At a high enough setting it could vibrate the Gunslinger apart and melt my boneless body. It would shake my townhouse and the neighborhood to pieces before that.

I used a trio of well-placed rockets to knock out the craft's primary and secondary engines, along with the emergency drive. It dropped from the sky. It bounced off the street. Atlantis made a quality product, and though scraped and dented, with smoke coming from its burning engines, it remained intact. An explosion might've been more satisfying, but the threat was neutralized.

For just a moment, I thought about drilling a few additional missiles into the cockpit, but that would've been a waste of ammunition. And petty, I suppose.

By the time I checked on Zala and Snarg, the situation was well in hand. My living room was sliced to pieces, but neither was harmed. Zala didn't have a scratch on her. Snarg had a few wounds, but nothing significant. The augmented armor of an ultrapede was made of sterner stuff.

"I kept one alive." Zala ground her heel into the assassin's chest. "For questioning."

Snarg brought a soldier's head, dropped it at my feet, and clicked sweetly at me.

"That's a good girl." I patted her on the thorax, took the head. "You can keep this one."

I tossed it across the room. She scampered gleefully after it, where she devoured it in loud, crunching bites.

Zala scowled.

"I didn't think you Venusians had such delicate sensibilities," I said.

"The dead deserve more dignity than to be fed to your pet."

"Hopefully, the dead are past concerns to their dignity."

She yanked her prisoner to his feet and pulled off his helmet. He had the slight orange skin and deep green eyes of an Atlantese citizen.

"I thought you had tamed these Terrans, Mollusk. How is it that they attacked you?"

"My invasion methods only pacified the Terra Sapiens, the

largest portion of their land-dwelling population. Atlantis, the mole people, the sasquatch nations, and other pockets of intelligent Terran life remain unaffected. But I never had any problems with any of them before."

Zala shoved the soldier against the wall and snarled.

"Who sent you?"

"Time out." I pulled her away from him. "There's no need for that."

She smirked. "I didn't think you Neptunons had such delicate sensibilities. If you only give me a few minutes, I can get him to talk."

The Atlantese tried to sneak away while our backs were turned. Snarg let him know it was a bad idea with a hiss.

"I can get him to talk," I said, "and it'll be a lot easier than whatever interrogation technique you were about to employ. I haven't found pain all that conducive to conversation. I've managed to make it work to my advantage, but it's just as often counterproductive. And I don't do that kind of thing anymore."

"Still trying to convince me you've changed?"

"I haven't changed," I replied. "I still don't get why Venusians respect the dead more than the living. And I still don't bother wasting my time knocking assassins around for information... when I can just bribe them."

She gnashed her fangs. "You're going to pay him? After he just tried to kill you?"

"And I'm sure this notion offends you in some way, but since this is my life we're talking about, we'll do it my way. If you have a problem with my methods..."

I left the sentence hanging, knowing full well that I was

offering her an illusion of choice. Her sense of honor and duty meant she couldn't abandon me. It was a very complicated set of rules she lived by, and while I found them ridiculous and unnecessary, I found some ridiculous and unnecessary rules people lived by to be useful.

And I rather enjoyed watching her squirm.

"How do you know he'll take the money?" she asked smugly.

"Because if he doesn't I'll feed him to my ultrapede." I addressed her, but I was clearly talking to him.

"A loyal soldier accepts death before tarnished honor."

"That's up to him now, isn't it?"

I turned to the prisoner. "So what's it going to be?"

Snarg snapped her hungry jaws.

"I'll take the money," he said.

"See how easy that was?" I asked.

Zala's feathers ruffled, and she snorted, obviously disgusted by his unwillingness to die horribly for the sake of his principles. But her mistake was assuming everyone followed her code.

The code of the Atlantese army was simple. Much more understandable than Venusian rules of honor. It was a profit-making venture. Not quite mercenaries, but close enough. This soldier's failure would go on his performance evaluation, and in order to minimize the damage, he wanted to bring something back.

My small army of maintenance robots puttered around fixing the damage while we hammered out the details. They reupholstered and straightened the furniture, extracted the hundreds of razor-sharp discs embedded everywhere, and began bricking up the hole in the wall. In a few hours, the townhouse would be restored. Except for the couch. The chief robot reported it as unsalvageable.

I deducted it from the payment. Only a few hundred dollars. But a Neptunon had his principles, and I'd really loved that couch.

I forked over a few million, enough to cover the retrieval and repair done to the craft, the training and hiring of new personnel, with enough left over for a small profit. It was a very generous offer, considering I had the advantage, but it was only money. I had unlimited assets and all manner of convenient currency tucked away here and there. I hadn't walked away from warlordship with a light shell.

The soldier called in a quick credit check, had me sign a cessation of hostility contract.

"Pleasure doing business with you, Lord Mollusk."

Zala stood in rigid disapproval of the whole affair. "Well, if you were just going to take a bribe, why did you bother trying to kill the Neptunon in the first place?"

"Contractual obligation," explained the soldier. "We're signed for one elimination attempt. We tried. We failed. If the client is unhappy with the results, he's entitled to file a complaint with the Atlantese Pecuniary Society."

"I doubt he'll complain," I said. "If he'd really wanted me dead, he'd have sent something more..." I searched for a word that would make my point without insulting the soldier. "...less frugal."

"No need to be polite on my account. I work in the discount division. Strictly low rent. When I'd heard they were sending us after *the* Emperor Mollusk, I knew we were taking on a suicide mission. But, hey, it's a living, right?"

"And you didn't wonder why they sent you?" asked Zala.

"I don't wonder. Mine is not to wonder why. Mine is to follow the work order."

His attitude irked her. I couldn't see why. She was a virtual slave to her own chain of command, and I doubted she'd ever questioned it. The only difference between her and this hapless soldier was how command chose to motivate them. Venusians thrived on honor and duty. The mercenary divisions of Atlantis worked on stock options and a bonus plan. In the end, both were merely tools of a manipulative central command that reaped the benefits of expendable lives.

Zala's patience was growing thin. "Who sent you?"

"Atlantis Executive Command," he replied. "Beyond that, I can't tell you."

She drew her scimitar.

I stepped between them. "Put that away."

"But he's already admitted that he knows nothing. You paid him for nothing."

"No, I paid for the right to negotiate a meeting price for Atlantis Executive Command."

The soldier smiled, counting the hefty commission check that would be coming his way.

"But that's robbery!" she said. "You paid him not to kill him and to tell you nothing. And now you're going to pay him to arrange a meeting with someone else? It's madness."

"It's good capitalism," said the soldier.

She nearly bowled me over and beheaded the poor bastard right there. Then she remembered the chain of command, with me on top, and backed down like a good little soldier.

After he radioed his commanders to be sure he was in a position to negotiate, the haggling began. It took the better part of an hour. I could've paid his first offer without discussion, but just because I had the resources didn't mean I wasn't looking for a deal. The best way to earn an Atlantese mercenary's respect was to be a shrewd negotiator. Meteor guns and death rays weren't cheap, and more than one conquering genius had been foiled by poor cash flow. Maybe I wasn't out to conquer anyone right now, but who knew what tomorrow might bring?

The deal was made. The soldier had me sign the appropriate forms. Atlantis had paperwork for everything. Then I told the soldier to make himself comfortable while I supervised the preparation of my mid-class saucer.

The robot workers marched through my underground storage space, loading equipment into the craft. Zala stayed by my side as I supervised.

"So after paying those who tried to kill you, you're going to fly into the heart of their empire," she said. "How have you survived this long?"

"By knowing my enemies, and Atlantis isn't my enemy. It's merely a tool of those who are. And as long as Atlantis is getting their money, it'll play by its rules."

"You are remarkably trusting, Mollusk."

A procession of exoskeletons on autopilot trudged into the saucer. A giant exo, bristling with weaponry, brought up the rear.

"Not that trusting," I said.

CONQUEROR

I chose Hayward, Wisconsin, site of the Freshwater Fishing Hall of Fame and home of the largest muskie, to make the announcement. I hovered my saucer over the muskie for several days. I maintained transmission silence until a good crowd had developed. When all the tanks, artillery, soldiers, and civilians were in place, I finally set down.

I lowered the hatch with much deliberation, turned on the fog generator, and stepped out into the chill December evening. It was important to make the proper impression, so I wore my formal exoskeleton, the Ambassador. The gleaming silver exo stood eight feet tall. I'd toyed with installing a cape, but that seemed too flashy. Didn't want to look like I was trying too hard.

I spoke, and my saucer blasted my voice across the crowd.

"Terra Sapiens, I am Emperor Mollusk of the planet Neptune. I am here, not as an agent of Neptune but merely as an individ-

ual. Please do not take my actions as in any way indicative of the Neptunon people or governments."

I paused.

"What I want to make absolutely clear is that I do not in any way represent the planet Neptune in any official capacity. In point of fact, they don't like me there. A bit of a mess. Too complicated to really get into. Neither here nor there."

A scan of the perplexed Terran faces convinced me I'd lost them.

"Sorry. I probably should've rehearsed this better. I'm not much of a public speaker. Regardless, I am here to announce that I am Emperor Mollusk, and I have conquered your planet."

The Terrans remained silent.

"So that is all," I said. "Just wanted to make it official. Carry on then."

A colonel stepped forward. "You don't think we'll just roll over for you and your Neptune masters?"

I sighed.

"Didn't I make it clear that I don't have any Neptunon masters? It's the first thing I said."

"You aren't the first alien to menace our world," growled the colonel. "We've repelled them all."

I advanced on him. "I see that we're having trouble communicating. I didn't say I was here to attempt to conquer your planet. I said I have already conquered your planet. Past tense. English isn't my first language, but I'm certain I have that part right."

The colonel put his fists on his hips, clenched his jaw, and glared with every ounce of military ferocity at his disposal. "We'll fight. We'll give everything we've got and more."

"Quiet."

He saluted. "Yes, sir!" He lowered his hand and squinted at it.

I pointed to a soldier. "Can I see your weapon, please?"

He rushed forward, handed me the rifle. A puzzled expression crossed the soldier's face. He wasn't quite sure why he surrendered his rifle so easily, but it was only a momentary bewilderment.

"Thanks," I said.

He smiled. "My pleasure, sir."

I tossed the weapon aside. "This is a battle you've already lost. Mostly because you didn't know you were fighting it. I had no intention of conquering you with ray guns and space armadas. And all the death rays and melting tanks and rockets and explosions would've been terrific fun. Who doesn't like a good epic war now and then?"

I threw my arm around the colonel.

"But it's all so... indulgent, isn't it? I got that out of my system during my conquest of Venus. And, if I can be honest with you, that didn't go all that well. It's just so labor intensive and wasteful. So much to keep an eye on. After a while, it just becomes a chore."

We walked toward my saucer.

"This time, I elected to go the more subtle course. Why bother battling and then oppressing the indigent population when there are simpler methods? I'm a scientist. I like to experiment. And I like to think I learn from my mistakes. And the mistakes of others. You Terrans are a stubborn bunch, despite your technological inferiority and primitive development. Did you know the Martians still scare their young with stories of Teddy Roosevelt? Or that there is a Viking colony on Ceres? Nobody knows how it even got there. All they know is that only Terrans would be foolish and obstinate enough to somehow live there.

"You're a capable species. So much so that all the other civiliza-

tions in the system have decided it would be better to just leave you alone. A hands-off policy. More trouble than you're worth."

I chuckled.

"That's what drew me to your planet. It seemed like a challenge. And it was. Believe me. It wasn't easy to set all this up. To keep your scientists and leaders in the dark while I saturated your water with certain perception-altering agents. And the mind twister... first, I had to steal the basic technology from the Mercurials. Then I had to adapt it to Terran atmospheric conditions. I practically had to reinvent the science from scratch, but I didn't know that would be necessary until after I'd already been put on Mercurial official enemy lists. I tried apologizing for the misunderstanding, but they didn't want to hear it."

The colonel said, "I don't understand."

"No, of course you don't. You're a soldier. You shoot things, and I'm sure you're very good at your job. Unfortunately, my choice of invasion didn't give you anything to shoot at. And I apologize for that. I considered even giving you a little bit of a war. Just something to make you feel as if you had a chance. But that would've been a farce, a silly little dance. In the end, we'd still end up here."

"Are you saying you've brainwashed us?"

"In a manner of speaking. I actually used a multipronged approach. Very technical. You'd find the details uninteresting. Mind twisters secretly built into various innocuous buildings, seeding the global water supply with rapidly replicating microbes with aggression-suppressing qualities, some subliminal messaging here, a few world leaders replaced with robotic duplicates there. And some other things I'd rather not get into right now."

"Our president's a robot?"

"Yours? No. Though most of your legislative branch is. And

the mayors of Scranton and Sheboygan. Don't ask why I needed Scranton and Sheboygan. It's complicated. Still, they're better off than Portugal. I had to place the entire population in stasis. The whole country is just one big holographic projection at this point."

"That's impossible."

"Have you recently touched any Portuguese national?" I asked.

"Not in the last fifteen years, I can assure you."

"We'd notice."

"If you did, that'd be some substandard mental reprogramming. Let's not even call it brainwashing. Let's call it, oh I don't know, something less aggressive. We'll figure it out later."

"I'm sure you'll come up with something great," he replied with a smile.

"You're too kind. But returning to the brainwashing thing, are you absolutely positive you'd know?"

"Yes. I'm positive." But a moment later, he wasn't so certain. "What do you think?"

"I think it's nothing to trouble yourself about."

"You're probably right."

"Colonel, could you have someone contact the U.N. and tell them I'll be along shortly. I'd appreciate it if you had them prepare some kind of coronation ceremony. Nothing too fancy. I don't want to make a fuss."

He saluted. This time, there was no hesitation. "Yes, sir."

*"Oh, and have them throw up some banners. Something pithy." I spread my hands in the air and gazed at an imaginary slogan. "'*Welcome Emperor Mollusk, Warlord of Terra.*' Or is that too much?"*

"No, it's perfect."

I tapped my dome. "Seems too much. Well, we can always hammer out the details later." I turned the colonel back toward his troops, boarded the saucer, and waved to the Terran forces gathered around me. Smiling, they waved back. The colonel had the biggest grin of all.

The Atlantese sent a craft to pick up their soldiers. They offered to act as an escort (for a nominal surcharge), but I didn't need one.

Zala's guard, who had arrived too late to do any good against the Atlantese assault, insisted on coming along as backup. As long as I got to take my own saucer, I decided not to argue. Someone was out to kill me, and while I'd never been one to hide behind bodyguards, I didn't see the harm.

My craft was mostly cargo bay and weapon systems. The cockpit didn't even have a chair because, for all practical purposes, I was either sitting in an exoskeleton or lounging in a saltwater tank while flying. Despite this, Zala demanded she remain by my side. If she was willing to sit in a folding chair in the corner not occupied by Snarg's coiled form and my tank, then it was fine by me.

"There would be more room if your pet wasn't here. Is there any reason she can't sit in the cargo bay?" she said.

"She's a nervous flyer," I said as I punched in coordinates.

Snarg gurgled. Her claws tore scratches into the metal floor.

Venusian warriors prided themselves on their fearlessness, but Zala backed away from the anxious ultrapede. "Wouldn't it be wiser to restrain the creature?"

"You wouldn't say that if you saw how she reacts to being caged."

Snarg arched her back and screeched unhappily.

I activated the navigation system. The saucer lifted off.

"I still don't understand what you're doing, Mollusk," said Zala. "This is foolishness."

"And what would you suggest I do?" I asked. "Surrender myself to Venusian protective custody and be hidden away while you attempt to get to the bottom of this?"

"It's sensible."

"I've never been the kind to let others solve my problems, Zala."

"So instead you fly straight into your enemy's open jaws. Perhaps the tales of your evil genius are overstated. Or does your ego make you assume that no one else can handle this problem?"

"Let's reverse the situation. Hypothesizing that you were the one who was the target of assassination. Would you feel comfortable sitting under guard while someone else... handled the problem?"

"I would do as ordered."

I chuckled. "You're sidestepping the question."

"As a soldier—"

Zala had spent enough time obsessing over me that she could read the unconvinced look on my face.

"Without the chain of command, there is only anarchy," she said.

"That's still not an answer."

And then Zala did something I never expected. She thought about it. It wasn't easy for her. Her gray brow furrowed and her blue lips pursed. She shifted in her seat several times. I had never thought Zala stupid, but imagination had never been her strongest attribute. But there must have been something buried under all that training, and it poked its head out to peer into the light for just a moment.

"Mollusk, if I were you, I would hope that I would be sensible enough to know when I was being foolish. But I know you, and I know that, aside from your need to be self-reliant and your complete lack of trust in the abilities of those around you, that you would rather die than be caged."

I pushed a few buttons that didn't need pushing. When I glanced behind me, she was sitting there, just smiling.

"It must be irritating," she continued. "To have that great intellect at your disposal and yet you're not sure what to do with it. I'd imagine it must be quite a burden finding challenges worthy of it.

"What I don't understand, Mollusk, is, if you're so smart, why aren't you satisfied unlocking mysteries of the universe. Surely, there must be some grand equation or amazing scientific breakthrough you could be offering the universe right now. But instead you're zipping around, fighting assassins. A bit unseemly for a genius of your caliber, if you ask me."

I'd created a monster. Now that Zala was thinking, she was on a roll. But I saw a chance to interrupt, and I took it.

"This is not the work of the Celebrants of Oblivion," I said.

"What makes you say that?"

I replied, "The Celebrants of Oblivion are a legendary cult of death-worshipping nihilists that haven't even been proven to exist. If such a cult exists it surely doesn't employ outside assistance from Atlantese mercenaries with questionable loyalty. It certainly doesn't launch halfhearted assassination attempts that are more likely to fail than succeed."

"You aren't telling me you were never in any danger, are you?"

"No, there was danger. I could've even been killed. But it wasn't certain, and the Celebrants wouldn't settle for anything less than that. Otherwise, they'd never remain the shadowy presence that may, or may not, exist. Furthermore, when the Celebrants do kill, they do so in such a subtle and unnoticeable way that no one even knows they did it.

"They're a legend. They don't go around leaving calling cards or blowing up their targets. If they were going to kill me, I'd already be dead. Most probably."

"It's a pleasant surprise to see you admitting you're not infallible and invincible."

"Did I ever say otherwise? I'm flesh and blood. I make mistakes. Just because I'm smarter than you that doesn't mean I'm perfect."

She glared.

"And when I say *you* I don't mean you specifically. I just meant the great majority of intelligent beings in the system." I rubbed my dome. "Although I guess that technically does mean I'm saying I'm smarter than you, which I am."

Blue and green freckles appeared on her neck and face. A sign of her annoyance.

I thought about apologizing, about pointing out that I was only speaking the obvious truth, but I was pretty sure that it would come out wrong no matter how I phrased it.

"But you're making assumptions, Emperor. If no one has ever proven the Celebrants exist, then it stands to reason their methods and goals remain even more mysterious."

"Yes . . . mysterious."

Zala narrowed her eyes. "What do you know?"

"I know the Celebrants exist," I said. "And I know they believe that entropy is the only irresistible force in the universe. But rather than be doom and gloom about it, they seek to employ the art of entropy toward productive ends. Aside from that, I can't say anything else about them."

"And how do you know this?"

"I can't say. And I do mean can't. If I were to share too much information with you about the Celebrants, they would kill me."

"I didn't think you feared anyone, Emperor."

"Now you know differently," I replied. "So don't bother asking. Just take me at my word that I know what I'm talking about."

I turned the conversation back to more pressing concerns.

"Whoever hired these mercenaries had every reason to expect them to fail. Anyone who knows the workings of the Atlantese army knows that their loyalty is only as strong as their contractual obligations demand. Therefore, I'm going to assume that the attack itself was only meant to get my attention and that there are larger machinations at work here."

"It's an interesting theory," she agreed, "but there's an old Venusian adage. 'The hungriest clug can eat frot-shaped stones all day.' "

"I'm familiar with the expression."

"Then I trust I don't have to explain it to you. Seeing as how you are so much smarter than I."

It was entirely possible I was creating conspiracy when incompetence was usually the more reasonable explanation. I couldn't deny the sense of invigoration that had been absent in the months since I'd foiled my clone's plot. Boredom had always been my most persistent enemy. An enemy I could only forestall. Never defeat. And I did worry about the day when there were no more challenges, no more scientific breakthroughs, no more enemies, as unlikely as that day ever seemed. But a sufficiently long lull could be just as worrisome, leading me to chase after phantoms of my own imagination.

"You have a point," I said, "but if I'm wrong about this then it won't hurt to take a look. But if I'm correct—"

"If you're correct then someone is manipulating you for sinister reasons you have yet to decipher, and you're playing right into their hands."

She waited for me to offer a rebuttal, but she wasn't wrong.

"You agree with me then? That this is a foolish course of action in either case."

Zala's pointed ears perked up.

"You agree then?" she asked again.

She wanted acknowledgment. A less secure intellect might have trouble allowing her this victory, but I was confident enough in myself to admit when I was wrong.

Although I wasn't wrong.

I remarked, "When all options are equally foolhardy, you might as well choose the more interesting one."

Zala leaned forward. "I didn't hear you say it."

"Yes. I agree."

She leaned forward some more, dangerously close to falling out of her chair.

I sighed. "Yes, I agree. With you."

She nodded. It was a small triumph, but sometimes, the small triumphs were the sweetest.

"Now that you've admitted it, what's to prevent me from plucking you from that mechanical suit and taking you into protective custody? For your own good, of course."

"First, you've sworn an oath, and we both know you aren't going to break that. Secondly, you're just as curious as I am to see where this is going. And thirdly..."

I pointed to Snarg. The ultrapede's antennae twitched, and she released a low hiss.

Zala sized up Snarg. In these cramped quarters with only a sharp Venusian sword and the small arm pistol on her hip, she didn't stand much of a chance. But I hadn't gotten this far by underestimating my enemies. She was a fine specimen of a warrior, and if anyone could do it, she could.

"Even if you managed to overcome all these obstacles and pry me from my exo, I should point out that Neptunons can exert enough pressure with our tentacles to bend steel. Or that our suckers can inflict terribly painful wounds. Not to mention that trying to hold a wet invertebrate is a lot harder than you'd expect."

She sat at the edge of her chair. She might be preparing to spring. Or she might be only thinking about it. If she got lucky, she could drive her scimitar through my head. She was fast enough. Snarg would kill Zala in kind. Or her gods would smite her. But either was a price she'd gladly pay.

But Zala didn't want me dead. She wanted me alive and well. That had always been my advantage, and it didn't change now.

She sat back, folded her arms, and smiled in a slight, unreadable way.

"Very well, Mollusk. We'll do this your way. But don't think you'll escape justice by dying by your own arrogance."

I tipped my hand to her. "Wouldn't dream of it."

Contrary to popular fact, Atlantis didn't sink under the ocean. Not entirely. Ten square miles of land of what had been the tallest mountain on the lost continent remained above the surface. It was prime real estate, and only the powerful and privileged lived the dry life.

Every square inch of surface area was occupied by skyscrapers, but a single high-rise in the center reigned over them all. The setting sun gleamed off the polished glass and steel and the thousands upon thousands of priceless stones set in the walls. At night, the spotlights would switch on and the gems would form a glittering tower of opulence.

Zala scowled. "Such a ridiculous display of prosperity."

I agreed. In principle. But when you had money and power and nothing else to do, studding a skyscraper with diamonds and emeralds could seem like a good idea at the time. I liked to think of myself as above such things, but in a moment of indulgence, I'd had my face carved in Mount Rushmore, so I wasn't one to judge.

A pair of Atlantese craft appeared and offered escort. They mentioned something about my Venusian ship, but their complaints ended when I promised to pay the extra parking fee for their trouble.

Our craft landed on the roof of the capitol building. Zala expressed her surprise that we weren't shot down immediately, and as we disembarked, her finely honed warrior instincts scanned for signs of an ambush. Her battleguard flanked me, and I'm sure it looked very pomp and circumstance as I was met by an Atlantese contingency led by a tall, rotund officer.

Atlantese had a naturally golden orange tint, but it was the fashion of the drys to dye their skin to enhance the color. And since they didn't have hair, wigs were very popular as well. The officer sported a black coif complete with spit curl. This, along with the sparkling white uniform, had the accidental effect of making him appear to be a colorful Elvis dictator.

"Ah, Lord Mollusk." He clasped my mechanical hands and waggled them a bit in a traditional greeting. "I'm Lieutenant Cal, and I shall be your liaison while you visit our wonderful nation. So good to meet you."

"Thank you, Lieutenant."

"Thank me? Oh no, it is I who should be thanking you. This is quite an honor. Quite an honor, indeed. To be entertaining the former Warlord of Terra will look great on my résumé. Confidentially, I'm bucking for a promotion, and this might just be the thing to push me over the edge."

Zala scoffed. Loudly.

"I see you have brought your own staff," Cal said without bothering to disguise his contempt. "You needn't have bothered. I've been ordered to see to all your needs while you're here, and I can assure you that the finest indulgences will be at your disposal. All you need do is ask."

"Thank you," said Zala, "but we won't be staying long."

Cal cocked his head to one side, as if acknowledging the

buzz of an insect he was only vaguely aware of, before addressing me.

"We have taken the liberty of preparing the finest saltwater treatment based on your previous visits with us. I'm sure you'll find it a most satisfying way to relax after your flight."

"Tempting," said Zala, "but we're in a bit of a rush."

He put his arm around me like we were old friends. "And we have a special order of Neptune sour kelp that the chef assures me is fresh and delectable."

It'd been a long time since I'd eaten anything other than nutrient extracted paste.

"It can't hurt to stay for dinner, I suppose. I wouldn't want to be rude."

Zala scoffed again. Louder this time.

"I didn't think it was possible to maintain Neptune sour kelp on Terra," I said. "Where did you even get it to begin with?"

"Ah, trade secret, I'm afraid." Cal smiled devilishly.

He turned and led us to our suite. The unspoken understanding was that none of this was free, but a cephalopod of refinement didn't comment on such things.

"Don't you find it a bit odd," asked Zala, "that they're so prepared for your arrival? Including a rare dish that even you don't have access to? It's as if they were expecting you."

"They were expecting me."

"Doesn't that concern you?"

"It would if it was surprising, but I told you already that the entire point of this attack was to bring me here. Isn't that right, Cal?"

The lieutenant didn't turn to face me, but I could hear his

unflinching smile. "I'm afraid I'm not at liberty to discuss it, Lord Mollusk."

I dispensed a few gold coins into Cal's hand. His fingers tested the weight and value of the metal although he did so with discretion. When it met with his satisfaction, he said, "Yes, sir. We were told to expect you, should you survive the assassination attempt."

I nodded knowingly to Zala, who only shook her head, annoyed.

"And how much is it going to cost to find out who your mysterious employer is?" she asked.

He did his best to ignore the question of an underling, but Zala wasn't so easily discouraged. She seized him, spun him around.

"You will answer me, you pompous excuse for a soldier."

The Atlantese and Venusians drew their weapons. Snarg hissed curiously.

Cal ordered his soldiers to stand down. "Now, now, that's no way to treat a customer. Though we would appreciate it if you could keep the help in line, Lord Mollusk."

"I don't work for him," she said through clenched fangs. She ordered her battleguard to lower their weapons.

I kept quiet. I'd never been good at diplomacy, and anything I said was just as likely to make things worse.

"How long do we have to play your game, Cal?" said Zala, very pointedly skipping over the space where she failed to acknowledge his military rank.

"I'm not at liberty to discuss all the details of the contract," he replied with equal disdain.

"This is nonsense." Zala threw her hands into the air. "One

doesn't negotiate with the enemy. One crushes the enemy with merciless precision."

"And yet, I'm considered the evil genius," I said.

She glared, proving that I was right about my ability to make things worse.

"I'm sure that we're here for a reason, Zala. And that reason will present itself when the time is right."

Her terse, accepting response was smothered by a tremendous shriek.

Toward the setting sun, a faint pink glow appeared, at first indistinguishable from the glimmer on the water's surface. A phosphorescent mountain rose from the depths, and the shimmering, seventy-meter creature unleashed a fearsome howl.

"By the Twelve Gods," said Zala, "what is that?"

"An unnatural combination of genetic enhancement that, in any reasonable ecosystem, would never exist," I replied.

"How do you know that so quickly?"

"Because I created it."

The bioluminescent behemoth strode onto the shores of Atlantis's capital. Its glowing mass dragged itself, with great clumsiness, across the land and toward the high-rise.

Zala wheeled on Lieutenant Cal. "What is the meaning of this?"

"I have no idea," he said.

She grabbed him by his collar. His soldiers were too shocked by the approaching monster to rise to his defense.

"How much are they paying you for this?" she said.

"Put him down, Zala. I doubt the Atlantis Executive Command was expecting this. They might be greedy, but even they would have a hard time convincing their citizens to allow a monster to destroy their prized capital."

"Why would you create such a thing?" she said.

"It's called a jelligantic. Never really liked the name, but I figured I'd change it later. But then I shelved the project and forgot about it."

"But you just said you created it."

"I researched the design. It was a thought experiment, an exercise in whimsy. I always assumed it would take too long, and I wasn't convinced it was a viable life-form."

The jelligantic (The gigantiglop? The slime-asaurus? The goopanormous?) was mostly a mound of quivering pudding, but it did have tremendous mechanical tentacles that allowed it to lurch across the ground. It wasn't very fast outside of the water (or very fast in it either), but what it lacked in speed, it made up for in inevitability. It was significantly faster than a glacier and far less forgiving.

Cal barked an order to scramble. Within minutes, aircraft were deployed. They strafed and bombed the creature with all the hardware at their disposal. It howled and roared, giving the false impression that they were hurting the thing.

"We should evacuate this location," said Zala.

"I can assure you," said Cal, "that we have this well in hand."

The jelligantic used cybernetic tentacles to swat a fighter from the sky like an elephant flicking its tail at flies. They could've blasted it all day with negligible results. The only vital point in the creature was its nucleus, protected by a bulk of highly absorbent flesh. The jelligantic never paused in its march toward the building, but it would be another few minutes before it would reach us.

I stared at the monster laying waste to the city. I moved closer to the window and studied the beast, a beautiful spawn of genetics and engineering. It was glorious, a triumph of science. If Neptunons could've cried, I would've shed a tear.

Zala shook me out of my delirium.

"We have to leave."

"Right." I forced myself to focus. "We have to get to my ship."

We ran back to our craft. Cal trailed behind us, offering weak reassurances, though nothing the Atlantese threw at the monster had any effect on it. I boarded my saucer with Snarg and Zala, lifted off, and flew toward the jelligantic.

"What are you doing, Mollusk?" she asked.

"I need to get closer," I replied.

The monster waved its tentacles at my saucer, but the craft's navigation system was able to avoid them with ease. The anti-inertia function kept the ride smooth as my saucer zipped among the deadly metal tendrils.

The jelligantic's every movement inflicted millions of dollars in property damage. The death toll should've been in the thousands, but if there was one lesson Atlantis had learned from its previous cataclysm, it was how to plan orderly evacuation. Escape pods were a standard of their architecture. Hundreds of the spherical pods shot into the sky and on to safety. So many, my ship was in more danger of being hit by a pod than a tentacle.

Zala said, "Mollusk, are you insane? Get out of that creature's reach."

"Just let me get a few more sensor sweeps."

The saucer zipped between a pair of tentacles, dodged another escape pod, zoomed beneath some falling rubble.

"One more scan," I said.

Zala turned me away from the monitor.

"Don't you get it, Mollusk? This thing is the perfect tool of assassination for someone like you. You can't resist it. Any sensible being would turn and fly away, but you can't. You have to get up close and take a look at it."

"Hmmm. You're probably right."

I was only half listening as I pondered the creature. It had stopped worrying about the Atlantese and focused its attentions on my ship. My original design wouldn't have allowed that because it would have had photosensitive pigmentation pools that allowed for the detection of light and dark but not distinct shapes. There was no need for more than that since the jelligantic had been intended for mass destruction. It was a weapon to destroy cities, not individuals, and being half-blind wasn't a problem.

"Attention, Atlantis Executive Command, this is Emperor Mollusk," I transmitted. "Have your fleet stand down. I will neutralize the hostile." I added with a smile, "We'll discuss my fee later."

"Are you mad?" asked Zala.

"I designed it. More or less. I can destroy it."

"I don't doubt you can," she said.

The jelligantic toppled a twenty-story building with the swing of a careless tentacle.

"Okay, I do doubt it just a bit. But if you know that this thing is a trap, why are you playing into it?"

"If I walk away, then I lose."

"But you get to live."

"True, but I'd rather not settle for the consolation prize."

I set the ship to maintain evasive maneuvers while leading the creature back the way it came—to minimize damage—and into the ocean.

"The jelligantic is too powerful a weapon to be in anyone's clutches, Zala. Unchecked, it could cause untold devastation."

"Since when do you care about that?"

"I will not tolerate outsiders using my own science to do harm."

In the cargo bay, a robot handed me a fifteen-pound cube. Another secured the rocketpack and microwave emitter to my exo. I opened the cube, pushed a few buttons, twisted a few dials until I was comfortable with the setting.

"What is that?" asked Zala.

"Silica bomb."

"You're going to blow it up?"

"Not exactly. If this device works—"

"If?"

"I don't have time to field-test everything." I opened the loading bay doors and stared into my opponent's sea of shimmering flesh.

"You're going to get yourself killed," she said. "I told you I can't allow that."

"I remember."

A robot grabbed her from behind. It failed to immobilize both her arms, and with her free hand, she drew her scimitar and sliced the robot in two. Several more jumped on her. She would make short work of them, but it gave me all the time I needed.

"I don't have time to program and arm a missile," I said.

Growling, she kicked aside the last robot.

I winked at her and jumped out. As soon as I was out of my saucer's artificial gravity and inertia dampeners, I plummeted into free fall. I engaged my rocketpack just in time to avoid being squashed by a towering tentacle. Evasion was easy because the tentacles were designed for crushing buildings, not a single fast-moving exoskeleton.

I punched through the monster's outer skin with minimal resistance and swam through the opaque pudding of the jelligantic's interior. Neptunon vision was adapted for murky waters, so I could see well enough. I switched over to my aquajets and headed toward the nucleus.

A blob of cybernetic protoplasm, the equivalent of a white blood cell, reacted aggressively to my invasion. Its mechanical limbs tried to drag me into its smothering mass. I burned it with the microwave emitter, shriveling it into blackened goo.

It wasn't the only one. Dozens of defending organisms closed in. Twice the globs managed to grab me, and I had to jettison my damaged legs, deadweight anyway, to avoid being dissolved.

It was slow going. The creature's thick pudding and the army of goo were troublesome. But there were no surprises. Everything was close enough to my original design that I had to stop myself from appraising the results to improve the next generation of jelligantic. Perhaps it was the rogue scientist in me, the same young squid who built desalination bombs and genetically modified six-headed piranhas for the simple joy of it, but there was something inspiring about the jelligantic.

I buried my scientific instincts and pushed deeper. I reached the nucleus, a pulsing yellow glob with a cybernetic mesh that acted as the mind, such as it was, of the beast. I paused. I'd never planned on building this monstrous weapon, but now that it was here, I hesitated to destroy it. Just for a moment.

It had to go. If I didn't trust something like this in my

tentacles, I couldn't trust it to anyone else's. The challenge had been posed, the gauntlet thrown, and if I didn't destroy the jelligantic then it would be a loss. I'd lost before. But never willingly. It wasn't in my nature.

I noticed a computer node on the jelligantic's nucleus that didn't belong there. It wasn't much. Just a small component, barely noticeable, along the wiring. It was probably nothing, a built-in redundancy, a simple modification, but in the very cursory examination necessity allowed me, it appeared to not only be unnecessary, but not even connected to the rest of the system. Upon closer study, I discovered it came right off with a simple twist.

The jelligantic's defenses closed in, returning my attention to my mission. I activated the bomb, threw it into the nucleus, and pushed my jets to their limit, not even bothering to avoid the defense slimes, just rocketing through them, taking the damage, pondering if there would be anything left of my exo to carry me out. I lost an arm, and my battery was barely able to power the jets as I burst out of the jelligantic. My rockets kicked in, sputtering and nearly useless, but they got me clear of the creature's flailing limbs. My remaining exo was nothing but deadweight. I grabbed the node in my tentacles and ejected the pilot dome as the exo fell from the sky.

The dome's emergency anti-graviton pods slowed my descent, but weren't good for much else. The jelligantic screamed as my bomb scorched the nucleus and burned its way through the protoplasm. It took a while for a creature of this size to die. It lurched from side to side, howled as its goop grayed and calcified.

Six minutes later, the jelligantic was a fossilized mountain.

* * *

I walked among the rubble left in the jelligantic's wake. All things considered, the destruction could've been worse. Property damage meant new construction projects on the island, which was almost a boon from an Atlantese mind-set. And casualties were minimal though there were those who had failed to escape unscathed.

A child, half-buried in rubble, cried out to Zala. She rushed to his aid.

"I wouldn't do that if I were you," I said.

She ignored the warning. It took her several minutes to clear away the debris, but she wasn't strong enough to move the better part of a wall.

"You could help," she said. "These people wouldn't be in this situation if not for you."

Sighing, I summoned several dozen worker robots from my saucer. They trundled among the damage, beginning the rescue work. A pair threw aside the wall, and Zala helped the child to his feet.

"Ow," he said. "You didn't have to pull so hard."

"We should get you to a hospital," said Zala.

"Yes." He rubbed his shoulder. "I think you wrenched my arm."

"Can you walk?"

"My legs are fine." He moved his right arm and winced dramatically. "But my shoulder feels dreadful."

"Yes, yes. I'm sorry about that. I guess I should've been more careful, but I was—"

"So you admit you were careless," said her charge.

"Well, I wouldn't go that far. You were half buried alive."

"But my shoulder was just fine before you helped me up."

Zala rolled her eyes. "Fine. I don't see how that's important, but it's possible I could've caused the injury."

"Aha!" The child pointed to several other people being dug out of the rubble by my robots. "You all heard her. You're my witnesses. She caused my shoulder injury."

"This robot stepped on my hand," said an old man.

"I think this one aggravated my tennis elbow," said another.

The other rescued victims registered their own complaints, ranging from broken bones to vague psychological trauma.

"What's your name?" the child asked Zala. "I need to know who to sue for my medical bills."

"You're still in shock. You don't know what you're saying."

Zala put her hand on his shoulder. He howled.

"Now you've exasperated it!"

"I saw her do it," said another. "Witness."

Zala stepped back as they advanced on us.

"Are you all mad?" she shouted. "Your city faces disaster, and you're all out to make a profit from it?"

"The Atlantese find optimism through litigation," I said. "If they can fatten their bank accounts then at least some good can come of this."

"Well, I am a native of Venus and not beholden to their stupid laws."

The citizens murmured among each other. It was a gray area. They might have been willing to fight about it, but why bother when the former Warlord of Terra was within range.

They showered me with their complaints, but I raised a hand to quiet them.

"As soon as the authorities get here, we'll discuss an equitable settlement."

Zala retreated to the shadow of my saucer, and I joined her.

The Atlantese rescue forces reached us. They had a lawyer with them as a matter of protocol. I left it to him to negotiate the two or three dozen settlements while discussing things with Lieutenant Cal.

"My superiors agree, Lord Mollusk, that this is unacceptable." He paused for effect. "Quite unacceptable. The rampage of this monster has unleashed at least three hundred separate wrongful injury complaints against the military."

By the end of the day, there would no doubt be several thousand more. Not just for loss of life and property either. If a fleeing citizen stubbed a toe, he was certain to find someone to sue over it. Citizens on the other side of the city would claim mental anguish. Some would sue because the warning horns were too loud, causing possible hearing loss. Others would sue because the horns were too soft, failing to give them ample time to escape. And there was the always popular escape pod–induced whiplash.

Cal wiped his brow with a handkerchief. "The profit margin of this venture has become—"

"Unacceptable?"

"Your frivolous reply doesn't diminish the situation."

I leaned down, took a sample of the powdery white substance on the ground. The petrification process was unstable, and the jelligantic was disintegrating. I opened my helmet to rub a tentacle across the powder.

"Who hired you?" I asked Cal.

He balked. "We haven't even begun negotiations on the terms of that information."

"I'll write you a check."

"I'm not authorized to act without a lawyer present."

I stood, turned on him. "I will write *you* a check."

"I, sir, am a member of the distinguished Atlantese army. I have pledged an oath to follow certain regulations—"

My patience was at its end.

"I will write you a check. And your distinguished army another check. And another check for every citizen who survived the attack with a healthy bonus for all their pain and suffering. And one more to rebuild the city. In the end, this won't cost you a penny."

Cal relaxed. "That's very generous of you, Lord Mollusk. Perhaps you would like to discuss the details over dinner?"

"I would not. I'm leaving in twenty minutes."

"But for a matter this profitable, I must consult with my superiors."

"Twenty minutes."

I walked away, leaving him to work out the details.

"Is that wise?" asked Zala. "What if he doesn't give you the information?"

"He will. Though it doesn't matter. Whatever the Atlantese know will be unimportant." I held up my hand, showing the powder on my fingertips. "This was the clue."

"Then why pay them at all?"

"Because I did destroy their city. None of this would have happened without me."

She nodded to herself. "For someone claiming not to be interested in reforming, that's a very responsible thing to do."

"No, it isn't. I have unlimited resources at my disposal. Money coming out of my gills."

"Still, I'm surprised you didn't just hypnotize them into forgetting the entire affair. Or threaten them with disintegration."

"Never occurred to me."

The rescue lawyer handed me a stack of settlements in need of my signature and a pen. I started signing.

"Well, maybe it occurred to me once or twice," I said with a half smile.

The Atlantese had been hired anonymously. A robot had paid for the assassination attempt with one ton of untraceable gold. The contracts were signed with an *X.* As long as the payment was big enough, the Atlantese were fine with not asking any questions.

I was allowed to watch the security video of the transaction. The robot had arrived in a small craft, alone. Both the robot and the ship were of my own design.

There was nothing else the video could give me, so I turned it off.

"So where are we going now?" asked Zala.

I projected a three-dimensional image of our destination.

"Less than a century ago, the Terra Sapiens discovered atomic energy. Like nearly every sentient race in the system, they immediately started seeing how big an explosion they could make with it. All very fun and a perfectly natural step in their technological growth. One of their tests was on an island in a graviton well-known as the Bermuda Triangle."

"Are they idiots?"

"They haven't figured out all the subtleties of gravity yet. In their defense, their development has been sporadic and confusing. They jumped onto geometry and engineering at a very young age, but it took them ages to put the steam engine to good use."

"What were they doing in the meantime?"

"Culture," I said. "Poetry, music, plays, philosophy. They're really good at that sort of thing."

I pushed a button and various images scrolled across the screen. Triumphs of architecture, art, and creative expression. It wasn't that the other races of the system were devoid of arts. But none spent nearly as much time on it as the Terrans did.

"They've produced a tremendous variety of the stuff," I said. "They argue over it, obsess over it, fight wars over it. They declare some of it all important and other bits of it to be stupid and pointless. And the most interesting thing about it is that they can't seem to agree on which bits are which."

Zala studied the images. "How do they get anything important done?"

"Don't judge them too harshly," I said. "I don't really get it either, but it seems to make them happy."

She shook her head. "How did they manage to remain unconquered for so long?"

"Tenacity." I smiled. "They're a very stubborn race. Also, lucky. The atomic blast interacted with the gravitons in a one-in-a-million way. Instead of blowing up their planet, it formed a space-time anomaly, a singular phenomenon in the system. Possibly the galaxy."

Zala said, "Its many and varied life-forms, its strange ability to defy every reasonable expectation of extinction, its ridiculous inhabitants. I'm beginning to see why this world captivates you."

"It is full of challenges. The anomaly was very near collapsing on itself, possibly destroying Terra, until I found a way to stabilize it."

"More of that Terran luck," she said.

I gave her a view of the island. "The anomaly sits on this landmass existing in a state of quantum flux, sporadically accessible, usually by accident. Or with the help of a quantum synchronizer."

"I wasn't aware such technology existed in the system."

"I invented it. The relative stability of the Terran anomaly made it easier to crack the problem. Although it was made considerably easier by my preliminary studies in space-time. I got a commendation for my work on wormhole theory. Primitive stuff, but not bad for a preschooler."

"Do you ever get tired of remarking upon your own brilliance, Emperor?" she asked.

"I'd remark upon it less if it wasn't such a frequent topic of conversation."

I pulled up a map of the island.

"The anomaly has allowed fauna and flora from Terra's past to slip into the present. The radiation has caused mutation to run rampant. I call the place Dinosaur Island."

She smirked. "Very creative of you."

"I'm an evil genius, not a cartographer."

Zala sat back in her chair. "I think I can guess the rest. You located a secret laboratory or storehouse or whatever on this island on the egotistical assumption that no one would be able to unlock entry to it."

She'd hit the word *egotistical* a little hard, but she wasn't wrong. I had made a mistake, and that mistake had unleashed consequences on Atlantis.

"No pithy response?" asked Zala.

"No pithy response."

I activated the synchronizer and transmitted instructions to our Venusian escort. A doughnut-shaped island materialized in the ocean below as all around the air took on an emerald hue. A volcano at the northern tip belched plumes of blue-black smoke.

The thick jungle hid most of the island's many dangers, though a family of speckled apatosauruses was visible on the closest beach, and a flock of pterodactyls soared nearby. Another flock flew in from the east. And another appeared from seemingly out of nowhere to surround our ships. Radar was unreliable on Dinosaur Island.

"They're just curious," I said. "Nothing to be concerned about."

My saucer's sensors beeped a warning.

"We've lost shields."

The pterodactyls' eyes flashed as they projected dozens of lasers at our craft. The armor plating held its integrity. One of the great winged reptiles collided with the saucer. It scrabbled for a perch, but its claws slipped across the alloy. The saucer's rotation flung the pterodactyl away.

The Venusian scoutship had eight or nine new passengers.

Without its shields, the attacking beasts were already burning and tearing their way inside.

I activated the starboard blasters, picking off the onslaught. The background radiation confused advanced sensors, forcing me to manually zap the reptiles. My defense of the Venusians was stifled by a sky darkened by attackers. I lost their craft in the living cloud.

Sensors screeched another warning.

Zala scanned the monitor. "Multiple incoming projectiles of indeterminate type."

"Now that's something to be concerned about," I said.

The sensor interference meant my navicomp's evasion protocols were hit-or-miss. The dozens upon dozens of obscuring pterodactyls made manual avoidance impossible. I punched in a standard evasive maneuver. Whoever was shooting at us had to be relying on unassisted targeting so it was worth trying.

A projectile zipped by the cockpit. Too fast to identify. Several more made contact with the pterodactyls and exploded. The craft trembled with the concussions. The swarm dispersed, clearing an opening in the sky big enough to see the several hundred missiles speeding toward us from the island below.

"Crude, but effective," I remarked to myself.

"For someone who claims to be a genius," said Zala with a scowl. "You certainly do make glorious mistakes."

"That's how genius works," I replied.

Several missiles hit my saucer, and we fell from the sky.

The computer informed us with cool indifference.

"Brace for impact."

Zala sat in her rolling chair, realizing it wasn't going to do her much good in a crash. I left her to her own devices, locking my exoskeleton in its crash brackets.

The crash wasn't so bad. At least, not in the cockpit, which had its own inertia dampener, a stabilizing gyroscope, and an emergency ejection system. At the moment of impact, we were catapulted a safe distance away. Our silver sphere rolled several hundred feet, propelled by the force unleashed, tearing a path through the jungle. The systems worked, keeping everything so smooth that to the passengers inside, it wasn't any more upsetting than riding a rough ocean wave. It took me a few seconds to notice we'd stopped rolling.

I disconnected from the brackets and checked exo functionality.

"You could've warned me that would happen," said Zala.

"Warned you about what?" I asked. "That my escape pod would work just as designed and that there was nothing to be concerned about?"

"Then why did you secure yourself?"

"I'm confident in my designs," I replied, "but I'm not stupid."

I performed a few scans of the outside environment. The radiation interfered with the pod sensors. The peculiar waves of Dinosaur Island made precise readings all but impossible. Right now, all I was getting were dozens of life-forms, but the readings were inexact, unreliable. The jungles were teeming with organisms, and there was no way to know what was out there without taking a look firsthand.

I pushed a button and the pod walls went transparent. Our ejection had torn a gash through the jungle. We'd crushed trees and flattened foliage, and seeing it after the fact gave me a certain pride in how well my design had worked. There were indications that we'd bounced several hundred feet without so much as a bruise to show for it. Aside from our path, we were enclosed by an impenetrable wall of green. The luminescent emerald skies above were clear, what little we could see through gaps in the canopy.

"Why aren't they pressing their advantage?" asked Zala, ever the strategist. "We're vulnerable."

"I don't know, but we can't wait here for my man to rescue us."

"You have someone stationed here?"

"Not really. He was already here when I set up shop, but I still rely on him. He knows the island better than anyone. Under normal circumstances, I'd say stick around and wait, but like you said, whoever attacked us probably isn't going to give up now."

"Tell me, Mollusk. Do you ever get tired of walking into ambushes?"

"It's becoming a bad habit," I replied, "but you have to admire their style, whoever they are. The real question we have to ask ourselves is whether they keep missing or whether they aren't really trying yet."

"Why would they be trying *not* to kill you?"

"Another good question. One I haven't figured out. Yet."

She noticed my smile.

"You're enjoying this, Mollusk."

"Some of it."

I remembered the devastation my monster, in the wrong hands, had unleashed upon Atlantis. It was at least partially my fault. I remembered Paris blazing as Saturnite warships littered her streets. I remembered Saturn.

Those were the memories I could do without, the things I no longer wanted any part of. I'd considered erasing them. More than once. But deleting past mistakes didn't undo them. Some things needed to be remembered.

I opened the emergency supplies compartment and handed Zala a few weapons.

"I'm already armed," she said.

"You'll want something bigger." I gave her the rifle. "The wildlife isn't going to be deterred by a sword and a pistol. You'll want this as well, to counter the radiation."

She took the shielding field bracelet and slipped it on. I had one already built into the suit.

Zala nodded to Snarg. "What about her?"

"Radiation just makes her hungry."

Snarg snapped her mandibles and uttered a low-pitched purr.

My exo had built-in defenses, but I slung a wave cannon over my shoulder. For good measure, I attached a protonic disentanglement pistol to my arm. There was a spare rocketpack in the store but flying was probably a bad idea with the pterodactyls on the loose. Better safe than sorry though, so I plugged it into my back.

We exited the pod. Zala, retaining her bodyguard role, insisted on being the first one out and telling me to wait until she signaled it was safe. I humored her, but what she failed to understand was that Dinosaur Island was never a safe place.

I trusted Snarg's senses more than anything else. The ultrapede scanned the jungle and gave the squeal that meant danger, but nothing imminent.

Something roared. The echoes made it difficult to place.

I squeaked a command to Snarg to scout ahead, then followed after her.

"I would feel better taking point," said Zala.

"Trust me. If Snarg doesn't see it, we won't see it until it's too late. You can take rear guard, if it makes you feel productive. I'm sure there are all manner of deadly mutants stalking up behind us as we speak."

I smiled as if I was joking, but the foliage rustled. A pair of red eyes stared out from the shadows and a tail (or possibly a tentacle) whipped into view as the creature darted away.

Zala attempted to contact her battleguard, but radiation rendered her comm system inoperable. The best she could manage was a few garbled sounds that might have been words. Or possibly just static.

"We should assume they are dead," I said. "If the pterodactyls and crash didn't kill them, the island will."

"We Venusians are sturdier than that. One can't even become part of the Protectorate until we've survived, naked and unarmed, in the harshest jungles of Venus. Only after a warrior crawls into civilization wearing the pelt of the fearsome screeching five-horned fiend do they pass the test."

"Sounds like fun," I said. "Then they can take care of themselves. Just as long as they don't do anything stupid like leave their crash site. Or drink the water. Or make too much noise."

"Standard protocol is to attempt to rendezvous with the leadership," said Zala.

"So I'll stick to my dead assumption then. In the unlikely event that they're not, we won't be doing them much good if we die trying to find them. At my compound, I have equipment and supplies for a proper rescue mission. If they're not dead, which they most certainly are."

We reached the crash site of my saucer. My hope, albeit slim, was that the craft would be salvageable or at least give us access to better equipment. But the pterodactyls swarmed over the wreckage, tearing it to pieces with their claws, beaks, and eye beams. There was no way to get to it without meeting the same fate.

"Didn't you know about those things?" asked Zala.

"They're not normally so aggressive, although the fauna mutates at such an advanced rate that there's no way to stay on top of it. But in this case, I think they were triggered." I pointed to a device, a small missile lodged in the side of the saucer. "That must be what shorted the force field. It's probably equipped with some kind of signal generator that gets the pterodactyls frenzied. Clever. The sensor interference makes the small device almost undetectable, and once the field is down, the reptiles do the rest."

"Don't tell me you made that too."

"I'd experimented with frequency sensitivity in the wildlife but hadn't done anything with the research. Someone must've carried it forward to practical application."

"Is there nothing you've touched that can't be made into a weapon?"

"Everything is a weapon," I replied. "It's just a matter of being creative enough."

Zala took aim with her rifle. "I'll destroy the device. The creatures should leave, and we might be able to salvage something of worth from the saucer."

"That could backfire on us. We don't know how the pterodactyls will react."

"No, but we do know that trekking through the forest with what we have is probably inadequate for our survival."

She made sense, but in a situation like this, it paid to weigh the variables. While I was pondering, she fired her rifle from the hip. The shot was dead on. The missile blew to bits. The pterodactyls responded with shrieks and a few lasers blasted in random directions. One came dangerously close to slicing off Zala's head. Another reflected off Snarg's thick armor. The ricochet killed a reptile. The pterodactyls took to the sky in a chorus of caws and screeches.

"Looks like you were right"—Zala snapped her fingers—"there was nothing to worry about."

Something fell from the sky, landing just a few feet away from us. The metallic polyhedral embedded itself in the soil. We remained still, waiting for more to fall.

"Another weapon?" asked Zala. "A bomb perhaps?"

Snarg extended the spikes along her back. She only did that when especially tense. My exo detected an ultrasonic whine signal.

"Destroy it," I said.

Zala fired several bolts into the device. They only blackened its shell without damage. The frequency remained, and Snarg clawed the ground and twitched.

The island rumbled. The roar of charging nodosaurids was much too close and getting closer. The canopy made direction impossible to figure, but we had only a few seconds before they would be upon us.

I grabbed Zala, activated my rocketpack. We flew upward just as the two-headed nodosaurids came crashing through the jungle, knocking down trees and crushing everything in their way. We hung suspended while underneath my ship was pulverized by the rampaging herd. The creatures' extra heads didn't make them smarter, only more likely to panic. And several hundred tons of panicked, armor-plated dinosaurs were enough to finish my saucer off. The nodos smashed it with their tails and butted it back and forth like a giant Frisbee.

It was several minutes before the device that had triggered their rage stopped emitting. Whether some stubborn nodo stepped on it or someone just cut the signal, the dinosaurs calmed. The herd milled about in the clearing and wreckage they'd created.

I'd hovered close to the canopy to avoid detection by any

zealous pterodactyls, but it was only a matter of time before they spotted something smaller than them to blast from the sky. I landed, set Zala down. The nodos brayed, gave us some room but otherwise ignored us.

"Oh, Emperor." Zala nodded toward Snarg, trampled into the ground. "I'm sorry."

"Don't be."

Snarg raised her head and spit out some dirt. She crawled out of the hole and coiled up at my side.

"By the Seventh," said Zala. "What does it take to kill that thing?"

"More than a few enraged nodosaurids." I bent down and picked out a piece of scrap I couldn't identify. Just junk now.

"We should get moving," I said.

We'd both seen the plume of smoke where the Venusians had crashed. They'd come down closer to the compound, but it was still faster to continue on our own. Zala didn't like it, but she had to admit it made more sense than trying to search a teeming wilderness.

The journey was slow, but it was better to keep moving on the island. Standing still usually meant death. If not from the assassins after me then from the irradiated monsters that called this place home. Moving wasn't really safer, but it felt more active, gave us the illusion of having some control over our fate. I'd never been very good at inaction. I liked to initiate. If we were going to stumble across something large and hungry, I'd prefer we were the ones doing the stumbling rather than being stumbled upon. Either way, we were likely to perish on the island, but I still found the former more satisfying than the latter.

Zala questioned me. I didn't mind. In point of fact, I rather liked being questioned. It was refreshing, a nice change of pace.

"Your compound's security has been compromised," she said.

"True."

"Someone is trying to kill you."

"Also true."

"And yet you continue to act exactly how they want you to."

"I don't see any alternative. We're unlikely to survive the night if we don't try. Unless my operative finds us first. In the meantime, it's better to keep moving."

A small predator jumped out of the jungle. Zala smashed it across the jaw with the butt of her rifle, and it retreated. She didn't lose a step.

"What if this ally of yours is in league with our mystery puppet master?"

"I sincerely doubt it. Although it's an interesting possibility."

"Your definition of *interesting* continues to elude me."

We stopped while Snarg sniffed the air. Her antennae twitched nervously.

"If he's not a traitor, then he could be dead," said Zala.

I chuckled. "If Dinosaur Island hasn't killed him yet, then it is safe to say he is nigh unkillable."

Snarg chirped a warning. Zala didn't have to be told to ready her weapon.

An obsidian boulder flew from the underbrush and came crashing at our feet. Zala swept the jungle with her rifle.

"Put it down," I said.

"But..."

"Put it down before they kill you where you stand."

"What kills me?" she demanded.

"If you don't put it down, you'll never get a chance to find out."

The next boulder flew inches from her head and shattered a thick tree trunk into splinters.

"There won't be another warning," I said.

Reluctantly, she lowered the rifle.

The jungle parted and twelve-foot-tall reptilian primates with sails running down their backs emerged into view. The creatures surrounded us.

"What are they?" she asked.

"At some point, they had been dimetrodons, but several generations of mutation have transformed them into hulking primates with a cunning higher animal intelligence. I call them primadons. Interestingly enough," I added, "dimetrodons are often thought of as dinosaurs by your average Terran, though in fact they are more closely related to mammals than reptiles and fall under the category of pelycosaurs."

"I don't find that very interesting," she said.

"Not a fan of terrestrial paleontology, I take it."

The alpha of the primadons, a great brute with a scarred body, pounded the earth with his fists and roared.

"What are they going to do with us?" whispered Zala.

"It remains to be seen, but they're carnivorous, so they're probably planning on eating you. They'll probably just smash me to pieces and, if they notice, lick up the pulped remains."

Her rifle hummed as she upped the damage setting.

"You'll only end up annoying them."

"A true warrior does not slide willingly down her opponent's gullet."

The alpha leaned forward and sniffed Snarg. She snipped his nose, and he jumped back with a fearsome howl. The primadons responded with their own dreadful cacophony, and no doubt every edible creature within a thousand yards was already running in the opposite direction.

"We'll have to risk flying to escape."

"I don't like being carried from battle like some helpless child," she replied with a snarl.

"Fine with me. I don't need to take you with me."

The dance of the primadons reached a fevered pitch. They punched and grappled with each other for the right to the first bite, and there wouldn't be a better opportunity. I seized her and rocketed upward. But the alpha, alert predator that he was, had other plans. He threw something. I didn't know what it was, but it was big and heavy and had enough force to cause me to spin around, smash through the trees, and come crashing to the ground.

I lost track of everything. My senses only cleared enough to see the hazy outline of the creature preparing to bash me into oblivion.

Then I heard the long, terrifying howl that filled every monster on the island with fear. A figure bounded from out of nowhere and put himself between the beast and me.

My squat and bulky rescuer stood barely five feet tall. His carapace was a rainbow of scarlet and blue. He had a knife sheathed at his side, but he didn't pull it. It wasn't necessary.

The savage raised his head and howled, beating his chest with his fists, a throbbing rhythm that warned of his arrival.

The primadons retreated. All except the alpha, who bull-rushed his opponent. Faster than the eye could follow, the savage wrestled with the alpha, turning and twisting and with a fluid motion, slamming the great beast to the jungle floor. The alpha shrieked his surrender, but the savage didn't let up until he heard the snap of bone.

He released the alpha, who growled at us one last time before loping mildly into the jungle along with the rest of the tribe.

The savage helped me to my feet.

"How goes it, Emperor?"

"Could be better," I replied. "Glad you could make it."

The savage didn't smile. It wasn't in his nature. He clasped me on the shoulder and nodded. "You'll have to forgive my people. They are rarely gracious hosts."

Zala stumbled into view.

"Good of you to join us," I said. "May I introduce Kreegah the Merciless. My man on the inside."

With Kreegah and Snarg escorting us through the jungle, the journey was much smoother. The diminutive but powerful Jupitorn spoke rarely. His trained senses focused on the environment, scanning for any threat.

"I would have been here sooner," he said, "but I was closer to the other skyship."

"Did you find my battleguard?" asked Zala.

"I found some people. They looked like you. Several were dead."

"But not all?"

"No, there were still living among them. I told them to stay where they were until I could come back for them. They had weapons. If they wait for me, they should be fine."

Kreegah tilted his head at Zala. He blinked his large blue eyes.

"Did I do something wrong?"

Zala shrugged. "No, but couldn't you have brought them with you?"

"They were too slow. If I'd waited for them, you would be dead by now."

He sniffed the air. He sprang through the canopy and disappeared. We waited for his return.

"How did a Jupitorn end up here?" asked Zala.

"It's difficult to know for sure," I replied. "I've seen the ship that brought him here. A pleasurecraft. It must have had drive problems. Possibly the gravity well caught them unaware. Wrong place, wrong time. Whatever the reason, the craft crashed onto Dinosaur Island roughly forty years ago. All the passengers must have been killed upon impact or fallen victim to the jungle. Except for one hatchling, adopted by a primadon female and raised as her own. Even then, he would've died if not for his superior strength and adaptability."

"I've never seen one with such a fully developed carapace."

"My guess is that the island's radiation triggered dormant genes while still in the egg."

"And he lives here?"

Kreegah dropped behind us, landing with barely a rustle. Zala jumped. She did her best to hide it.

"Where else would I live?"

Before she could answer the question, he held up his hand.

"You should be quiet now."

Something thumped through the underbrush. It had the throaty respiration of a full-grown stegosauroid, a dim-witted but easily startled beast, but when it shrieked, it sounded more like a siamotyrannus. We didn't see it, and it passed without noticing us.

We made it to Kreegah's home just as night was falling. It

was never dark on the island, only an emerald twilight. The flora glimmered with faint light visible when the sun went down, and the radioactive sky shimmered.

He lived in a small mountain. In the dim green glow, it was difficult to spot the shape of a Jupitorn pleasurecraft covered in moss and vines. Kreegah rolled a moss-covered boulder from an old airlock.

He said, "Wait in here. If your friends are still alive, I'll bring them back."

After we were gone, he sealed the entrance.

"What if something happens to him?" asked Zala. "How are we supposed to get out of here?"

I ignored the question. Jupitorn craftsmanship meant the interior still had a few working lights. Kreegah had also taken to scattering luminescent grass on the floor. We moved down a corridor. There was a noticeable tilt in the floor, but nothing to slow us down. We reached the bridge, where the emergency lights cast a soft yellow glow that mixed with the green of the grass to cast sparkling emerald hues on the walls. Most of the consoles and terminals were broken. A few creeping vines and stubborn roots had pried cracks in the hull and a thin layer of dust covered everything. Bones of all shapes and sizes littered the floor, and judging by the way Zala winced, the place probably had quite an unpleasant odor. Sealed in my exo, I was spared that experience.

"He lives like an animal," she said.

"Oh, I don't know," I replied. "I'd say he's done very well for himself, all things considered."

She sat in a chair, gently at first for fear of its snapping with decay. "He doesn't belong here. You should take him home, Emperor."

"I've offered. He's not interested."

"So we're staying here for the night then?" she asked.

"You don't want to be out in that jungle at night," I said. "There are... things out there."

"There were things out there earlier."

"These are different things," I replied. "Worse things."

She passed the next hour checking and double-checking her weapons. When I suggested she take off her armor and make herself comfortable, she dismissed the notion. I amused myself studying a sample of grass.

"You can't stop it, can you?" said Zala.

"Stop what?"

"Analyzing and studying and thinking. It's a compulsion with you."

I paused to note the energy yield of the sample. "You make it sound like a bad thing."

"For you, it is. You've already probably managed to think of twelve ways to use that grass for some nefarious scheme."

I laughed. "You flatter me, Zala. I'm not that good. It's only six so far." My exo beeped as it added more data. "Oh, seven."

She pointed her rifle at me. "Wrath of my gods be damned, I should kill you right here."

"And only five of these uses could be classified as *nefarious*," I said. "The sixth and seventh are merely *morally dubious*."

She lowered the weapon, placing it across her lap. Her eyes glinted, two pinpoints in the dark. Her scales caught the peculiar lights, and she almost glowed herself.

She continued to polish her gun until Kreegah returned. He had only three Venusians with him.

"Where are the rest?" she asked.

"Dead," replied one of her soldiers. "Some were killed in the crash. The rest we lost when we ventured into the jungle to find you. We were able to fend off the creatures until night. Then something came out of nowhere and carried off several of the others."

"I warned them," said Kreegah.

"We were following protocol," said the soldier.

"Protocol is for people without common sense," I said softly to myself.

Zala glared. "We wouldn't even be here if you hadn't led us into an ambush."

"You're free to abandon this misguided bodyguard mission anytime you want."

There was a moment of silence. I couldn't know what Zala was thinking, but I assumed it was something about honor or justice or some variation of them.

As for me, I wasn't certain how I felt about the idea. I'd grown fond of Zala over the years. I didn't have many friends, and while our relationship had always been tinged by a few past misunderstandings, there was something reassuring about having her around. In a chaotic equation, she was among the constants. It was nice to have something to rely on.

She gave her remaining battleguard permission to relax. They found places to sit and check their equipment. Like good soldiers. There was something comforting about that too. They were woefully underequipped for the threats of Dinosaur Island but were still determined to make the most of what they had. I enjoyed their optimism.

"We'll be safe here until morning," said Kreegah. "Care for something to eat?"

He bent down, grabbed an unidentifiable slab of raw meat, and presented it to us.

"I can't eat Terran foodstuffs," I replied.

"Oh, yes. I forgot about that. Perhaps the Venusians would like a piece?" He tore strips of flesh and offered it to each. They accepted.

Snarg eagerly swayed and clicked at Kreegah. He laughed and threw her a few pounds of rotting flesh. Squealing with delight, she skittered over to a corner to tear into her dinner.

Zala and her soldiers removed cylindrical devices from their belts. It hummed as they waved it under the meat.

"What's that for?" asked Kreegah.

"It cooks and purifies," she said.

He gave her a curious look. "Why would you do that?"

"To avoid contaminants, parasites, and the like."

Kreegah took a big bite of his raw dinner. "But the parasites are the best part."

Snarg chirped her agreement as she crunched into tasty bone.

"Venusian biology is... delicate," I said.

He nodded, chewing and wiping his greasy hands on his thighs.

"Where did you learn to speak?" she asked. "Did Emperor teach you?"

"The computer taught me."

He pushed a button. It took several presses to get a response. The only working screen crackled to life, the lighting went blue, and a klaxon sounded.

"Attention," said a static-filled voice. "Attention. Unauthorized life-forms identified aboard bridge. Unauthorized—"

Something shorted, and the blue switched off. The klaxon attempted to continue, but only came out as a muted bass thumping.

Kreegah pushed the button several more times. The blue came back. The computer sounded its warning.

"Intrusion acknowledged," he said. "Authorized visitors." This satisfied the computer. It returned the lighting to normal once again, and the bass thump disappeared.

"Hello," said the computer.

After a few moments, when we didn't reply, it repeated itself.

"Hello."

"Greetings," said Zala, taking pity on the underpowered device.

"Hello." The computer's voice squealed. Zala covered her ears.

"You remember Emperor and Snarg, don't you, computer?" asked Kreegah.

Deep in its core, the computer processed the question. Wisps of smoke rose from its cracked screen.

"Emperor Mollusk and Ultrapede Snarg identified. Hello, Emperor."

"Hello, computer," I replied.

The machine shrieked an ultrasonic greeting to Snarg, who stopped eating just long enough to bat her milky yellow eyes and shriek back.

"I am Zala of the—"

"Please designate unidentified life-form."

Zala tried again, but the computer cut her off, demanding designation.

"I'm trying to supply designation," said Zala. "If you'd just let me—"

"Designation, please."

"Zala of the Venusian—"

"Designation, please."

"Zala of—"

"Designation, please."

"You stupid malfunctioning piece of technology—"

"Unacceptable levels of hostility detected. Deploying pacification."

A panel in a wall opened very, very slowly. By all rights, it shouldn't have worked at all, but it was able, after several seconds of determined creaking, squealing, and cracking, to part and allow a pair of hovering robotic security devices to list clumsily into the bridge. One of the robots only made it a few feet before it popped, caught fire, and fell to the floor. The second managed to reach Zala. It extended a small prod and jabbed her in the shoulder. There was a tiny spark, but not enough to warrant a response from a hardened Venusian warrior.

"Unidentified hostile life-form pacified," said the computer with just a hint of self-satisfaction.

The robot then chugged its way back to the panel, where it quietly deactivated. The panel creaked and groaned its way closed.

"Designation, please."

Zala sighed.

The computer made a grinding, whirring noise.

"Designation assigned: Zala."

The computer snapped off.

"She's not what she used to be," explained Kreegah, "but she was functional enough to give me an education."

"Then you know where you come from?" asked Zala. "Where your home is."

"This is my home. Jupiter is a planet I don't even remember."

"And you don't want to go back there?"

"Why would I?"

"But it's your origin, where you belong."

"I wasn't raised on Jupiter. I only know what the computer has shown me about it. But I would be a savage on that world, a thing to be pitied and mocked. Here, I'm happy. I don't belong on Jupiter."

"But don't you get lonely?"

"I'm too busy surviving to be lonely," he replied. "And I have the computer and my adopted people to keep me company. Why would I need anything else?"

"But there's more to life than surviving," she said.

"Like what?" asked Kreegah, genuinely interested.

"Like honor and service."

"I'm unaware of these concepts. The computer has never mentioned them, and they've never come up among my people."

"Because your people are uncivilized beasts."

She paused.

"I'm sorry. That was disrespectful."

"Was it? You were just saying what you were thinking. Is that considered rude? But isn't that honest? Is honesty less important than respect? Is deceit a part of honor?"

"No, but I didn't mean to offend you."

"But I'm not offended. I'm more troubled by lies than by truth. In the tribe, if one member doesn't like another, they say so. Then they fight until the matter is settled. To the death, if necessary. Are you saying you don't like me? Though I'm not offended, I will fight you if that's what your honor demands."

She said, "No, you misunderstand me."

Kreegah nodded. "I see. If I've offended you, then should we fight?"

"I don't want to fight you."

"I'm afraid I don't understand honor then. It seems... ridiculous, a way to be offended by others and to offend others."

"No, it's not like that. It's complicated."

"I've heard this before," said Kreegah. "It seems to be a word people use to avoid explaining something. Perhaps I'm too uncivilized to be offended."

Zala hesitated. They weren't easy questions, and I doubt she'd thought much about them in the past. Venusian warrior society wasn't given to philosophy.

"I wouldn't know about that," I replied. "I'm civilized and don't understand it myself."

She snorted, mumbling to herself.

"Don't mind her. She thinks I'm a criminal."

"You are a criminal."

"Depends on who you ask," I said.

"Who could I ask that would not consider you a dangerous menace?"

"The Terrans like me."

"Only because you've brainwashed them."

"A technicality. It's not as if I'm imposing my will on them anymore. They're free to go about their lives."

"You can't just decide not to be a criminal, Emperor," said Zala.

"Why not?"

"Because that's... because..." Her gray brow furrowed, and she frowned. "Because it doesn't work that way. You have to pay for your crimes."

"Even if I'm no longer doing them?"

"You can't just wave a tentacle and pardon yourself from all your past sins."

"Sure, I can. As a matter of fact, that was one of my last acts as Supreme Warlord. Remind me to show you the document sometime. It's on official government stationery and everything."

Zala sighed.

The ship rumbled as a tremor shook the island.

"The island has been shaking at night. Ever since the other one came," said Kreegah. "My people fear it. They say the new tribe has enraged the volcano. But now that you're here, Emperor, I can tell them not to fear."

"What's this other one look like?" Zala asked.

"He's small. Like Emperor. And uses robots and creatures to do his work."

"A Neptunon?"

Kreegah shook his head. "No, I've only seen him from far, but he isn't like Emperor."

The ground quaked.

"This shouldn't be happening," I said. "Not unless someone has tampered with the stabilizing unit. But without the stabilizer, the anomaly could collapse into a singularity that could endanger this planet and eventually the whole system."

"Endanger how?"

"Black hole how," I replied.

"That's bad."

"Very bad. We should probably do something about it," I agreed. "Well, good night."

"Are you mad, Emperor? You're going to sleep now?"

"No, I'm not going to sleep. I don't need to. But you really should because we have a big day tomorrow, and you'll be no good to me tired. In the meantime, I'll be studying this."

I held up the node I'd taken from the jelligantic that I'd been storing in an exo compartment.

"What's that?" asked Zala.

"Possibly something important," I said. "Or just something I think is important. I'll know after I take a closer look."

The screws holding the blackened, half-melted node together were melted and blackened. I used a laser to carefully cut it open. The internal circuitry was damaged, but oddly, it didn't look like they'd ever been switched on in the first place. I began disassembling the unit, laying out the parts on a clear spot on a console.

I gave Snarg the ultrasonic command to rest. She found a dark corner to curl up in. Kreegah plopped into an old chair and was immediately asleep. He could sleep or wake on a moment's notice. Such was the requirement of his life.

Zala, despite her protests, understood this too. An exhausted soldier was a liability, and she'd slept on her fair share of battlefields.

"I understand that it annoys you to be at the mercy of an

inhospitable situation with only me to guide you," I said. "But you'll get used to it."

She glowered. "I don't take orders from you."

"Don't think of it as an order. Think of it as a helpful suggestion from someone who should be in charge by default. Unless you think you know the best way to avoid a space-time disaster from consuming the galaxy. In which case, you're more than welcome to rush headlong into the night by yourself."

"I thought you said the threat was limited to the system."

"Did I? Let's hope so. I'll keep my tentacles looped."

Zala shook her head. "You enjoy tormenting me, don't you?"

"I'll admit to some small pleasure."

Dinosaur Island quaked its approval.

EXTERMINATING TOPEKA

Mutant insects were eating Kansas.

Again.

My saucer and its fleet of automated fighters waged war with the giant creatures. Huge radioactive hornets engaged in dogfights through the streets of Topeka while forty-foot fire ants belched flames, setting anything and everything ablaze.

It wasn't as devastating as it might first appear. This was the fifth attack in as many weeks. The citizens of Topeka hadn't moved back into their city after the second. Nor had they started repairs on the ruins. There wasn't much left of the city to destroy at this point. Which meant that if I didn't stop the insects here and now, they'd probably march on in search of more appealing hunting grounds. From there, they'd spread across the globe.

But the real danger of the bugs wasn't in their ascendance to dominance, but in the radioactive waste left in their wake. It was even more difficult to contain than the insects, and if enough of it contaminated the water supply and air, the native Terran life-forms were due a painful death.

I'd rather not have my reign over Terra end with her as an unlivable wasteland. Though if the Terrans went extinct, they wouldn't be around to hold it against me, and the rest of the system already considered me an irredeemable criminal. So it wasn't as if I had to worry about damage to my reputation.

But it would've still been a lousy way to end my warlordship.

Several jumping spiders pounced on my saucer. I pushed a button and electrocuted them. A praying mantis snatched a fighter out of the air and devoured it in three bites. The ship self-destructed, blowing off the mantis's head. I blasted the tide of fire ants, but there were more.

There were always more.

I couldn't help but think myself somewhat responsible for keeping this doomsday from happening, and it probably had something to do with the fact that the bugs were an unintended consequence of my own entomological research. My design had been some genetic tweaking, the creation of a new breed of insect that could excrete a useful power source as a backup should the molluskotrenic ever fail. A simple splice of some Mercurial queen wasp genetic material in a few native species. A carefully controlled experiment until a few ants escaped into the wild.

I still didn't know what caused the gigantism. The Mercurial insects weren't this large. But some of science's best discoveries came from happy accidents. I was ever optimistic that this research could be salvaged. Though at the moment, I was more concerned with keeping it contained.

While my automated tanks and fighters waged their battle, I hovered over the city, scanning it block by block. There had to be a queen to this insect empire, a prime carrier to infect the other creatures. There always was. Every time before, I'd destroyed the queen and hoped that was the end of the problem. It had yet to take.

If it didn't work this time, I'd have to vaporize the state.

My sensors pinged, detecting unusually high levels of radioactivity. It had to be the prime queen's nest. My research suggested that she was likely to be a vast, virtually immobile creature whose sole function was to spit out the mutagenic contagion. The swarm would defend her to the death, but they were outgunned. And once the prime was gone, it would be easy to clean up the mess.

The nest was under a building barely standing. I toppled it with a blast and then used a tractor beam to clear away the rubble. The buzzing of the insects grew angrier. My defense forces kept them at bay while I dug deeper.

A sonic shriek rattled the air as a geyser of dust kicked up. Sensors went wild. A shadow blotted out the sky. The prime queen was seven times the size of my own craft. And she was unhappy.

She was also far from immobile. She was too massive to fly with her vestigial wings, but her three pairs of legs worked. A volley of rockets exploded against her natural armor plating, inflicting some minor wounds. She barfed up a ball of slime that I weaved under. It exploded against the ground with tremendous force. At least the energy source idea had proven viable.

She spit a stream of unstable mucus across a row of tanks, destroying them in a burst of flames. She hunched over. Orifices along her back sprayed the air with a hundred pellets. Bugs and fighters alike disintegrated under the indiscriminate attack. My saucer shields absorbed the brunt of the force, but they wouldn't hold up to another.

The queen turned her attention toward me, the only thing still flying after her blitz. She scuttled forward with surprising speed, but I flew up and out of her reach. The enraged prime shrieked as she belched round after round. I dropped my payload of rockets and bombs on the creature, then burned out my pulsar and blaster cannons. The queen was wounded but showed no sign of falling.

Finally, I got the creature to spit straight up. Gravity did the rest. Her mucus struck her between her multitude of eyes, and her head exploded. She stumbled through the city another three hours, rampaging blindly in the ruins, before succumbing to her injuries.

The Terrans already had banners and a parade at the ready as I set my saucer down outside the city limits. I stepped out to the sounds of much rejoicing. Reporters pushed microphones at me.

One asked, "Lord Mollusk, how does it feel to have saved the city of Topeka for the fifth time?"

"Perhaps saved *isn't the right word," I replied.*

"Nonetheless, the people of Terra are indebted to you once again. Surely, you must feel a sense of tremendous pride. Or are you simply too humble to realize how amazing you are?"

"I'll get back to you on that."

I approached the podium. A hushed awe fell over the crowd.

"That should do it, everyone," I said. "I'd probably wait another week or two before starting any serious rebuilding. Just to be on the cautious side. Now if you'll excuse me..."

My exo communicator beeped.

"Excuse me one moment. I need to take this."

The voice on the other end said, "Lord Mollusk, we've lost China."

"Define lost.*"*

"It's not there anymore, sir."

"Well, that's no good, is it?" I said.

"No, sir. We thought you should know."

"Yes, I'll look into it. Mollusk out."

"Hail Lord Mollusk!" shouted the voice in the speaker.

"Hail Mollusk," I agreed quietly.

I waved good-bye to the crowd and boarded my saucer.

I did end up finding China, though getting it back from the transdimensional cat people who stole it was almost more trouble than it was worth.

Zala awoke to find me hunched over a console.

"One second," I said. "I'm almost done here."

I used the spot welder in my exo's fingertip to finish a final repair, then closed the panel.

"I'll need you to throw that switch over there when I give you the signal." I pointed to a jury-rigged circuit breaker by her on the wall.

She folded her arms and glared. "You can't command me like one of your robotic drones, Emperor, and just expect me to jump to your bidding."

"I'll need you to throw that switch over there when I give you the signal... please."

She noticed the patchwork repair job, exposed wires, and rerouted systems I'd been up to while she slept.

"What did you do?"

"Got bored," I replied. "Did some repairs."

"Why?"

"Why not?"

"I would've thought the node, which may or may not be important, would've kept you busy."

"It wasn't. Only took me forty minutes to see that it didn't work. There was no data in it."

"Not important then."

"I wouldn't say that," I replied. "There were a few peculiar components in it. Things that seemed unnecessary, though considering it wasn't being used, the whole device could be considered unnecessary. But I saved the parts that seemed uniquely out of place."

"Why?"

"Why not?"

Zala grunted. "That's not an answer."

"It's the best answer I have at the moment."

She appraised the mess of wires I was working on. "I'm surprised you didn't wake me."

"I'm a quiet worker."

"I don't care how smart you are, you can't take a decayed derelict spaceship buried under the ground for decades and make it functional."

"Well, I'm very smart," I said. "And anyone can fix something when they have all the parts. You don't need a genius for that. Just a skilled worker. But taking half of a broken computer and turning it into something useful...that takes talent." I examined a few more systems. "Is there some morally questionable dilemma I've failed to notice from fixing an old computer? Because if there is, I'm sure you can't wait to tell me."

"No, there's nothing wrong with it," she said. "Although if you're doing it, I do have some suspicion that it could be wrong in some manner."

"You wound me, Zala. Not everything I do has a sinister purpose. Actually, nothing I do has a sinister purpose because *sinister* implies *deceptive*. And I'm never that. I'm up front about what I've done, and I was mostly up front when I did it."

"Mostly," she said.

"You can't conquer a world without lying or the occasional half-truth. At least, I haven't devised a realistic plan to do so, and if I can't think of it, then it's unlikely. But I do like to think I keep my deceptions to a minimum."

She glanced around the dim room. "Where is my battle-guard?"

I nodded toward another chamber. She marched over there to find her loyal soldiers locked in stasis. She came back with her scimitar drawn.

"That would be a lot more threatening if you didn't pull it out at every opportunity," I said.

"What did you do to them?"

"Saved them from a death by radiation poisoning," I replied. "I apologize if that was too presumptuous on my part."

"They wouldn't have just allowed you to stick them in those pods."

"Oh, I wouldn't hold it against their honor. I waited until they were too sick to put up much of a fight. One of them, the female, did give me a kick. Considering she could barely breathe, that's probably worth a commendation or something.

Bravery in the face of foolish shortsightedness or something. I assume there's such an award on Venus, though it probably has a less accurate name."

"Let them out."

"Let them out yourself." I paused twisting wires. "Without protection, they'll be dead in a matter of hours. I can't claim to understand all the nuances of your particular warrior code, so I leave it to you to decide if a pointlessly agonizing death is part of it."

Zala put away her sword. Her tail swished in sharp, annoyed snaps. "Will they be well?"

"Eventually. I had to retrofit the stasis pods to cleanse radiation and repair the cellular damage. It's a patchwork job, but if the process is uninterrupted, they should be fine in nine or ten days."

"That's too long."

"They're in stasis. It'll be like a light nap for them."

She put her hand on her scimitar but didn't draw. She chewed her lip. Her scales darkened.

"And before you ask," I said, "no, the pod won't transform them into mind-controlled slaves. Or implant self-destruct codes in their DNA. Or turn them into living bombs. Or transform them into cannibals. Or give them an embarrassing stutter. Or any other crazy, inane evil thing you're about to accuse me of."

She relaxed, though her version of relaxed always struck me as only marginally less tense, but maybe that was only while around me. "You could've asked me first."

"I didn't think I'd need permission to save lives. And I was hoping to avoid a long, unnecessary conversation about it. The kind we just had. You're welcome."

Zala's lips barely moved as she forced a grunt through them. It was the closest I would get to a thank-you.

I connected one last wire. "On my count, I need you to throw that switch. If you would be so kind."

She threw the switch. The lights went out, and the glowing green grass kept the bridge from becoming pitch black. I sorted through the multicolored tangle before me.

"Aha." Zala chuckled. "So even the incredible Emperor Mollusk has to accept his limits."

"Your obsession with my failures borders on obsessive. I never claimed to be perfect. Merely brilliant."

"So now you're only *merely* brilliant."

"Being brilliant isn't difficult for me," I said. "Most Neptunons could do what I've done. Perhaps without the grace and aplomb that I so effortlessly incorporate, but it hardly matters. In the end, all that matters are results."

I twisted a red wire in the colorful tangle of cables sitting before me. The bridge lights snapped on. The ship's computer crackled to life. I hadn't been able to fix the speakers, and a bit of feedback screeched as the computer spoke.

"Hello, Emperor. How may I help you?"

"I'll need a general scan of everything within thirty miles," I said. "In just a moment."

I performed a few small adjustments on the improved sensor array I'd cobbled together from spare parts. I gave a squeaked order to Snarg. She skittered over from her corner to take the array in her pincers and dashed outside. The cable spooled out behind her. It would stop when she found a sufficiently high perch.

"Where is Kreegah?" asked Zala.

"He went out at dawn. I'm having him run a few errands."

She used her purifier on some less rancid meat to make her breakfast. "Aren't you hungry, Emperor?"

"I can go for weeks without eating."

"Don't eat. Don't sleep. Aren't you the veritable superbeing?"

"Actually, I do sleep. Just not my entire brain at once. Only a small percentage at any one time."

"How convenient for you."

The cable stopped. I ordered the computer to perform the scan.

"Pity you couldn't fix the monitors," said Zala.

"I was able to improvise a work-around."

A hologram of the island projected at our feet.

"I apologize for the monochrome. Best I could do with what I had to work with."

"Didn't you say the island's radiation made detailed scans impossible?"

"Not if you know what you're scanning for. My previous experience with the space-time anomaly gave me a jumping-off point. You'll excuse the imprecise nature of the measurements."

I pointed to a blip. "This is us. And this..."—I indicated a second blip in the northern tip of the island—"this is the heart of the anomaly. It's at the base of the volcano, where the tear in space-time is geographically tethered. My research on the anomaly was unable to yield the secrets for closing it, but I was able to stabilize it."

I highlighted a few ripples in the hologram.

"Time distortion isn't much different than gravity manipulation when you get right down to it. As you can see by these radiating deformations in the graviton spread, you'll no doubt observe a noticeably stronger wave here indicating—"

"Yes, I can see the thing with the thing on the thing. And I'm sure it means something very important. Why don't you just tell me what that is?"

"Time travel."

"You have a way to travel through time?"

"My own experiments proved that this was impossible. The anomaly only works one way. Any matter from this universe, aside from a few exotic subatomic particles, is instantly destroyed if it attempts to move backward in time, as we traditionally measure such things."

"Maybe someone has figured out something you haven't."

"Possibly," I said. "Or more likely they're poking the universe in the eye without thinking of the consequences. In either case, we need to put an end to whatever misguided experiment they're performing and restore the anomaly to constancy."

The computer asked, "Would you like me to commence further analysis of the pattern?"

"Do that." I rotated the hologram to study it from a different angle. "You might want to brace yourself, Zala. We can expect a minor quake now."

The island shuddered. It shook loose some dirt, and the lights flickered.

"We should be fine for the next few hours, though I'm estimating complete collapse in six hours."

"Complete? What does that mean?"

"An excellent question," I replied. "Could be anything, really."

"Define *anything.*"

"The anomaly could repair itself, leaving Dinosaur Island permanently stabilized. Or it could lead to the eventual collapse of the universe. That's a worst-case scenario, mind you. And it's really not that bad because it would take a few billion years to complete the task. We'd be killed instantly, of course. As would everything within several light-years."

"And Venus? What about Venus?"

"I'm less concerned with the planet than our own predicament."

"There are billions of lives at stake, Emperor."

"I'm aware. And if I'm killed then it's unlikely I'll be able to solve the problem. Ergo, my life is rather important."

"I trust you have a plan," she said.

"I'm working on one. I'm sure I'll have something soon. Something with antigravity. Or possibly lasers. I do enjoy working with lasers."

"Whatever you can come up with, Emperor. Just make it quick."

I grinned.

"What is it now?"

"It's funny, isn't it? You're so eager to place your trust in my scientific genius now."

"That's not funny. It's a situational demand, and I'm not eager. Or even very happy about it, but a warrior adapts to her situation." She slung her weapons over her shoulder. "I trust you're ready to go."

"Almost."

I welded the casing shut on a small device, gave it a quick double check.

"What's that?" she asked.

"Portable weather machine I invented last night with a few leftover parts. Might come in handy." I secured it via a magnet on my hip. "Did I mention I was bored?"

"Good luck, Emperor," said the ship's computer. "I will relay any important information my analysis determines."

"Thanks."

We exited the access tube to the surface. Yellow clouds churned in the glowing green skies.

"I don't see your Jupitorn savage anywhere," said Zala.

"Did you look behind you?" I asked.

She turned.

Kreegah waved. "Hello."

"You really shouldn't do that," she said.

"Do what?"

"Sneak up on people."

"Sorry. It's a habit. I thought I was being quite obvious. I'll try to make more noise if that would relax you."

She grumbled.

"Did I do something wrong?" Kreegah asked me.

"No, she's just out of her element and grumpy about it."

"Should I apologize?"

"That would be ill advised," I replied. "Better to just leave it alone."

"I see."

"You'd have to be civilized to get it," I said.

Kreegah nodded. It was all the explanation he needed. Of all the beings in this universe, I liked Kreegah the most. He was without guile, good-natured but merciless to his enemies. Some might mistake his lack of sophistication for stupidity, but Kreegah was the rarest of creatures, a being perfectly fitted for his world. I envied him. All my brilliance had yet to solve that most universal of desires.

He unleashed a howl, beating his chest. His armored skin echoed with a deep bass thump. The ground trembled. It wasn't another earthquake. A hecteratops burst through the foliage. Zala pointed her rifle at it. The dinosaur lowered its head and focused all eight of its eyes on her. It thumped the earth with its six legs, flapped its great feathered wings, and its scales shifted to a threatening shade of red.

"Unless you want to get stepped on," I said, "you'll probably want to lower your weapon."

The hecteratops brayed. It shook the rattle on the end of its tail.

Kreegah put his hand on the end of the dino's snout. He playfully tugged at the two horns on the dino's nose, and he bleated back.

"He will get us to the volcano much faster than on foot," said Kreegah. "Much safer too. Few predators on the island want any part of Old Broot."

The hecteratops bull snorted, stamping the ground with earth-shaking force.

"I don't see how we're going to sneak up on anyone riding this thing," said Zala.

"Sometimes, it's good to sneak," answered Kreegah. "And sometimes, it's better to be heard coming."

"Shock and awe." Zala grinned. "That's something I can get behind."

Kreegah offered to help her get on the bull's back, but she insisted on doing it herself. It took her several minutes to scale the massive creature. She managed to grab hold of one wing and hoist herself into position. Kreegah gave his customary *I don't understand* expression. I gave my customary *You're better off not understanding* look, and used my rocketpack to boost to a seat ahead of Zala.

"Where's your pet?" she asked me.

"Did you look behind you?" I replied.

Snarg squealed and playfully wrapped her pincers around Zala's head. She pushed the ultrapede away.

"You should be nicer to her," I told Zala. "She likes you."

"You'll excuse me if I don't want drool rusting my helmet." She tried to clean the slime sticking to her armor.

"She was coating you with a waxy resin that hardens with the tensile strength of titanium. It dries very quickly, but I guess you just found that out."

Zala tried and failed to remove her hands from the helmet she held. I sprayed a neutralizing agent on the resin, and she was able to pry her sticky hands free.

"It's a sign of affection."

She scowled at Snarg, who batted her milky yellow eyes and cooed.

Kreegah howled again. Several primadons lumbered into view.

"I've told my people that Emperor Mollusk has said that the future of this island and all the islands beyond the sea are at stake. They don't understand. I'm not sure I do either. But the braver males have agreed to venture with us to the mountain of fire."

He barked a few orders to the tribe, and they disappeared back into the jungle. Kreegah vaulted onto Old Broot's back, and with one more primal roar, the hecteratops rotated. The dinosaur wasn't agile, and the extra legs weren't cooperative. But once Broot managed to turn around, he plunged into the forest with a burst of speed.

The island zipped by in a blur. We crouched low, clinging to Broot's back to avoid getting thrown off our lurching mount or knocked aside by the whipping branches. I didn't try to absorb any details from the journey, trusting in Kreegah's expertise the way he trusted in mine.

The jungle parted, and we lumbered through a swampy clearing. A herd of telekinetic iguanodons scattered and levitated out of our way, which was a good thing, considering Old Broot wasn't interested in stopping. A Chinese junk mired in the muck (a relic from some forgotten adventure) wound up in our path, and rather than go around it, the hecteratops plowed through, trampling the ship and long-dead sailor bones beneath his hooves.

The yellow clouds glittered with strange colors, and a B-52 Stratofortress pierced the churning veil. The plane plummeted from the sky to crash on the far side of the island.

I checked the latest readings from the computer scan. "It's getting worse."

"I thought you said we had hours," shouted Zala over the thunder and howling winds.

"Time is relative, and the closer we get to the anomaly, the quicker it passes. Relatively. Hours can become minutes as we approach the focal point."

The island quaked and a chasm opened in front of us.

Clumsy Old Broot barely avoided falling into it, but tripped, burying his snout in the dirt. I was thrown to the ground and by the time I stopped tumbling, I was just glad I hadn't been crushed beneath the hecteratops's bulk.

Zala, Kreegah, Snarg, and even Old Broot were nowhere to be seen. The island was quiet. The skies were cloudy but calmer. A quick scan of the data confirmed that I had fallen into a temporal distortion, a pocket of displaced time. It was like going to Mars by staying where you were and having the planet come to you. Zala and Kreegah must've been minutes, maybe hours, in the relative past. Possibly days or years.

I needed to find the edge of the phenomenon, either temporal or spatial, to escape it. The result would snap me back in sync with proper space-time alignment. This was only a hypothesis, but my own studies in theoretical time manipulation had suggested this possibility. Admittedly, I was more of a time travel hobbyist, but there was nothing like a little practical field observation.

I obviously hadn't stayed put otherwise I would've been waiting for me in the clearing before the pocket hit. I could stick around and see if it would be possible to create a paradox. As appealing as that sounded, it came fraught with peril by causality, and while under normal circumstances, challenging the space-time continuum sounded like fun, I had a planet to save.

I rocketed into the air, sticking close to the trees. It afforded me some degree of stealth, on the chance that it was warranted. Exo sensors guided me to the anomaly, although I didn't need them. It was exactly where I'd left it, at the southwestern base of Dinosaur Island's turbulent volcano. My attempts at sneakiness were rendered pointless when a flock of pterodactyls flanked me. An unusually large specimen with the striped fur pattern of a tiger spoke to me.

"So good of you to join us, Emperor," it said. Rather, the speaker built into the apparatus strapped to its back said it. "We've been expecting you."

He gave the other winged reptiles an ultrasonic command. They shrieked. Their laser-projecting eyes flashed, waiting for the kill sign.

"I trust you won't try anything foolish." The lead pterodactyl was incapable of expression, but since its face was always a terrifying scowl of teeth, it matched the threat very well.

"I assume you're not here to kill me or you'd have done it already," I said.

"You assume correctly. Come along, Emperor. And do play nice."

They escorted me to the volcano. As we drew closer, the clouds grew more violent. The island's trembling worsened. I detected the sudden data input of the Jupitorn ship I'd repaired earlier, confirming that I was in the past. Perhaps only a half hour from the point where I'd lost Zala and Kreegah. I was on my own until then.

We landed in a clearing around my stabilizer, a device that took up most of the volcano's southwest side. Two dozen robotic workers marched about completing tasks. Someone had modified the stabilizer with a few components added here and there. And there was a machine the size of a great horned reef shark positioned beside the shimmering distortion.

Even at its most agitated, the anomaly was mostly invisible. Sometimes, at the right time of year under the right conditions, it would glow soft red. It took a lot of science to pry open space-time. The machine sparked and smoked. The robots sprayed it down with coolant to keep it from exploding.

The striped pterodactyl landed beside me. “Impressive, isn’t it?”

“How did you correct for the tachyon feedback?” I asked.

“There will be time enough for questions. First allow me to change into something more practical.”

Worker robots brought over a lumbering tyrannosauridae with an apparatus similar to the pterodactyl’s wired on its back.

The mesmersaurus was the apex predator on the island. I’d catalogued only one specimen. An albertosaurus, smaller cousin to the more famous tyrannosaurus, it was a fat, sluggish beast. There were fiercer and stronger creatures, but the mesmersaurus didn’t need to be fast or crafty when all it had to do was wait for its prey to look into its third eye. Any animal would be rendered catatonic, helpless as the clumsy predator lumbered in for the kill.

Despite its impressive powers of mental dominance, the mesmersaurus was possessed of a single-minded stupidity. Hardly surprising, considering it fed itself mostly by waiting for something to look it in the eye.

“I suppose you’ll want me to surrender my weapons and deactivate my exo,” I said.

“That won’t be necessary.” The pterodactyl skulked over to the mesmersaurus. The apparatus opened, revealing a Terra Sapien brain encased in a clear spheroid. The spheroid extended several mechanical limbs and scuttled up the mesmersaurus’s tail to settle into the connection on its back. The apparatus buzzed. The mesmersaurus blinked, flexed the stubby fingers on its stubby arms. It arched its back in a stretch and clawed the ground with its hind legs.

The same voice issued from his speaker.

"So good to finally meet you, Emperor. Face to face."

The toothy dino turned its hypnotic eye in my direction.

I locked stares with the mesmersaurus's third eye, and a tingle ran through my nervous system. The tips of my tentacles went numb.

His teeth glinted. "Still with us, Emperor?"

"Funny thing about life on Neptune," I replied. "Hypnotic predators were all the rage at one point. All Neptunon life-forms are naturally resistant to psionic manipulation as a result."

The Brain shrugged the small shoulders of his borrowed body. "As I suspected. It doesn't make a difference though because you will work for me."

"I'm flattered," I said, "but I'm independently wealthy and not very good at taking orders, so I think I'll have to pass."

"Oh, but you haven't heard my offer."

"World domination."

He snarled.

I sighed. "It's always world domination."

"My purpose is so much greater. Why stop at a single world when we can rule the entire system? And from there... who knows? One day, the galaxy..."—he spread his tiny arms—"... no, the universe itself shall bow to our rule."

"You have ambition. I'll give you that."

He chuckled. "You doubt it's possible."

"Anything's possible," I said.

"Yes, yes," he replied. "If you only believe it bad enough and set your mind to it and work hard and blah blah blah. We've both heard that believe-in-yourself claptrap before, and we both know it for what it is. The wishful fantasies of lesser beings, of fools and idiots who think they can be more than the witless chattel they were destined to be."

He cackled. His attempts to wring his hands together failed due to the limitations of mesmersaurus anatomy.

"If you want some advice," I said, "you should probably try sparing the sinister laughter. It loses its punch after a while."

"Doesn't it bother you, Emperor, to walk among these pathetic Terran morons as if they were your equals? Don't tell me it doesn't because I know what it's like. I know the frustration and rage that builds up inside of you while you watch these irrational creatures bumble about in their wretched lives."

He trudged to me and bent down to look me in the face. "Don't tell me you've never thought it."

"Oh, I end up thinking that at least once a day. Usually several times a day."

"So you admit it then. Deep down, in your heart—"

"Neptunons don't have hearts. We circulate our blood via a system not unlike osmosis. Even if we had hearts, we'd avoid assigning them any functions outside of strict biological design. So you probably are trying to appeal to my basal ganglia."

The Brain rolled his eyes. "Very well. Deep down, in your basal ganglia, you know you are destined to rule over these—"

"The basal ganglia aren't in charge of perception. They're more of an action and inhibition system."

He glared. "You're trying my patience, Emperor."

"It's only fair," I replied, "seeing as how you're trying mine. I don't need to hear your offer. I'm not interested."

"You doubt my capabilities? You think I can't accomplish the unthinkable, achieve what no other being has managed? But history is full of great life-forms who have done the incredible because they dared to imagine what lesser creatures thought impossible."

"I didn't say I doubted. I said I wasn't interested."

He leaned in closer, having to tilt his jaws to one side to look me in the eye. "Where is your conqueror spirit, Emperor?"

"I'm over it."

He pulled away and performed a mock gasp. "Oh, you're reformed now. I keep forgetting."

"Not reformed. Retired."

"Is there a difference?"

"I'm not out to make amends for past sins. I couldn't give a damn about the past and the crimes, as some might label them, I've committed. I did what I did, and now, I don't do it anymore."

He grinned sinisterly. "You can't walk away from your destiny."

"I've never believed in destiny. My personal philosophy is one of feigned entropic denial."

"You can't change who you are."

"So everyone keeps telling me."

The island quaked. The volcano rumbled. The sky started to turn yellow again. All signals that the anomaly neared critical collapse.

"Do you want me to tell you that I think the universe is run by stupid beings?" I asked. "Fine. I think it. Do you want me to admit that I think things would be better if more worthy leadership was in charge? Yes on that too. Do I think that my time as Warlord of Terra, despite some tumultuous moments, left the planet better off than when I got here? Without a doubt.

"But even if I wanted to rule the universe, I don't see why it's necessary to team up with you to do so. You'd only get in my way. But none of that changes anything because I don't want to do it. I had my world domination fling. If you want to go out and conquer the universe, be my guest. Have at it. Just don't expect me to tag along."

The machine beside the anomaly exploded. Only a little. The shimmering hole in time turned a bright shade of orange, and a robot that was too close decayed into a pile of rusted parts within a few seconds. The other drones struggled to keep the machine in one piece.

"You should probably let me take a look at that before the galaxy implodes," I said.

He stepped aside. "By all means..."

The worker robots moved out of my way as I inspected the machine. "You've really gone and made a mess of things."

"Nothing you can't fix, I'm certain." He chuckled. "Don't you see, Emperor? You already work for me. It was your initial research into the anomaly that gave me the foundation to build the time-ray receiver. It was your genius that allowed me to unlock the secret of reverse time projection."

"You didn't unlock it," I said. "You stole it. From me."

He grumbled. "I'll admit that much of the groundwork was laid by you, but it was I who had the will and the vision to complete what you were too spineless to dare."

"You do realize that certain insults don't translate into invertebrate culture?" I asked.

He scowled. "You get the idea."

"I do. You've taken science you don't understand and are now making terrible mistakes with it."

"Listen to yourself. There are no limits to what science can accomplish in the right hands."

"Oh, I agree. I think we just disagree on who has the right hands."

The anomaly radiated a blast of heat and friction that nearly knocked the machine over. The Brain backed away a few steps.

"Nothing to be concerned about, I assure you," he said.

"Now that I'm here," I replied, "but you already knew that, didn't you?"

"Yes. The receiver works. It works! Once we removed a few needless safety features in your original design, we were able to accomplish the greatest feat of modern science. Communication through the very fabric of time itself! Can your limited imagination grasp the fantasticalness of this achievement?"

He laughed as the yellow-green skies seethed. Lightning flashed, and the volcano roared. I had to give him points for style, though I was too busy keeping the receiver from overloading and destroying the planet to appreciate the show.

"Has my violation of the feeble limits of knowledge rendered you mute with awe and terror, Emperor?"

"You wouldn't happen to have a wrench on you?" I asked.

A robot handed me a tool, and I smacked the trembling receiver until its shaking stopped.

"Sometimes, you just have to remind science who is boss," I explained. The machine rattled, but another whack quieted it to a dull roar. "It's all in the wrist actuator."

The robots brought me a variety of toolboxes, both reliable old favorites and cutting-edge devices, and I rummaged through them as the Brain watched.

"As for my limited imagination…haven't we established that this machine was invented by me? And, by the way, I prefer to call it an anti-time radio."

He nodded. "Yes, yes, you did create most of the basic design."

"Mmm-hmm. Not to be a jerk or anything, but what exactly did you add that improved it?"

"Lots of things," he said.

"Lots, you say?"

"They're mostly little things. But vitally important to make the machine, *the reverse temporal receiver*, work."

"Like removing the safety override that kept the *anti-time radio* from triggering singularities?"

"Yes." He nodded. "Things like that. It was that needless override that kept the *reverse temporal receiver* from working."

"Granted. But that was because I wasn't certain it was worth the peril of destroying the galaxy to get the *anti-time radio* operational. There are limits to even what I'll risk for science."

"And those limitations are your weakness, Emperor."

"I was Warlord of Terra," I reminded him.

"You were," he replied with a smug grin. "But you aren't anymore, are you?"

He had me there, so I instead focused on using a screwdriver and a handheld particle accelerator to keep the anti-time radio from melting into a pile of slag.

"You might be the most brilliant mind in the system," he said. "Next to mine, of course. But your refusal to risk everything means you can never accomplish what I will."

"Your genius coupled with your ruthlessness make you the superior being. I get it, and I'm not interested in debating the subject. I couldn't care less if you conquer the rest of the system. Have at it. It's all yours. But you won't do it with my science. Get your own. And you can't have Terra. I conquered it first. And even though I let it go, it's still mine in every way that counts."

"Oh my," he said. "Have you grown a soft spot for this little planet in that heart...osmosis-based circulatory system of yours?"

I turned from the machine. "I don't get this."

He smiled. "Do you need me to explain the finer workings of the device to you?"

"No, this"—I banged the machine—"this I get. I don't get what we're doing here. What is this conversation about?"

He smiled. "I'm taunting you."

"Why?"

His smile dropped. "Because it's part of how this is done. You're at my mercy, so now I taunt you. I subject you to a game of verbal cat and mouse until you have no choice but to admit I am your superior. Or maybe I am slowly peeling away the layers of your psyche to expose a mental weakness, some crippling vulnerability that I can exploit."

I thought back to the beginnings of my conqueror career. I had done some taunting then. It seemed so immature now, so self-indulgent.

"Or maybe you're wasting my time," I said.

The anti-time radio rattled, and I gave it a few smacks to calm it down.

"If you're going to conquer then just do it. There's no need for drawn-out speeches and veiled threats. Or at least aim those speeches at your minions and armies, if you insist. Although I always preferred robots, specifically for the reason that they didn't require any of that."

A robot handed me a tool, which I took.

"See? And I didn't even have to worry about thanking it."

I adjusted a few technical things on the anti-time radio while continuing to speak. "You're obsessed with conquering the universe, but you don't know why. Well, I'll tell you why. It's because you're an insecure little brain with an inferiority complex who can't think of a better way to get people to like you than to rule over them and force them to like you. Or at least pretend to like you.

"But even that won't be enough for you. Because you're not unhappy with the universe or the people in it. You'll never be happy. And I can empathize a little, but it doesn't mean I have to listen to you drone on and on about how incredible you are when it only demonstrates the differences between us and how you're not much different than the chattel you look down upon.

"And, yes, I'm aware of the irony of me saying this, so don't bother pointing it out. But consider it a warning because I've been where you're going, and I wish you better luck with it. Although I only mean that in a very general sense because I will stop you."

The dumbstruck Brain scowled. But at least he was quiet.

"I take it back," I said. "Maybe I do see the point in taunting sometimes. Now keep quiet and let me get back to work."

It took me fifteen minutes to convert the anti-time radio into a makeshift stabilizer. I had to jury-rig a few parts on the fly, but space-time repair via graviton manipulation was an art, an instinct. When it came to stuff like this, I usually relaxed and let my nervous system do the work. Thirty percent of Neptunon brain is distributed in little pockets here and there, and my primary and tertiary tentacles were pretty darn smart all on their own. My secondary tentacle was no slouch either, having once drawn up improvements for an exo while I slept. When a Neptunon hits the right rhythm, when every neuron is working in unison, it was a rare and beautiful thing. And repairing something as trivial as a hole in space-time was childishly simple.

The mesmersaurus watched me intently. He didn't dare ask questions, not wanting to own up to his ignorance, but every so often I'd explain what I was doing because it annoyed him. I found this very satisfying.

"Now I'm stabilizing the gravimetric waves via a series of timed proton bursts," I said.

"Obviously," said the mesmersaurus.

"And since we're dealing with anti-time here, of course we're using Quorg's Theorem on parallel universe convergence."

"An interesting choice."

"Granted, Quorg didn't take into account the hyper-time paradox proposed by Rusk, but in a situation like this, it's easier to just ignore that detail and trust it will work itself out on its own."

The Brain failed to completely cover the confused look on his host's face. He must have been woefully mystified to manage that with a dinosaur's limited powers of expression. He should've been, considering that Rusk's paradox had been resolved over a century ago. Trans-quantum physics humor always put a smile on my face.

The island shuddered as I turned one last dial. Then the anomaly became invisible again. The volcano went silent. The clouds drifted apart.

"That should do it," I said. "All I had to do was reverse the polarity. That fixes ninety percent of most superscience problems."

"Yes, a very fine job, Emperor."

I dropped the tools, leaving the robots to pick them up. "So now that I've prevented you from destroying the universe, would you tell me what you've learned about the future?"

"Surely, you can't expect me to reveal all my secrets."

"Why not? If you have knowledge of the future, if you were able to manipulate me to arrive at this time and place at the exact moment of your choosing, then what possible danger could I pose?"

The Brain waved his arm. "Well, that knowledge isn't absolute yet. You understand the nature of the process requires a sophisticated filtration and enhancement process to clarify it. This is an addition to my own coding measures to ensure that the messages would not be easily deciphered on the very unlikely event that someone with their own receiver intercepted the messages."

"A bit paranoid, but a wise precaution. So how much have you unscrambled?"

"Enough to get you here to repair the device. And a few more bits here and there. Things that would indeed intrigue you, Emperor, and no doubt soon will. But since I am the master of time, you have to admit that any resistance on your part would be pointless. Nothing can surprise me. No plan, no matter how clever you might think it is, can catch me off—"

The fearsome battle cry of Kreegah the Merciless split the air, and Old Broot, the mighty hecteratops, burst through the jungle. Zala sat atop his back, firing her weapon into the robots. Kreegah vaulted through the air, springing like a giant red cricket to crush more drones beneath his feet. Snarg and the primadons followed up the rear, finishing off any other robots not pounded to scrap by the lead.

Old Broot charged the Brain, who, despite his earlier claims of infallibility, appeared very surprised. He brought his hypnotic stare down upon Broot. The entranced juggernaut slowed to a stop, his five horns inches from piercing the mesmersaurus's belly.

Kreegah pounced on the mesmersaurus's head. Zala, with six bounding steps across Broot's back, had her sword unsheathed and leapt. The clumsy dinosaur moved just in time to avoid being stabbed in the throat. Zala's scimitar sliced only a few inches from the dino's jugular vein. The mesmersaurus retreated while Zala destroyed robots.

I sighed.

Snarg skittered beside me and snipped the heads off the robots on either side of me. She cooed and chirped until I patted her between the antennae.

"Thanks, I suppose."

The mesmersaurus's thrashing sent Kreegah hurtling into the underbrush and knocked Zala to the ground. He locked eyes with her, and she could only lie prone, helpless, as he moved to crush her underfoot.

I pushed a button on my portable weather machine. Several lightning bolts struck from the sky, pushing the Brain back. Zala jumped to her feet, ready to continue the battle. I adjusted a dial on my machine, and strong wind kicked up. Miniature tornadoes whipped around us. Exact control was impossible, and the tornadoes ricocheted around in random patterns. One swept up Zala and threw her to the ground. Another button press and a larger tornado rushed forward, hurling the mesmersaurus into the distance.

"Why did you make me do that?" I asked as I helped Zala to her feet.

"Make you? I was saving you! How did you get ahead of us, Emperor?"

"Long story."

A triangular craft, one of my own designs, passed overhead. It paused over where the mesmersaurus had landed. A tractor ray beamed the Brain from the mesmersaurus and drew him aboard. Before we could react, the craft blasted into the horizon, gone in a flash.

The primadons howled and screeched as they continued to demolish thoroughly broken robots.

"You can tell them to stop, Kreegah," I said.

The jungle lord grunted, and his tribe fell into place.

"What did you think you were doing?" I asked.

Zala glared. "We saved you."

"It's almost endearing that you think that," I said. "It'd be more endearing if your hastily planned and gratuitously violent *rescue* wasn't, in actuality, a triumph over harmless utility robots."

"But we thought—"

"You didn't think. You just charged in, every bit the headstrong warrior who lets her weaponry substitute for her intellect."

"But the army of robots. And the dinosaur."

"Do these robots look armed? And I was talking to the dinosaur. Were you worried he would discuss me to death?"

I pushed aside my annoyance. There was no point in worrying about what had already happened.

"It's not your fault, Zala. Your training hasn't equipped you for subtlety. And I appreciate what you were trying to do, misguided as your intentions might have been. But thanks to your headstrong rush to stab and shoot something, our enemy escaped.

"All you managed was to destroy a borrowed body. Like smashing one of my exos, except instead of an exo, the mesmersaurus was an irreplaceable specimen. So that's something worth recording in your mission report. Might even earn you a promotion."

She protested, halfheartedly, but I cut her off.

"This is why I work alone."

I passed the next half hour double-checking the stabilizer. I rarely doubted my genius, but given the stakes, a little doubt was prudent. I'd have hated to implode the Sol System because of a dropped integer or loose screw. I needn't have worried. Everything was in working order, and while improvements on the makeshift device would be necessary at some point, there were more pressing concerns.

I used a remote signal to open a secret door in the volcano.

Zala readied her weapon.

"You can put that away," I said as I entered. She and Kreegah followed me down a short hall illuminated by soft white light.

"How did you know that was there?" she asked.

"I put it there. This is my facility."

"The same facility that has been compromised?"

"The very same."

We approached a set of sliding doors. Zala grabbed me by

the arm. "And now you're just leading us into another ambush or some sort of booby trap?"

"There won't be any ambush."

The doors slid open, and Zala leveled her gun at whatever threat she imagined waited for us. But it was only the entryway, a room I'd modeled after the Silver Palaces of the dukes of Mars. The Second Symphony of Gugugugug Roost, Mercury's greatest composer, gently wafted from the speakers.

Gugugugug had always been a favorite of mine, and the Mercurial use of living creatures for instruments gave their music an edge. Gugugugug had died a noble artist's death when he'd been mauled by a viviphonork, the Mercurial equivalent of a tuba but with a lot more teeth and a taste for blood. The mauling had been an accident, but the critics agreed that Gugugugug's dying shrieks had elevated the piece to heights of genius. It remained Mercurial tradition to feed a baritone to a viviphonork at the third crescendo, and while it was a barbaric practice, it was hard to argue with the visceral appeal of the composition.

A utility robot approached. "Hello, Lord Mollusk."

I blasted the robot. It collapsed into a pile of scrap.

"Why did you do that?" asked Zala.

"The compound has been compromised. All the robots will have to be dismantled, inspected, and repaired." I blasted another robot. "I don't have time for a subtler method."

"I thought you said everything would be fine."

"I also thought storing my most dangerous technology on a dimensionally unstable island full of mutant dinosaurs would be safe. Much as it pains me to admit it, I do make my share of mistakes."

I instructed the forty-two remaining robots to assemble and gave Snarg an order to destroy them. She gleefully carried out the command, devouring the robots. She loved exotic alloys though they did sometimes give her indigestion. I left one robot functional and by my side for the moment.

We checked on the archives, a room full of filing cabinets. Zala opened a drawer, flipped through the files.

"Seems a bit inconvenient," said Zala.

"That's precisely the point. Electronic files are more easily copied and stolen," I explained. "I keep the more radical research stored in hard copy form to prevent that."

"Nothing looks disturbed," she said.

"Why would it? If the Brain had control of my utility drones, he could get anything he wanted without having to look for it."

I requested a schedule of archive maintenance. I flipped through a report handed to me by the robot. The anti-time radio, the jelligantic, the earthquakerator, the 501 models of death ray, the atomic cappuccino machine, the xylophonic mutantifier, the positronic terrarium. All these and every other file had been scanned and uploaded. Most were only in the theoretical stages, and others were half-finished ideas. But they were the foundations of dangerous superscience.

Despite the stoic nature of a Neptunon's face, Zala must have noticed something.

"What's wrong, Emperor?"

"I just armed a megalomaniac with the tools to conquer and/or destroy the system."

As mistakes went, it was a big one.

* * *

"The Brain has everything it needed."

"But you're still alive."

"I was never in any real danger. No one was ever trying to kill me."

"Then why did they hire mercenaries? Or the jellyfish monster? Or lure you into an ambush on this island?"

"All a calculated manipulation meant to get me here at just the right time to stabilize the anomaly."

"That's absurd," she said. "It's impossible to control everything so perfectly. Those mercenaries weren't holding back. The jelligantic could've easily squashed you by accident. And this island is full of beasts that could've killed you at any moment. No mastermind could arrange everything so perfectly. There are too many variables."

"Under normal circumstances, you'd be right. But the Brain has one advantage. He's been getting instructions from the future. It's much easier to control chaos when you know the end results as you set things in motion."

"You mean to tell me our enemy knows how everything will end before even starting it?"

"Theoretically."

"You had access to such a device and didn't use it?" she asked skeptically.

"I designed it mostly for the scientific challenge. As I neared completion, I realized that the radio, coupled with my intellect, would render conquest of the system, even the universe itself, a foregone conclusion. What's the point in that?"

"If you were as smart as you think you are, you would've destroyed the research."

"Why would I do that?"

"To keep it from falling into the wrong hands. Like it just has."

"Destroy knowledge?" I said. "The only point of existence, if there is one at all, is in the accumulation of the collective intelligence of the sentient beings of the universe."

"Even dangerous intelligence?"

"Intelligence is neutral. Application is everything."

She sighed. "Says the evil genius."

"*Evil* is a relative term."

"Exactly what I would expect an evil genius to say. So if the Brain has used this radio of yours to gain knowledge of the future then what is the point of any of this?"

"We can only hope he has made a mistake. He appeared genuinely surprised by your frivolous *rescue*. The nature of the communication means there may be holes in what he knows. And then there's the question of whether or not the flow of time is stable or can be altered by the mere act of transmitting information to the past."

"It's worked to his advantage so far," she said.

"So it would appear," I agreed. "But all it takes is one seemingly tiny miscalculation to change everything. It's unlikely he has considered all the possibilities of anti-time transmission."

"But you have," Zala said. "Did it occur to you that the Brain is every bit as intelligent as you are? He discovered your island, stole your technology. And if I understand this anti-time radio of yours correctly, he did those things without any knowledge of the future at that point."

"You understand it correctly. And I'll grant that the Brain is a formidable opponent. But aside from finding Dinosaur Island, something he might have done by accident, he hasn't displayed any true creativity. He understands the science he's stolen, but his application is uninspired."

"Having seen the damage you've been able to do with your science in the past, I don't find that comforting. And let's assume that he is as intelligent as you are. For the moment, let's assume he is *more* intelligent."

"Very well. Let's assume that. I admit it's an intriguing possibility."

"What does it mean?"

I shrugged.

"It means we lose."

WRECKING PARIS

In hindsight, it had only been a matter of time before someone gazed down upon my world and decided to take it from me.

That moment came while I was sunning myself on the terrace of my manor in the heart of Paris. Hundreds of Saturnite warships, their distinct corkscrew design filling the sky, descended over the city.

The lead ship spiraled its way into a landing, burrowing its needle-like tip deep into the ground, destroying my topiary garden. A hulking Saturnite commander disembarked with his personal guard. The commander had the craggy gray complexion of a weathered veteran.

Several bodyguard robots attempted to intercept. They were blown into piles of scrap. My loyal Terra Sapien servants, though unarmed, moved to my defense. I waved them away.

"Emperor Mollusk?" asked the commander.

He was a few feet taller than my exo, so I extended the legs to look him in the eye.

"Yes."

"I am here as a duly authorized representative to notify you that Terra and all her resources are being commandeered by the nations of Saturn. Any resistance on your part will be considered an act of rebellion and will be met with all necessary force."

"I see."

"I have also been instructed to allow you a subservient position should you cooperate."

"What kind of position?"

"The title is irrelevant. You can come up with whatever you like." The commander shrugged, and you could hear the tectonic plates in his shoulders rumble together. "You'll have no actual authority, but will be allowed to remain for as long as you cooperate fully with the Saturnite ruling council."

"How very generous."

"You'll find we are benevolent conquerors."

"I can see that. May I speak to you a moment, Commander?"

The Saturnite leader adjusted his sash and nodded. "Certainly, Warlord Mollusk."

We strolled to the other side of the veranda.

"I understand that this is not an arrangement to your liking," he said, "but you must admit it is a generous offer. I would've preferred to take you to the Red Halls of Conquest, where you would've been put on display for the amusement of gaping rocklings. But I'm not in charge of such things."

"You're a good soldier, Commander. I can see that. Before I accept your offer though, I'd like to show you something."

"No tricks, Mollusk. At the first sign of resistance, I am authorized to employ deadly force."

"No tricks," I said. "Just a short lesson in Terran history."

I pointed to the tower in the distance.

"That structure is the vision of a Terran named Gustave Eiffel. Eiffel was obsessed with defending his world from alien invasion. At the time, it'd been seen as the quaint paranoia of an eccentric genius. Terra had faced and repelled conquerors from space many times throughout its history. The hordes of Genghis Khan, armed with spears, horses, and brutal determination, had repelled the Slors of Titan. Leonardo da Vinci defeated the Comet Monster in 1499 with nothing but a sketchpad, a gyroscope, a harmonic resonator built with a few scraps of bronze and iron, and the reanimated corpse of Joan of Arc. There is strong archeological evidence that the Assyrians trounced an incursion of the Emirates of the Negative Dimension. No easy feat."

"Is there a point to this?" asked the commander.

"Yes, there is. You can understand why the Terrans felt a certain fearless disregard for the defense of their world. No one listened to Gustave Eiffel, and his great defense grid prototype had become a mere curiosity. But Gustave was truly ahead of his time, and with a few modifications on my part, I was able to get it up and running. Granted, it doesn't have the range and power to disable an entire fleet, but any nonterrestrial craft within a few thousand miles is quite vulnerable to it."

Understanding glinted in the commander's eyes, just a moment too late. I activated the Eiffel Tower. The skies over Western Europe crackled a bright green as Saturnite ships exploded. They came crashing down to Terra, smashing into Paris and the surrounding countryside. The commander's ship burst in two. Half of it remained standing, while the other half fell into my lawn, destroying my favorite fountain.

The commander rushed me, but I unleashed a vibrating uppercut to his chin that pulverized his stony head. Pebbles and dust flew everywhere, and he collapsed into a heap of rocks.

"I know you're just doing your job," I said to his guards. "Surrender now, and I'll go easy on you."

One young soldier reached for his weapon. I blew a hole through him where he stood.

The three remaining Saturnites disarmed themselves and raised their hands.

"What are you going to do with us?" asked one.

"You'll be free to return to your fleet."

"But we'll be humiliated," he said. "We can't just go back with nothing to show for it."

I blasted his hand to gravel.

"Is that better?"

"Yes, thank you."

After maiming the other two, I had the butler escort them away.

I studied the City of Lights. The armada might have been destroyed, but the damage to Paris was unfortunate. It was my first taste of the bitterness of conquest, to see that which I'd worked so hard to obtain be destroyed because of me.

And it would only be the beginning.

Relations between Terra and Luna had been strained since the Lunans had eaten Neil Armstrong in 1960. Diplomacy remained stalled even after the Terrans established their first moonbase. It was no doubt the never-back-down attitude of the Terrans (not to mention their irresistible deliciousness) and the bite first, ask questions later policy of the Lunans, which were the heart of the problem. Life on Luna had been hectic and unpleasant for everyone with the arrival of the Terrans.

I'd fixed all that. I'd updated the Terrans' primitive space technology and given their moon a light atmosphere. Nothing too showy. Just enough air to make it convenient. There wasn't much on Luna for Terrans to see, but they still enjoyed coming to see it. Since time immemorial, the Terrans had dreamt of reaching their moon and when they discovered there weren't many wonders there (aside from the four great Lunan pyramids and the Horrible Shothog slumbering in its subterranean depths) they went ahead and created their own wonders. More of that never-say-die spirit I enjoyed so much about them. Tourism was Luna's number one industry, with amusement parks, spas, and all-inclusive resorts. Moonbase One had grown from a struggling colony to a thriving resort town.

Kreegah stared at Terra below as we left the atmosphere. "It's so small."

"Yes, it is," I said.

"The computer told me the universe was big, but it's different to actually see it."

"Seeing it isn't the best way to comprehend its size," I said. "I find graphs demonstrate it best. I have a pie chart that shows just how vast and indifferent the universe is."

"Maybe we'll take a look at it later," said Zala. With Kreegah now with us, she had less room in the cockpit, and she wasn't happy about it. But I couldn't make him stay below and miss the view.

We shot toward Luna, but I took our time, allowing Kreegah to enjoy the journey.

"You still haven't told me why we're here," said Zala.

"I didn't think it was vital for you to know."

"Maybe I want to know."

"You'll just find it uninteresting."

She folded her arms, leaned back in her chair. "Maybe you should let me decide that."

I displayed a line chart on the viewscreen closest to her. She studied it for a few moments before giving up.

"What am I looking at?"

"It's the gravimetric readings from Dinosaur Island. Specifically, the distortions caused by the anti-time radio."

She glanced at the chart again. It wasn't fair of me to throw it at her. A lack of education, not stupidity, kept her from understanding the data. But she took such pleasure from mocking my intelligence, I couldn't help occasionally irking her with it.

"The variance is within expected parameters." I highlighted a single line among many. "Except for this reading here."

Zala slouched. "Uh-hmm."

"I'm not boring you, am I?"

She straightened and forced the glaze out of her eyes. "Not at all."

"This reading doesn't belong. It's almost like the anti-time radio was designed to generate the signal in the background, unnoticed. An analysis found that the variation matches the frequency profile of the extinct Neptunon great speckled porpoise."

"Okay, you were right." Her tail went limp. "I don't care."

"Too late. Once I get started, I like to finish. From there, it was a simple matter of translating the signal into binary code and then converting that binary code into a set of standard universal coordinates."

"And those coordinates lead to Terra's moon," she said.

I smiled. "Nice to see you're paying attention. It translates to a specific address and suite number."

Zala pointed to the screen. "Assuming you're right, who put the signal there for you to find? Someone had to put it there, right?"

"I would assume so. Unless I'm reading too much into it. It's not impossible I imagined the pattern."

"Assuming you haven't," she said, "then who put it there?"

"An excellent question. If we're going to keep building on assumptions, which is dangerous but necessary at this point, then someone has managed to compromise the Brain's security and plant a clue for me to follow."

She traced the line on the screen as she mulled it over. "And who would that be?"

"I'd rather not venture a guess on that just yet."

"There's another possibility, Emperor. The signal was deliberately planted by the Brain, just like the Atlantese assassins and the slime beast, to lead you on a merry path of distraction."

"If you're right," I asked, "what do you recommend we do instead?"

She said, "We should investigate."

I smiled.

"What?" she asked.

"I'm just surprised you didn't suggest going into hiding," I replied.

"If you're right about this Brain, hiding wouldn't do any good. Charging into a battle you are destined to lose is still better than retreating from a battle you might win."

I docked my saucer in my private hangar. A crew of Lunans greeted us upon disembarkment. Lunans came in two sizes. Very, very small and very, very big. The females stood ten feet high, had shaggy gray fur and anywhere from three to seven limbs. The arrangement of arms and legs varied by individual.

The males of the species were barely ten inches. Their fur was shorter because when cold, they would simply hop on the nearest female for warmth. They always had two arms, and they rolled and jumped everywhere.

A Lunan female with three legs and three arms shambled toward me.

"Hello, Blug," I said.

"Lord Mollusk." The round, lipless mouth of the species made speaking difficult for some, though she managed to be fluent, aside from a touch of spit with every *S*. "This is an unexpected pleasure."

The males hopped around Snarg while squeaking and chirping. They scampered up her long back and groomed loose bits of dirt and fuzz collected in the crevices of her exoskeleton.

"Your standing suite is ready, should you need it," said Blug.

"It's not an extended visit," I replied. "Business, I'm afraid."

"Ah, unfortunate to hear. It's the height of moonslug-watching season."

I explained, "The males use their phosphorescent slime trails to create miles-long patterns on the dark side of Luna. The designs are based on symplectic geometry. I haven't quite figured out if they do it on purpose or if it's pure instinct, but either way, it's very beautiful. Next time you're on Luna, you should book a tour."

"I'll do that," said Zala neutrally.

"I'll stay by your side, Emperor," added Kreegah.

"If not the moonslugs, then what brings you here, Lord Mollusk?" asked Blug.

"Private business, I'm afraid," I said. "Can't really talk about it. I'll need transport to the business sector. And I want a gamma-level security squad on standby."

Check Out Receipt

Hagerstown
301-739-3250
www.washcolibrary.org

Friday, January 11, 2019 5:42:03 PM

Item: 32395006219915
Title: Patrick : son of Ireland
Call no.: FIC LAW
Due: 02/01/2019

Item: 32395009989381
Title: Emperor Mollusk versus the sinister brain : [a novel]
Call no.: FIC MAR
Due: 02/01/2019

Total items: 2

Visit us online at www.washcolibrary.org
to manage your account and renew items.

She nodded, which for a Lunan involved a general bob of the entire body. “I’ll see to it immediately.”

We passed Terran tourists going through customs. Several of the children waved to me, and I waved back.

“Doesn’t it bother you, Emperor?” said Zala. “What you’ve done to them?”

“I don’t see why that should matter,” I replied.

“No one likes you. Not really.”

“Blug likes me,” I said. “Isn’t that right, Blug?”

“Yes, Lord Mollusk, but you are very likable.”

“She’s an employee,” said Zala. “She hardly counts.”

“Kreegah likes me,” I said. “Snarg likes me.”

The ultrapede chirped.

“Very well. Kreegah and the insect do indeed like you,” agreed Zala. “But in every other way, you’re alone. An outcast among your people, a criminal in the rest of the system. Even the Terrans only accept you because you control them.”

“I find myself less concerned with the method than the result.”

“Don’t act like you don’t know the difference, Emperor,” Zala said. “I’m beginning to understand you. You aren’t as cold and ruthless as you would appear. You care about these Terrans.”

I said nothing.

Zala chuckled. “Did I just render you speechless?”

“It’s true,” I said. “Why bother denying it?”

“I wonder why though. Why of all the worlds you’ve attempted to conquer, of all the crimes you’ve committed without hesitation, that this is the one that you finally care about? I see nothing wrong with the Terrans, but not much special about them.”

She paused, waiting for me to answer. I remained silent. It was only after Zala and I were in the back of a limousine, cruising on its way, that I finally answered her.

"They need me."

She shook her head. "You said it yourself. The Terrans can take care of themselves."

"They could," I replied. "But then I came along and rendered them passive. I didn't count on the absolute success of the process. Don't get me wrong. I enjoy the Terrans and their adoration, artificial or not. But there's a problem that comes after you've conquered a planet."

"And what problem is that?" asked Zala.

"What do you do with it?"

"But surely you must have thought about that beforehand."

"Actually, I can't say that I did."

"But all the crimes you've committed, all the plotting and scheming, the enemies you've made, the damage you've caused. You expect me to believe it was just a mental exercise. Some sort of twisted game?"

"Have I mentioned I get bored easily?" I said. "Conquering a planet seemed like a good way to kill the time."

"Your crimes against Venus, against the entire system, were nothing but the by-product of boredom?"

"When you put it that way, you make it sound rather childish."

Zala's mouth tightened. Her nostrils flared. Her tail thumped against the seat.

"And now that you've conquered the Terrans, you're bored again."

"A bit," I replied. "Although I find myself in a difficult position. I have wealth, power, and unlimited resources at my disposal. It's more than I could ask for. But without limitations, how does one find satisfaction?"

"You could always turn your intellect toward the betterment of the system," she said.

"It's a little late for that, isn't it? Who would trust me at this point? And I've never been very good at constraining my scientific pursuits. I've tried, but I just can't help myself. And you've seen what happens when my research falls into the wrong hands."

"And of course you can't destroy it," she said sarcastically.

"Of course not. We've already covered that."

Her lip twitched. Her scales darkened. "You could always conquer another planet."

"I did consider that. But if claiming one world didn't satisfy me, I doubt two will. And Terra keeps me busy enough."

Zala said, "According to Venusian intelligence, at least half of the threats you protect Terra from are a by-product of your own activities. Our current adversary, for example."

"I've had a few experiments get out of my control from time to time. But I've kept them from doing too much damage."

"So far," she said.

The limo arrived at our first destination. The small home sat in a block of quaint cottages. There was a flourishing timeshare industry along the Sea of Tranquility.

I had Blug and Kreegah stay with the limo.

Zala and I approached the front door. She drew her gun.

"You won't need that. This is only some personal business I thought I'd get out of the way since we're on Luna anyway. It shouldn't take long."

I knocked. A pudgy little Terra Sapien with a bushy mustache and a sloppy haircut opened it. He adjusted his glasses.

He grinned. "Emperor Mollusk, you old son of a nautilus, what brings you by?"

"Business, I'm afraid."

"Business business?"

"Business business," I confirmed.

He pulled a handkerchief from his coat pocket and blew his nose. "Then come in, come in, by all means."

He showed us to the study. There wasn't much to it. A desk crowded with papers, a data bank, and a liquor cabinet.

"I know that Emperor doesn't drink," he said to Zala, "but can I offer you something? I have a fine selection of Venusian brandies. They play havoc with my intestinal tract, but I do love them."

"No, thank you." She went to the window and pulled the shades.

"Don't mind her," I said. "She's just paranoid."

"Don't mind him," she said. "He's just overconfident."

The Terran poured himself a drink and sat at the desk. He took a long drink, blew out a breath, and rubbed his round chin. "So I take this has something to do with the Celebrants."

"Yes, I'm afraid so."

Zala said, "What does he know about the Celebrants of Oblivion?"

"He's well versed in their affairs."

"Are you a scholar?"

"The Celebrants have no official history," he replied. "You don't remain a mystery by leaving records behind."

"Then how would you know anything about them?"

He took a sip and ran his fingers along the edge. "I'm privy to certain oral traditions among the Celebrants."

"How would you become privy to the cult?"

He smiled slightly. "We don't like to use that word. We find it... insulting to our calling."

She took in the short, round man in the off-the-rack suit and bright yellow tie. Her skepticism was obvious and not entirely misplaced.

"You're a Celebrant?" she asked.

He held up his hands and shrugged. "I hope it's not too disappointing."

"I don't believe you."

"Oh, that's a bit rude," he said. "You don't hear me questioning your qualifications."

"He's the seventh deadliest assassin in the system," I said.

"Sixth," he corrected. "But who's counting?"

Zala circled him. "You don't look like an assassin."

"Good assassins don't look like assassins." He clinked the ice in his drink. "How could I prove it to you? Would you like me to kill you?"

She smirked. "I'd like to see you try."

He chuckled. "You wouldn't see it."

"I hate to interrupt this chest-beating contest," I said, "but I didn't bring Zala here to be killed."

"Really?" He reached into his pocket and put a small red vial on the desk. "Then she should probably drink this."

She picked it up. "What is it?"

"Antidote for the poison I gave you."

Zala drew her scimitar.

"Well, it won't do you any good to kill me now," he said. "Drink the antidote."

"How do I know this isn't poison?"

"You'll have to take my word for it. I may be an assassin, but I'm not going to lie to you. Or you can give it a minute and drop dead. It will be quite painless."

She looked to me, but I said nothing.

"You understand, Emperor. It was an honest mistake," he said. "You don't bring a visitor to meet a holy assassin without certain assumptions being made."

I said, "No need to apologize. I should've made it clear from the start."

Zala unscrewed the vial and drank it. She slammed the vial onto the desk. "I'll play along and assume you're who you say you are. How do you know, Emperor?"

"I'm a member," I said.

"And you neglected to tell me this."

"Would you have believed me?"

"I still don't believe either of you," she admitted.

"I'm only an honorary inductee," I said.

"Don't be modest," he said. "What you did on Saturn still has yet to be matched among the order."

I didn't like to remember Saturn.

"I'm not here to reminisce," I said. "I'm just here for information. And could you give Zala the antidote to the poison you just gave her?"

"But he just gave me the antidote."

"No, he gave you the poison. He was lying before that."

She scowled.

He laughed. "Sorry." He opened a drawer, withdrew a

bottle, offered a small red pill to Zala. "You'll want to take this."

She held it in her fingers. Delicately, as if she didn't trust it.

"Take it," I said. "I'm almost certain it won't kill you."

"Almost?" she asked.

"He is a death-worshipping assassin," I said.

He smiled. "Guilty as charged. So if you didn't drop by to have me kill your companion, then why are you here, Emperor?"

"I need to know if you're trying to kill me."

He chuckled. "If I were trying to kill you, you'd know. Actually, you wouldn't know because you'd be dead."

"Is any member of the Celebrants trying to kill me?"

He tapped his fingers on the desk. "It's possible. It is against the rules, though how seriously a league of entropists follow rules is always up for grabs. Still, if you aren't dead yet, then it probably answers the question."

"I suspected as much." I stood. "Thanks for your time."

"No problem. It's good to see you again. We should get together for lunch sometime soon. I'll call you." He turned to Zala. "It was a pleasure to make your acquaintance."

"I didn't catch your name," she said.

"No, you didn't." He stood and straightened his tie. "I hate to be rude, but the vice president of Pluto is probably not going to have a seemingly ordinary heart attack all on his own."

We left the cottage. Zala watched him walk away.

Zala said, "I still don't believe it."

He stood beside her, a silent shadow appearing out of nowhere.

She jumped, drawing her scimitar. "Don't do that!"

"My apologies," he said. "Force of habit. So are you telling me for certain that you don't want her dead, Emperor?"

Smiling, I hesitated to answer.

"No, I guess not. She's proven useful so far."

"Because I just want to be clear on this," he said. "Make sure I'm not missing a wink or secret signal that's meant to say you don't really mean it."

"We really should work out some official sign," I said.

"I'm in complete agreement. Maybe a hand gesture or a code phrase." He glanced at Zala. "So not dead?"

"Not dead," I replied.

"Then you shouldn't take that pill I gave you," he told her.

Her eyes flashed. "I already did."

"No problem. I have the antidote here somewhere. One moment..."

He fumbled through his pockets until he produced a hypodermic injector.

"You'll want to use this on your pituitary gland in the next forty seconds." He handed it to her. "It's located just below your third rib—"

"I know where it is," she said softly.

"Right, right. Have a good day then." Whistling to himself, he walked away.

Zala scowled, unbuckling her armor. "You keep such interesting company, Mollusk."

The next stop on our Lunan tour was the address I'd deciphered. It belonged to a suite on the fourteenth story of an office building in the business district. There weren't many tourists here. Just Lunans and Terrans going about their daily lives. The streets were busy, but the advantage of being former Warlord was I never had to worry about parking.

The security team was already waiting for us. Three Terrans, four Lunans, and a Saturnite decked out in combat gear. They saluted. Everyone except the Saturnite.

"This is the finest team on Luna, sir," said Blug.

The Saturnite and I locked stares. "What's your name, Officer?"

"Gorvud," he replied curtly.

"An exemplary record," said Blug.

He saluted her. "Thank you, ma'am."

"Per your orders, the building has been evacuated and the block secured."

"Very good. I will be going in first. If there's a problem, I'll signal you."

"As you wish," said Blug.

Zala, Kreegah, Snarg, and I entered the lobby of the building.

"A Saturnite on your own security team," said Zala. "I sometimes wonder if you don't have a death wish, Emperor."

"He has to work, doesn't he?"

We rode the elevator to the fourteenth floor. The office we were interested in had been rented last week, but records indicated it hadn't been used. The door didn't even have a stenciled name on it.

It was unfurnished except for a small table with a four-by-four cube, wrapped in a featureless chassis, sitting on it.

"What is that?" she asked.

"The next clue," I replied. "No doubt left for me to find."

A cursory examination of the cube revealed no obvious way to open it.

"Could you use that prized Venusian steel of yours?" I asked.

She balked. "It would be undignified to use the sacred steel as a glorified can opener."

"I can open it." Kreegah took it in his hands.

"Wait," said Zala. "How can you be certain it's not some kind of explosive?"

"I can't, but it would be a needlessly complicated method of assassination."

"And if you're wrong?"

"An intriguing hypothesis."

She grabbed the box, but Kreegah held on to it. They both clutched it.

"Emperor, if you were as smart as you think you are, you wouldn't be despised by every civilization but one in the system."

"You make a valid point, Zala. And it's possible that this box is a trap. In fact, I assume it is. But I'd be surprised if it turned out to be something as uninspired as a bomb."

"Why touch it at all?"

I squinted. "I'm afraid I don't understand the question."

"You don't have to poke and prod it," she said. "You can just leave it alone."

"Why would I do that?"

"Because a bomb in a box would be the perfect weapon to use against you."

"But it's so dull," I said.

"Yes. It's dull and pedestrian and simplistic. But it works. Most beings in the system would simply elect to shoot and stab their enemies. It's not technically impressive, but it gets the job done. And it would exploit your biggest weakness: your curiosity. Anything complicated you would figure out almost immediately. But something simple like this is a trap you can't resist."

"You make an interesting point."

Before she could protest, Kreegah tore the top off the box.

"Hmmm. No bomb," he said.

"Too bad," I said. "I thought you were onto something there."

"You sound disappointed," she said.

"Do I?"

"If you thought I might be right, why did you let him open it?" asked Zala.

"An excellent question."

Because I didn't have an excellent answer, I didn't say anything more than that.

"You do realize that if I'd been correct," she said, "we'd all be dead now?"

"Yes, but you weren't." I removed a spheroid from the box. "That bomb-in-a-box idea. You didn't come up with that all by yourself."

"A proposal from the Venusian Covert Service. Back when we were considering merely assassinating you for your crimes."

"Good plan."

The spheroid clicked and whirred.

"What is it?" she asked.

"Some sort of pressurized vapor-release device," I said.

"A gas bomb?" Zala coughed.

I set the device down. "Something like that. Although why anyone would think gas could be much of a threat to me, sealed in my own exo, is a puzzle."

Zala wiped her tearing eyes. "Damn it, Emperor. Did you stop to think that maybe it's not meant for you?" Her coughing grew louder. Her gray scales flashed slightly different shades of green and blue.

"Well, that doesn't make any sense," I said. "They're not trying to kill you. Even if they were, there is any number of gases that could result in instant death."

Coughing and swearing to her gods, she exited the room.

Snarg chirped. Her forcipules twitched. Centuries of specialized breeding had made ultrapedes immune to nearly all poisons and toxins. Yet she reacted, which in itself proved unusual.

Kreegah just stood there. I waved a hand in front of his face, but he didn't react. The gas had rendered him catatonic.

I ran the air through my exo's analyzer. Since this was a general-purpose exo, results would take a few minutes.

Zala entered the office. She no longer coughed or sputtered, though her scales were a darker shade of gray than usual. Almost a deep green.

"You should probably stay outside until I've identified the nature of the gas."

Zala drew her gun and fired it. The blasts struck me in the chest. I stumbled backward. She kicked me with enough force to crack the window behind me.

Snarg was too busy twitching on the floor to be of much use, and Kreegah remained immobile. Zala fired as she advanced. Her aim was dead on, but her instincts were off. She kept shooting me in the exo when a good shot through the dome was all it would've taken.

I shot her with a stunbolt. It should've knocked her out, but it only caused her to drop her gun. She still had her scimitar.

"Kill Mollusk," she growled, spraying spittle.

I blocked the swing with my arm. The blade sliced several inches into the limb. She wrenched the sword free, and her next swing nearly split my head. Instead, it pierced my shoulder, nearly shearing off the limb.

The gas had affected Zala's fighting skills. Her attacks were powerful, but sloppy. On her third swing, I was able to land a punch across her jaw. It stunned her long enough to push her back. I fired several more stunbolts. It put a wobble in her legs, but she didn't fall down.

"Kill. Mollusk."

With unlikely speed, she charged. Zala hurled herself into me. The force shattered the window behind me, and we went tumbling toward the street fourteen stories below.

Zala wrapped her hands around my exo's neck as she howled, splattering saliva across my dome.

My thoughts were fractured at the moment, and I'll admit that too much of my attention was directed toward the vaporized catalyzer that had transformed my reluctant bodyguard into my enthusiastic assassin. Triggering mindless fury via chemical stimulation wasn't difficult. But outside of unleashing anarchy, the applications were limited.

Zala wasn't just enraged. She was enraged in my direction, and that was impressive, scientifically speaking.

I set aside my curiosity and shoved Zala away. My exo attempted to twist itself to land on my feet, but I was only halfway through the maneuver when I struck the pavement. The impact knocked me senseless. I assumed that Zala had landed on her feet. Luna's artificial gravity was weaker than Venus, and while she could've sprained her ankle with a bad landing, her rage no doubt allowed her to ignore the possibility.

She lurched toward me. "Kill. Mollusk."

The security team aimed their weapons at her.

"Hold your fire!" I said.

My exo wasn't in perfect working order, but neither was Zala. She staggered on shaky legs.

Another stunbolt caused her to collapse. She crawled. Unable to even hold her sword, she crept toward me with drooling determination.

"Kill."

She twitched and hissed, probably fantasizing about chewing me out of my exo with her own teeth.

Blug approached. "I thought she was on your side, Lord."

"Not exactly," I replied, "though this isn't her at her best."

The security team restrained Zala. Meanwhile, traffic patrol redirected vehicles and kept gawkers at a distance.

"Is this strictly necessary?" asked Gorvud as he slapped handcuffs on Zala's limp, semiconscious form.

"Better to not take any chances," I replied.

Zala raised her head and scowled in my direction. She sprang, but Gorvud kept his hold on her. She growled and thrashed.

"Kill Mollusk!"

Gorvud smiled. "Yeah, yeah. Get in line, lady."

He threw her in the back of a security carrier. After the hatch was sealed, the carrier rocked as she threw herself, screaming, against the interior.

"Is she going to be okay?" asked Blug.

"She should be fine once the gas wears off," I said. "We'll have to isolate her until then."

The carrier rattled after a particularly hard charge.

"Oh, dear," said Blug. "I hope she doesn't hurt herself."

The vapor stimulant wasn't likely to be permanent, and if necessary, I was certain I could synthesize an antidote. But I did imagine Zala, a maddened, frothing creature, spending the rest of her days locked in a cell. It wasn't the end a proud Venusian warrior deserved.

The ground quaked as something tremendous fell from above and smashed into the limousine. The security team pulled their guns and surrounded me.

Snarg scampered from the wrecked vehicle. I'd forgotten about her, but she hadn't forgotten about me. There was murder in her milky yellow eyes. She shrieked, barreling toward me.

The team fired their weapons, but nothing they had could penetrate her enhanced armor. She batted them aside as if they weren't there. Only Gorvud could grapple with her, and even that was a losing proposition.

She ignored my ultrasonic commands.

Kreegah landed light as a feather beside me. I dodged a punch that shattered my dome and nearly mashed me into goo. A guard tried to restrain the Jupitorn, but his great strength meant he didn't even have to bother shrugging them off.

I sprayed him with a healthy dose of sedative gas. Four times the regular dosage. He swayed, fell to his knees, and then collapsed.

Blug ushered me into a security skimmer. The vehicle rocketed down the road. I saw Gorvud falter. Off-balance, he was shrugged off by Snarg. Her undulating segments chased after the skimmer.

I ordered the pilot to get us airborne. We jumped into the sky, but not before something thudded against the bottom of the vehicle. The skimmer rocked.

"I'll shake it off," said the pilot, executing an extended barrel roll.

Pincers tore through the undercarriage. Snarg pushed half

of her head through the hole. Warbling, she snapped her jaws as she drew closer. The pilot struggled to keep the skimmer flying, but we entered a steep dive.

I latched on to the vehicle's roof. Snarg yanked my exo out the hole. She devoured the heavy alloy like tinfoil.

The pilot managed to pull up, and we bounced off the street below. The vehicle skidded, spun, and flipped once before coming to a stop. My grip on the roof kept me from getting tossed around within the cabin. I did get smacked once or twice by Blug's flailing limbs, but I could hardly hold that against her.

The light refracting through the broken windows added to my disorientation. I heard Blug moan.

"Are you okay, Lord Mollusk?"

"I'll live," I replied. "Are you in one piece?"

"More or less," she said. "I might have broken an arm."

Snarg sheared off the skimmer's door, and with a hiss, she wrapped her maxillae around me. It was my own damned fault for making her so indestructible. But I could think of no end more appropriate than to be done in by my own brilliance.

She ran her long black tongue across my face. Her antennae no longer twitched, and while her many eyes blinked irregularly, the worst of the gas must've worn off.

I stroked her pedipalps. "That's my girl."

Zala's system, being less efficient than Snarg's, took three more hours to get over the effects of the gas. She lost most of her energy after an hour of banging against the walls of her cell and spent the next two sitting in the corner, snorting and glaring.

I used the time to analyze a vapor sample and the delivery device. The design was simple. The gas triggered aggression while the device had a psionic transmitter that implanted an image of the target. It wasn't very subtle, but it didn't really need to be.

The lab door opened and Gorvud, the Saturnite security officer, entered.

"Your Venusian bodyguard is asking for you," he said.

"All better now?" I asked.

"She can say more than 'Kill Mollusk' if that's what you mean, sir."

I took a few minutes to reassemble the aggression catalyzer.

"Can I ask you something, Gorvud?"

"Yes, sir."

"You don't hold it against me. What I did to Saturn?"

Gorvud's face remained as inscrutable as the rock it was made of.

"You can answer the question honestly," I said. "Without fear of reprisal."

"It's not that, sir." He frowned. "It's just…I'm not sure how I feel about it."

"Intriguing."

"What you did to Saturn was horrible. Sir."

"Agreed."

"But you didn't start the war. And war is brutal business. I can hardly criticize you for defending yourself. My own ethics aside, you won. And it would be hypocritical to cite your own atrocities while ignoring the horrors of my own side. If we'd seized control of Terra, we would've plundered her resources, enslaved her people. Just because we didn't get the chance to do so doesn't change the fact that we would have. A bit silly to claim the moral high ground on this one."

"The boulder at the top of the hill is one good push away from the bottom," I said.

"Precisely, sir."

I screwed together the two halves of the device. "But you did save my life, Gorvud."

"Well, that is my job."

"So it didn't occur to you for one moment to let my ultrapede eat me?"

"I can't say that it did, sir. Afterward, yes, but at the moment, I was on duty."

"I admire your work ethic, Gorvud."

"Thank you, sir." He grinned. "But I'll admit that if I'd been off the clock, things might have been different."

I grinned back. "Fair enough."

I held up the sphere.

"You missed a piece." Gorvud pointed to a single part, a disc the size of a quarter.

"No, I didn't. It doesn't serve any internal purpose."

"Then why was it in there?"

"An excellent question." I tucked the disc into one of my exo's storage compartments. "One that we'll have to save for later."

Gorvud escorted me to the medical suite where Zala was being treated and then excused himself to check on his team. They hadn't been seriously injured, but even a casual backhand from a regressed Jupitorn was going to cause some bruising.

Zala was strapped down in a bed. She snarled at me when I entered. The vitals monitors beeped insistently with my arrival.

"We're having regression," said the Lunan doctor. "Prepare the sedative."

Zala scowled. "Emperor, if you allow them to inject me with anything, you'll wish I had killed you."

"She's fine," I said. "You can release her."

"Are you certain, Lord Mollusk?" asked the doctor. "We're getting elevated levels of activity in both her primary and secondary adrenal glands."

"That's as calm as she gets while I'm around," I said.

The medical staff undid the straps and began treating her injuries.

"Don't worry," said the doctor. "We have the finest medical facilities here. You should be good as new in another hour."

Wincing, Zala sat up. "What happened?"

"You tried to kill me," I said. "We'll attribute your failure up to the catalyzer's negative impact on your fighting skills, if that makes you feel better."

"You had to open that box, didn't you?"

"And you had to stay by my side while I did it, didn't you?"

"I'm here to protect you from yourself, Emperor."

"And a terrific job you did of it too. Except for the trying-to-kill-me part. But nobody's perfect."

Zala pushed away a nurse and tried to stand.

"I wouldn't recommend that," said the doctor. "You have severely sprained both ankles as well as your right knee."

She grunted, testing the weight on her ankles.

The doctor scratched her furry head. "Amazing. I can't believe you're able to stand."

Zala laughed. "This is nothing. I once fought a razortail trukyut while recovering from three broken ribs, a lacerated aorta, and the vor lung pox."

"And we're all very impressed," I said, "but if you're to be any good to me at all, you should let the doctors patch you up. If I have to look after you, then it defeats the purpose of having a bodyguard, doesn't it?"

She knew I was right, though she didn't admit it aloud. But sat back in the bed. When the doctor approached her with an injector, Zala asked, "What's that?"

"An all-in-one pick-me-up," I said. "Designed specifically with your biology and injuries in mind. It's really quite something. You'll be on your feet in no time."

She said, "That's all?"

"That's all," I replied.

"It won't have any side effects?"

The doctor said, "They'll be some incidental stiffness. And the acceleration to your metabolism might mean a marked increase in appetite along with dry mouth and possibly trouble sleeping for a day or two."

"And that's all?" repeated Zala.

I said, "Oh, and there's also a nanite that will attach itself to your aorta and self-destruct upon my command."

She glowered.

I chuckled. "Really, Zala, when will you trust me?"

Her blank expression answered the question, but she allowed the injection. While we waited for the serum to do its work, Zala lay in her bed.

"Where's Kreegah?" she asked.

"He'll be asleep for a while. At least a week. Possibly more. I sprayed him with the concentrated extract of the striped tulip. Harmless to most life-forms, but a powerful sedative to a Jupitorn. It's usually fatal in the wild as the tulip sucks out its victim's juices. But in this environment, it'll just be a refreshing nap, followed by a moonslug-watching tour as my way of apologizing."

"And you just happened to have that sedative at the ready."

"It pays to be prepared," I said. "It wouldn't make much sense to bring a powerhouse like Kreegah along without taking precautions."

"And what about me?" she asked. "Do you have precautions to deal with me, should it come up? Or am I not privy to that information?"

"You're easy. I'll just kill you when I have to."

"Good plan," she said. "Although shouldn't that be *if* you have to kill me?"

"I think we both know where our current leads, Zala, and neither of us seem very interested in swimming against it."

We shared a knowing smile.

"But you didn't kill me this time."

"It wasn't necessary. This time." I shrugged. "I wasn't about to allow the Brain to deprive me of an asset. You're just the right ratio of usefulness to expendability that makes you so handy to keep around."

"I'm touched, Emperor. Truly, I am. So did you design the gas bomb?" she asked.

"It possesses certain design elements that I'm partial to," I said, "but it's not something I've done much research on. It seems to use some very simple research as a jumping-off point, but it's mostly an original design."

"Do you know what that means? The Brain is getting smarter. At first, he was merely aping your scientific malevolence. But how long will it be before he is taking it in his own twisted directions?"

"You sound like you're more worried about him than me."

She smiled ruefully. "As much as it pains me to admit this, Emperor"—Zala winced as she shifted in place—"you have always been bound by a certain bizarre sense of fair play. There are things you've done that are insane and homicidal, but you can usually be expected to follow a code of conduct. You've never been enamored of needless destruction. And while you are ruthless in achieving your goals, given the choice, you will still usually seek the subtler path in reaching them."

She paused, but I didn't respond.

"Do you disagree?" she asked.

"I hadn't really thought about it before," I replied.

She laughed and then bit her lip as a pain ran through her side.

"It's amazing that someone who claims to be as intelligent as you are has spent more time designing doomsday machines and time radios than contemplating his own motivations. Don't misunderstand me. You are still a menace to the civilized universe. In the grand scheme, your methods make you far more dangerous than the Brain. But in the short term, the Brain is likely to do something even you wouldn't imagine doing. Who knows what possible irreversible damage he could do in a moment of ambitious stupidity?"

"Wait. Are you saying he's smarter or stupider than me?" I asked.

"I'm saying he's both. He's already nearly destroyed this planet using your research. And if the idea of your science in the hands of someone unfettered by even your flawed ethics doesn't frighten you, then you're not as bright as you think you are."

I pondered the various technologies I'd unlocked in my studies. Thousands of devices and ideas that could devastate a city, a country, a planet, the system. A handful that could endanger the entire universe. It was perhaps a bit foolish of me to have laid the groundwork for the star smasher or the penultimate nullifier, even if only as intellectual amusements. Perhaps even more foolish to put them down on paper at all. But it was my nature.

I'd convinced myself that all the truly dangerous ideas

were only ideas. The half-rendered musings of a superior intellect. Unfinished and unlikely to lead anywhere. But they didn't have to work exactly as expected to do immeasurable damage.

I was on the other side of this evil genius scenario. I didn't like it.

"What do we do next?" asked Zala.

"I'm surprised you haven't suggested going into hiding yet again."

"Your arrogance has unleashed this maniacal would-be conqueror on the system, but you may be the only one who can stop him before he does something terrible. For the sake of my precious homeworld and every other planet in the system, my personal desire to bring you to justice must become secondary to that."

"This is more serious than I imagined," I said.

"It's every bit as serious as you know it to be, Emperor. And that's why I know you have some sort of plan formulating already."

I handed her the small disc.

"A holograph disc? That's a bit dated, isn't it?" She turned it in the light, showing the almost imperceptible indentations in its sides. "This one doesn't look to have much data on it."

"I haven't read it yet, but I'm guessing it's a simple message. I found it in the catalyzer."

"The same device that nearly drove me to kill you."

"Yes."

"Let me guess. Another secret message from your mysterious inside agent? The very same mysterious agent who led us into a trap in the first place."

"No, the decoded message on Dinosaur Island was obviously planted there by the Brain."

Zala sat up. The serum must've been working.

"If the Brain laid one false trail, what makes you think he didn't just lay another for you?"

"An educated guess. The Brain probably wouldn't expect me to follow a second clue after giving me a false one."

"So your reasoning is that he wouldn't bother dropping a second false clue after giving you the first one? Because he wouldn't believe you'd follow it. Except that he has access to knowledge from the future and already knows everything you're going to do before you do it anyway. How can you possibly do anything he doesn't expect?"

"It's not as if the anti-time radio gave him a minute-by-minute recount of how things would unfold. He's like a starship navigating with an incomplete chart with certain events marking the way while trusting there won't be an exploding supernova found in the blank spaces."

I could see she was unconvinced, but she shrugged. "Fine. I'll pretend like I understand that."

Again, I was surprised. "You don't want to argue some more about it?"

"Why? It's not as if I have any suggestions myself. Even if I did, you'd just dismiss them. So let's skip the debate and get on with it."

"Very sensible," I said.

Half sneering, half smiling, she gave me back the disc. "Just decrypt the damn thing already."

HAUNTED SATURN

The war against the Saturnites had not been going as well as I hoped.

The pointed Saturnite spacecrafts were not the most powerful craft in the system, but they were cheap, efficient, and expendable. Saturnite tactics were usually limited to overwhelming force, and an endless swarm of disposable fighter craft had won them many a war against more nuanced opponents.

If that didn't work, they would bring out the Glorious Triumph, *the flagship of their fleet. The functional rectangular craft was little more than a flying weapons platform. Cannons and missiles and blasters and ballistic meteor guns and moon-melting heat rays were mounted on every inch of the thing. The craft had three separate doomsday weapons aboard her, including the dreaded System Killer, a bomb so powerful it could destroy all nine planets with the push of a button. Or so the Saturnites claimed.*

Given their love of firepower, few doubted it existed.

The debate over the bomb's plausibility was usually a secondary concern, considering that even without it the Triumph *could ruin a planet in a few minutes. Saturnites had won wars just by mentioning the* Triumph *in casual conversation.*

And after three months of war with the Saturnites, the Triumph *orbited Terra, a technological god of death and destruction.*

My saucer and its automated fighter escort approached the flagship. A small fleet of Saturnite craft encircled us. It would have been simple enough for the enemy to blast me, but what would have been the fun in that? The Saturnites were here to watch me grovel.

I landed in the Triumph*'s only docking bay. Barely big enough for a dozen ships. Anything larger would've required removing one of the countless starboard polar de-atomizers.*

I exited the ship. The Saturnite Warmaster General himself greeted me. Along with an attachment of imperial guards. The Warmaster measured nine feet tall with a turquoise complexion. Medals covered his dress uniform, and he stood with his arms folded behind his back and a glint in his obsidian eyes.

He smirked. "You're Warlord Mollusk?"

"I brought my Conqueror model exo. It's very tall and shiny with gratuitous spikes. But it just seems like so much glitter. Are we here to pose or to negotiate the terms of surrender?"

The Warmaster nodded. "I see that you're very direct. I can respect that. Did you bring any security?"

"I have a few robots aboard my ship, but they won't be necessary."

He chuckled. "I didn't think you'd be so relaxed about this."

"It's not personal," I replied. "Just two civilizations hammering out a mutually beneficial arrangement."

We were shuttled to a meeting room. I didn't question why the room was so far from the craft's only landing bay. The Triumph *wasn't a diplomacy ship, and Saturnites weren't a diplomatic people. Even their meeting room was a small gray chamber with a table and a few chairs. There was a viewscreen with an image of Terra. It was a very small screen, no doubt there to remind me how tiny my world was in comparison to the vast Saturnite war machine.*

"I'd offer you a tour, Mollusk," said the Warmaster, "but of course, the inner workings of the Triumph *are a classified military secret."*

"Yes, it's a very fine giant space gun you have here. Very intimidating. Very frightening. Impressive, if a bit conventional. But it does get the job done."

The Warmaster scoffed, which was difficult for a Saturnite to do, given his craggy stone face. "The Triumph *is the greatest weapon the system has ever known. The bloodsucking fiends of Dread Planet V took one look at this ship, and rerouted their fleet into a black hole rather than face her in battle. Even you, the great and feared Warlord of Terra, Emperor Mollusk..." He stifled a chuckle. Or pretended to stifle it. "... trembles at her mere arrival and gave up your senseless fight against us."*

"Oh, I think there's been a miscommunication. I'm not here to offer my surrender. I'm here to negotiate the conditions of yours."

The Warmaster and his guards laughed.

"Emperor... if I may call you Emperor..."

I nodded.

"Emperor, you've put up a hell of a fight for this little world of yours. Given your resources, the limits of the Terran population and technology, you've managed the impossible. You've forestalled the inevitable. And we salute you as a worthy opponent."

They slapped their right shoulders with their left hands. The Saturnites had an elaborate system of salutes. The right shoulder slap was reserved for respected enemies. Though I was a touch insulted I hadn't been given the double-chest thump offered to feared adversaries. But that was a bit ambitious, even for me.

"Our intelligence reports that you are stretched to your limit, Emperor. You could still fight, of course. But we both know where that would go. More damage to the world, more Terran casualties. In the end, this war will still end the same."

"There are those who say there's nobility in fighting to the very end," I replied.

"There's nothing noble about fighting a war you've already lost. Not when your opponent is polite enough to offer you an alternative. Surrender now, and we will allow you to remain Warlord of Terra. We really don't care about the Terran population. You can continue to rule over them as you wish."

"And all you want in return is the right to take whatever you desire from the planet," I said.

"We'll leave you enough for your own needs."

"And what about the Terrans?" I asked.

The Warmaster intertwined his fingers, deliberately rubbing his stone skin together to produce a grinding noise.

"What about them? You conquered them. We conquered you. By my calculations, that puts them two steps below my own concerns."

"But not my own," I said.

"Forgive me, but haven't you programmed the Terrans to adore you, regardless of circumstances? If you tell them to do what we say, they'll gladly do so, won't they?"

"They'd cheerfully hand over their world with a word from me. They'd even throw you a parade, create an international holiday."

"A pleasant thought," said the Warmaster. "We'll have to keep that in mind."

"Here's my counteroffer. You will agree to complete, unconditional surrender. You will withdraw your fleet and cease all hostilities."

I leaned forward and imitated his pose. Even intertwined my delicate fingers through the sound of metal against metal wasn't quite as intimidating.

"And in return, I won't destroy Saturn."

He smiled but didn't quite laugh. "Your bravado is almost endearing."

"I don't do bravado," I said. "And if you want to make this about who can twist the powers of science toward the better doomsday device, I'm afraid it's a game you can't win."

"Am I expected to believe that you have a weapon capable of disabling the Triumph*?"*

"Oh no. I have something better."

I overrode the small viewscreen, replacing its image of Terra with one of Saturn.

"I don't have to defeat your giant space gun. I just have to defeat you."

I pressed a blinking red button on my exo's arm. There were easier ways to activate my weapon, but nothing quite so dramatic. I was here to make a point.

Nothing happened.

"You'll have to give it a few minutes," I said. "The de-gravitators probably need to warm up."

The Warmaster said, "What's the meaning of this?"

"I'd think it would be obvious," I said. "I'm about to scatter your world across the system as so much cosmic dust."

He marched over to me. "You dare threaten Saturn."

"I didn't know that was against the rules."

His hands balled into fists indistinguishable from boulders.

"I wouldn't do that," I said. "If you kill me, the process will be irreversible. Within minutes, Saturn will disintegrate. Four minutes, by my calculations."

The Warmaster waved his hand with a chuckle. "You're bluffing, Emperor. You know that if anything were to happen to my world, I'd have no choice but to order the destruction of Terra."

"Mutually assured destruction," I said. "It's not ideal, but it is functional."

I pointed to the slight wobble in Saturn's ring formations.

"Of course, this is built upon the assumption that your giant space gun actually works."

"What are you implying, Neptunon?"

"Oh, nothing. Only that I've never found any records of the Glorious Triumph *engaging in battle. Outside of a single demonstration on one of your own moons, Mimas, I can't find any record of her even firing. Rather a small moon, wasn't it?"*

My exo beeped. Again, unnecessary but useful for demonstration purposes.

"At this stage, the atmosphere will begin to disperse." I zoomed the view for a better look. "Observe the funnel effects on the poles. A peculiar phenomenon. Rather beautiful though a bit inconvenient for those on the planet itself."

I took a seat.

"I can stop this at any time. It's up to you."

The Warmaster pounded his fist into the table, breaking it in two. "This isn't war. It's genocide. These aren't even your own people you're defending."

"Does it make any difference?" I asked. "The Terrans are my responsibility."

"And Saturn is mine!"

"Then do what you have to," I said. "Surrender. In forty seconds, the process is irreversible. Your family, your friends, everyone you know and billions you don't know will die. I expect a few million are already dead."

"How can you be so cavalier about this?"

I wasn't, but I had to appear to be. I had just killed millions and was possibly about to destroy billions more. And if Saturn perished, then the remaining Saturnite fleet would certainly take its wrath out on Terra below, leading to billions more deaths.

It was all just numbers. Statistically insignificant, really. A few million life-forms snuffed out with the push of a button. It didn't feel like that anymore. It wasn't fun. It wasn't science. It was just ugly, indiscriminate death.

Everything I'd ever done had inevitably led to this moment, and in another, I would discover where it would end. I was already a monster. How great a monster was yet to be determined.

My exo beeped. "There's nothing noble about fighting a war you've already lost. Not when your opponent is polite enough to offer you an alternative. Fifteen seconds, Warmaster."

The countdown beeped with each passing second. The Warmaster wrestled with his pride. I pondered the lives of untold trillions of life-forms being decided by the actions of two beings sitting in a gray conference chamber.

With only three seconds to spare, the Warmaster, his small black eyes narrowed, his jaw clenched, grunted.

"We surrender."

I pushed the button.

The Warmaster slumped in his chair. A great and powerful general, now rendered impotent. "What are your demands?"

"The viewscreen doesn't show the cities in chaos, the floods, the aftermath of quakes. And you'll have to contend with disrupted weather patterns, a shattered biosphere, and inevitable and disastrous tectonic shifts. Saturn will survive, but it will be many long years of struggle ahead of your people. Go home, Warmaster. Rebuild. But above all, stay away from my world."

He said nothing, but one of the guards stepped forward.

"That's all?"

"Isn't that enough?" I asked.

I left the Glorious Triumph *without incident, but I didn't leave alone.*

Its ghosts would be with me a long, long time.

The decoded disc had coordinates. They pointed us in the direction of Antarctica. I didn't have a secret compound there, and as far as I knew, there was little of interest on the frozen continent. But it couldn't hurt to check it out. Terra was a world of mysteries.

My saucer set down at the landing site, surrounded by an endless white expanse. We disembarked. Venusians were warm-blooded, but it was, evolutionarily speaking, a new development in her species. Ice and snow still put them on edge. Zala adjusted the heat setting on the containment softsuit.

The helmet obscured her face, rendering it unreadable. "This is it?"

"According to the coordinates, yes," I replied.

Snarg skittered across the ice. A stiff breeze kicked up, and ice was already forming on her armor plating. The crunch of frost accompanied our steps.

"There's nothing here," said Zala.

Snarg shrieked. She'd found something of interest. We pushed through the wind to see a cave entrance she'd discovered.

The mouth and the tunnel just beyond were barely big enough for us to squeeze through. It would've been the perfect spot for an ambush, but Zala suggested we enter. Her dislike of the frozen landscape overwhelmed her warrior training. She did insist on going first. I followed. Snarg brought up the rear.

It grew warmer as we went deeper. There was a slight incline in the cavern, leading us down into the subterranean mystery. Perhaps it was some long-lost entrance to the Undersphere. The kingdom of the mole people extended beneath the Americas, the Atlantic Ocean, and most of Europe. There was a second, more primitive mole culture under Asia and Australia, but as far as I knew, there was nothing of the sort under Antarctica. Admittedly, I hadn't given it a thorough survey yet.

"Shouldn't it be dark?" asked Zala. "Where's the light coming from?"

It was a good question. There was no visible source of illumination, but the cave was getting brighter, not darker, as we plunged on.

We reached the end of the tunnel, emerging on a ledge above a vast cavern overlooking a sprawling city carved from the stone. Hundreds of tubular creatures moved through its streets. Zala ducked down, but we were so high up, I calculated it was unlikely they'd see us.

"Have you seen these creatures before?" she asked.

"They resemble nothing I've come across," I replied as I zoomed my exo sensors on the creatures. I'd catalogued thousands upon thousands of life-forms throughout the system and beyond. Terra was uniquely populated by a diversity of intelligent beings, and one more wouldn't have been surprising. But the discovery of yet another new species was an unexpected pleasure.

They moved via bending end over end on their stalks. They had rudimentary feelers on either end that served to balance them. I noticed spots and orifices in the center that probably served sensory purposes.

Something shuffled up behind us. Zala whirled, her gun already drawn.

A contingent of two dozen creatures approached us. They produced peculiar whistles and chirps as they advanced.

I put my hand on Zala's gun, forcing her to lower the weapon.

"They could be hostile," she said.

"They might be thinking the same thing about you," I replied. "This is a first-contact situation. Let's not assume we have to shoot anyone until we see otherwise."

The crowd divided, and a beast lumbered forward. It appeared to be little more than several thousand pounds of protoplasm wrapped in a greasy sheath of skin. An especially thick and tall worm slid off the beast's back. This particular worm had a pair of underdeveloped wings growing from its center.

I assumed it was a leader.

There was no way to know how these creatures communicated. Or how they viewed the universe. The sentient helium entities of the Sol Collective, for example, had no concept of sound and communicated via flashes of colored light. Jupiter and Sol had nearly gone to war over a Jupitorn ambassador wearing an accidental assortment of clothing that translated into *Your mothercloud has a high melting point.*

It was impossible to tell these creatures' intent. They had no faces to read, and their bodies were so alien there was no way to glean anything from their body language. But they had yet to exhibit any obvious hostility.

"Greetings," I said. I had to start somewhere.

The leader flapped his wings. His reply, coming from somewhere in the center of his stalk, was perfectly spoken.

"Are you Emperor Mollusk?"

"I am."

The creatures erupted in a cheerful chorus. A contingency erupted into a whistling rendition of my favorite Neptunon composition, Scrog's *Ode to Bell Curves.*

The leader said, "I am called Hiss, and it is my honor to welcome you. We have been waiting for you for a long, long time, Emperor Mollusk. It was foretold in the days of old that a savior would appear. And that he would have a body of metal and a divine intellect."

"I don't believe it," mumbled Zala.

"And now, at long last, you have finally come," said Hiss. "We had never given up hope, but some of us did wonder when you would get here."

"Wait a minute!" shouted Zala. "Wait one second!"

The chorus stopped singing. The crowd stopped cheering.

"Who told you this?" she asked.

"Oracles," replied Hiss.

"And seers," added another.

"And at least one soothsayer," said a third.

"For it was written on the Great Stone of Prophecies," said

Hiss, "that a warrior of legend, a conqueror of worlds and master of the primal forces of the universe itself, would appear in the Crack of Revelation. And it is written that all on the Great Stone shall come to pass."

"Written where?" asked Zala.

"Why, on the Great Stone, of course," said Hiss.

"It was written on the stone that things written on the stone would come to pass," she said. "And you know this is true because it was written on the stone."

The crowd of things murmured their approval.

"That really doesn't make any sense," said Zala.

"It was written that you would not understand," replied Hiss.

"So now I'm on the Stone of Prophecy too?"

"It is written that Emperor Mollusk would be accompanied by a glorious beast and a hideous warrior companion." He slumped. His wings drooped. "No offense intended. It wasn't I who transcribed the prophecy."

"Don't mind her," I said. "She's just upset that she gets third billing."

Snarg chirped and clicked her mandibles. Zala grumbled.

"Your prophets said I'd be emerging through this hole today?" I asked.

Hiss chuckled. "The Great Stone doesn't specify time. So ever since your name was first inscribed on it, we've gathered here, waiting for your arrival."

"There's not much else to do down here," said another creature.

"Yes, ours is a simple life," said Hiss. "Graze the fungal fields, offer a sacrifice to our savage god, read the Great Stone, wait at the Crack of Revelation. It's not much, but it is deeply rewarding in its stoic beauty."

"Hear, hear," said a follower.

The chorus blasted the cavern with more singing.

Zala pulled me aside and turned away from the crowd. She whispered, "I don't like this. It's clear that this is all a trap and these creatures, whatever they are, were briefed by the Brain."

"It is the most obvious explanation," I replied. "Though the obvious explanation isn't always the right one."

Zala sighed. Her breath fogged up her helmet, so she snapped it open. "Don't tell me you believe these creatures have actually been waiting for you."

"It can't hurt to hear them out, can it? Isn't that why we're here?"

She shrugged. "Just as long as you don't believe this prophecy nonsense."

"Oh, I don't," I said. "Although wouldn't it be intriguing if it were true?"

"Your curiosity is going to be the death of you yet, Emperor."

"There are worse character flaws to die for," I said.

We turned. The creatures stared at us. Or at least they bent forward on eager stalks.

I asked, "So how can I save you today?"

Because the creatures had no official name for themselves (and indeed the very concept seemed to elude them) I settled on calling them Stalks. They seemed confused by the concept of needing an identifier, and from snippets of conversation, I surmised that they were the only form of life, aside from a red fungus they fed on, in the cavern. Even the fleshy pudding beast we rode was one of them. Less of a beast of burden and more of a peculiar mutant offshoot. It lumbered its way down a winding trail into the cavern's depths.

"In the beginning, there was the Great Seed," Hiss said.

"How many *great* things do your people have?" asked Zala. "Maybe you should get a thesaurus."

Hiss continued without trace of insult. "The Great Seed spawned the Great Gynoecium, which in turn spawned all life. It spread throughout the universe and for a long time, there was prosperity throughout. The fungal fields provided sustenance for all, including the Gynoecium.

"But then, the Great and Terrible Gynoecium's hunger grew beyond the ability of the fields to satisfy. In order to appease it, it was deemed necessary to offer sacrifices. As time passed, the Gynoecium demanded more and more of us. Now it devours at least thirty or forty a day, and if something is not done soon, then we are sure to be driven to extinction, leaving only an empty universe in our passing."

"You do realize there's more to the universe than this cave, right?" asked Zala.

Hiss chuckled. "There are those who say there is a place beyond where the fungus is damp and plentiful."

"Heretics!" shouted several Stalks.

"Most of us are wise enough not to believe such foolishness," said Hiss. "For if there were such a place, it would surely be written on the Great Stone."

"How long have your people lived down here?" asked Zala.

"It is written that we have lived here since the dawn of time."

Zala laughed. "If you've lived underground your entire

existence, then explain to me why you have the concept of dawn. It should be meaningless to you."

"We telepathically extract the appropriate words from your primitive minds to facilitate communication. Our own natural language has no such expression."

"Isn't that convenient?"

"Yes, it really is," agreed the thing.

"But where do you think we came from?" asked Zala.

"You came from the Crack, of course."

"Yes, but what do you think is on the other side of that crack?"

"What do you mean?"

Zala said, "If we came through it, it must lead somewhere. It's not like you believe we just materialized out of nowhere."

The Stalks murmured.

"You'll have to excuse my companion," I said. "She's a bit peculiar."

Zala snarled. If it had been more convenient, I might have suggested to her that this was neither the time nor place to challenge the Stalks' view of the cosmos. Instead, I turned the conversation toward more productive ends.

"So there haven't been any other visitors from the Crack?" I asked.

"None," said Hiss. "As it was written."

If he wasn't lying, then it meant that the Brain had nothing to do with the Stalks. Deception was possible but I deemed it unlikely. These creatures appeared to be largely incapable of deception. Or perhaps they were so very good at it, aided by their strange bodies and unreadable natures, that I was entirely wrong.

"So I'm assuming you need my help with the Great Gynoecium," I said.

"Yes. The Gynoecium's hunger threatens to destroy all life."

"So you need us... Emperor to kill it?" asked Zala.

The Stalks exhaled in a great high-pitched wail I took for a collective gasp.

"The Gynoecium is the source of all life. To destroy it would be to doom everything."

"Then what is he supposed to do?" she asked.

"He's here to save us," said Hiss with a chuckle. "How he does so has not been written."

"It's a vague prophecy," admitted another.

"The details are unimportant." Hiss wobbled in a circular motion. "It is not the way to question what must come to pass."

Zala wasn't going to let it go that easily, but then we entered the city of the Stalks. Cheering, they parted for our procession. Several of the Stalks placed oddly shaped metal instruments against their bodies and unleashed a discordant celebratory tune. The citizens of this hidden civilization danced and undulated, spraying colorful bits of mucus like confetti.

I waved to the little ones, hoping the gesture translated into something friendly.

"You're enjoying this," said Zala.

"Perhaps a bit."

"Just don't allow yourself to become careless, Emperor. We can't afford to..."

Her voice trailed off as we rounded a block and found ourselves before a giant statue carved in my likeness. It wasn't my biggest statue on Terra. Nor particularly well sculpted. But it did look like me in the broadest strokes.

We dismounted to get a closer look.

"Where did that come from?" asked Zala.

"The taller buildings must've hidden it," I said.

The statue's base was the immense rock formation from which it was carved. It was covered with strange pictographs.

"Behold, the Great Stone!" declared Hiss while whipping back and forth.

The lowest carvings were primitive in design, little more than squiggly lines. But the glyphs grew more sophisticated as one's eyes moved up the stone. Near the top, the scene of our arrival, with the Stalks surrounding us, was apparent for all to see.

"This is absurd," said Zala.

"You have to admit that it's a striking resemblance," I said.

"Of course it is, Emperor. The Brain could easily have set this up."

"Easily," I agreed. "But why? And if not, how? These are also questions worth asking."

She narrowed her glittering eyes. "Don't tell me that you believe any of this."

"No, not really. Although if I ran an analysis on the carvings, I could probably date their original creation and be sure."

"Only you would need scientific confirmation that you weren't a messiah."

"Never hurts to double-check," I replied.

The cavern city of the Stalks rumbled. Squealing, they ran in all directions.

"Behold! The Great Gynoecium rises!" shouted Hiss.

The ground burst, and a purple-and-yellow thing rose like a tower of writhing vegetable matter. Its head, so to speak, was a ring of barbed petals and snapping thorns. It pounced on the muck beast, and the poor creature was devoured in the Gynoecium's grinding jaws.

"Good luck, savior," called Hiss as he fled, flipping end over end. "Though I'm sure you won't need it."

The terrible vegetable turned its dark, unblinking eyes upon us.

The Gynoecium attempted to scoop us up into its jaws. Zala jumped to one side, and I used my jetpack to take to the air. It caught Snarg, but her armor proved too tough for its whirling teeth. It struggled to choke her down while Snarg clung to the colorful petals.

I regrouped by Zala's side. She didn't shoot at the thing, allowing Snarg to serve as a distraction.

"Any idea how to kill that with what we have?" she asked.

"I'd rather not kill it," I said.

"You don't really believe in that prophecy, do you?"

"No, but I have this reluctance to destroy unique lifeforms," I said. "Or are we in for a repeat of the mesmersaurus incident?"

Zala and I moved to one side as a root smashed the ground where we had stood only moments before.

"You killed the jelligantic without hesitation," she said.

"Not the same thing. I can always make another of those."

"But you won't."

"Probably not," I replied.

She glared.

"This isn't the best time to have this discussion," I said.

The Gynoecium abandoned its efforts to swallow Snarg. It spit her, along with several gallons of green bile, onto the ground. Then it convulsed, regurgitating several Stalks.

It spent the next minute gulping them back down.

Zala aimed her pistol at the monster, but it was unlikely to do anything more than annoy it.

"I knew I should've brought something bigger. If you can find a way to stop this thing without killing it, I won't object."

"Zala, I find your lack of faith disturbing."

She smiled mirthlessly. "Just shut up and stop that beast already."

The Gynoecium's roots broke through the ground. They probed blindly, snatching up any Stalk they could catch. Zala blasted a tendril, causing it to drop a few citizens. Others were not so lucky. The giant plant devoured them by the dozens.

I grabbed Zala and rocketed into the air and out of the reach of the hungry creature. She didn't protest.

The monster cracked open a stone building and slurped down its inhabitants like an aardvark attacking a termite nest.

I set Zala down a safe distance away and flew in for a closer look. It wasn't the monster's teeth or appetite that intrigued me. It was the dozens of pods hanging from its central body. While it gorged itself on the Stalks, I zipped close enough to tear one of the larger pods loose. The Gynoecium didn't notice.

I flew back to Zala and put the pod on the ground between us. It was a milky green color, and there was something wiggling inside. I used my laser to slice open the pod. A small Stalk spilled out. The creature rolled around in an effort to stand up.

"The Great Gynoecium," I said. "The source of all life."

"It's eating its own offspring?" asked Zala. "Where's the sense in that?"

I scanned the cavern. Once I knew what to look for, it was obvious. The fungus was sparse, but the smoothness of the walls and edifices showed that the Stalks had scoured everything else. The Stalk population, and the Gynoecium that had birthed them, had become unsustainable.

"It can't stop reproducing," I said, "so it's forced to devour its unwanted children in hopes of balancing its ecosystem. But it's too late for that."

"Can we destroy it then?" asked Zala.

"We're not going to kill it," I said.

"I'm surprised you're so squeamish. Or are you just reluctant to kill a specimen that could be used to further your own—"

I rocketed away before she could finish the question. I shot the monster with several blasts, but my exo's weaponry barely irritated the Gynoecium. I fired several mini rockets. Black sap oozed out of the wounds, extinguishing any potential fires. My final effort was to blast it right in its flowering jaws. The explosion burned away its stigma and whisker-like filaments. It swallowed its mouthful of Stalks and lunged at me.

I flew higher to draw it out of the ground as I kept shooting harmless, but irritating, lasers into its face. Its vines and roots whipped around me, but I was just fast enough. My plan worked perfectly until I hit the cavern ceiling. I had nowhere else to go and the Gynoecium had yet to expose its most vulnerable portion.

Roots wrapped around me and prepared to throw me into the monster's snapping maw. I tossed a bomb down its throat. It exploded, spraying sap and vegetable matter. The fearless Gynoecium howled. Its limp roots released me, and it retreated into the ground. Gone in a matter of seconds, along with every root and tendril. Only the destruction was left in its wake.

I flew back to Zala.

"You did it," she said.

"I only scared it," I replied. "It's not gone. It's just hiding."

The cavern rumbled. The subterranean cry of the wounded thing echoed from all directions.

"We should get out of here while we can," said Zala.

"Not yet. We haven't solved the problem."

"Don't tell me you believe that prophecy nonsense."

"No. But regardless, the Stalks and the Gynoecium are my responsibility."

I issued an ultrasonic command, and Snarg chirped, skittering down one of the chasms left by the Gynoecium.

"Is this some foolish attempt to make me believe you've changed?" she asked. "Or just your inability to resist any scientific mystery, no matter how unimportant?"

"We can have this conversation later. Or not," I said. "Preferably not. All I know is that there is no such thing as an unimportant scientific mystery. And I can't allow a unique form of life to perish, Zala. Not here. Not on Terra."

"You let this world go."

"It's a gray area," I said. "At least, for the next fifty or sixty years."

My exo pinged in response to a sonic chirp from Snarg. She'd found her prey. I gave her another command.

The ground quaked. The Gynoecium roared. The rocky formation beneath us threatened to crumble and fall into a deep black pit.

The colossal serpentine plant burst into the open. Shrieking, it flailed about, smashing against the cavern walls. A massive stalactite fell from the ceiling and crushed several Stalk buildings.

"By all the gods, Emperor," said Zala. "If you keep this up, we'll be buried alive."

The Gynoecium collapsed, writhing on the cavern floor. At last, the colorless vines and roots, the parts always below the surface, appeared. And on that vulnerable portion, several tons of pulpy, pink-and-white vegetable matter grew. Snarg coiled around the growth. She dug into it with her many claws while simultaneously gnawing. I regretted the pain, but it was the only way to get the monster to expose its vulnerable point.

Snarg ceased her aggressive massage at my command. I flew Zala down to get a good look at the incapacitated creature. Its vines throbbed. Its petals twitched. There was still some life left in its thorny roots, though nothing too dangerous.

The immobile Stalks drooped all around us.

"What's wrong with them?" asked Zala.

"Wrong pronoun," I said. "The Stalks aren't a group of individuals. They're simply extensions of a single, immense life-form. They were right. The Gynoecium is the Stalks, and the Stalks are the Gynoecium.

"Snarg is wrapped around its central *brain*, for lack of a more accurate term that would only confuse you."

She rolled her eyes. "Thanks."

"No problem. Basically, Snarg has overstimulated the brain, rendered the creature *unconscious*, for lack of a better—"

"Just because I'm not a scientist, it doesn't make me an idiot, Emperor."

"I apologize if I'm condescending."

"Apologizing for condescension is usually condescending in itself," said Zala.

"Usually," I agreed. "But I haven't figured a way around that."

She prodded an immobile Stalk. "But they talked to us."

"A telepathic parlor trick, I assume. The Gynoecium was responding to our own thoughts and producing alluring sounds. Perhaps it's an old adaptation from when it needed to lure prey to it. Its own primal grasp of the situation figured in as well. So it took its own instincts and turned them into something to pique my interests. In a strange way, it really was asking for my help."

Zala noticed that the statue in my honor was now only a rock shaped nothing like me, and that the carvings on the stone had vanished. They'd never been there in the first place. It had all been psionic tweaks in our own perceptions.

"Why did it pick you?" she asked.

"Most probably, it was responding to my own force of will."

She glared.

"Or perhaps it sensed that I was the leader of the expedition.

Or that I had the intellectual creativity to possibly solve its problem."

"Or maybe you were just easier to manipulate," she said. "Admit it. You liked the idea of being a savior."

The Gynoecium had tapped into something deep within me. There was a part of me that expected to be adored. I didn't rule Terra anymore, but it would've been a simple thing to resume where I left off.

Consciously, I wasn't interested. But unconsciously, I couldn't rule out a part of me missed it.

I said, "Regardless of the reason, it takes a tremendous telepathic field to control such a large life-form spread out in so many discrete pieces. It must be fairly powerful to get past my own innate psionic resistance."

"The Stalks were right. If I'd destroyed the Gynoecium, it most probably would've been the end of them. My theory, and this is a very loose theory, so assume it will have to be heavily modified after a thorough investigation..."

"I'll be sure to mention than in my report," she said.

"Be sure to. Sloppy science doesn't do anyone any good. I'm assuming that the central mass spawns the Stalks with the purpose of collecting fungus to feed the prime plant. The fungal supply became strained. The Gynoecium tried to reabsorb its biomass, but it wasn't evolutionarily equipped with a shutoff switch, so it kept spawning Stalks. The results were unsustainable."

"How could you possibly have guessed all that?" asked Zala.

"Does it genuinely surprise you that I have an extensive knowledge of botany? Uranus has evolved similar forms of massive flora. None is as mobile as this, but there's a parallel evolution. Uranacs have to actually dig to get to the brain. It's quite the delicacy there. But I guessed that it would be easier to get the Gynoecium to do the work itself."

Zala said, "You could've brought the whole cavern crashing down on us on a guess."

"It was an educated guess."

She laughed. Her scales brightened. "I should be angry, Emperor. But what should I expect at this point? It was a reckless and foolish plan that could've easily gotten us killed."

"You keep saying that, but we're not dead yet." I sliced off a chunk of the Gynoecium's brain for a study sample and used my laser to melt the rest. The tremendous plant went still.

"I thought you didn't want to kill it," said Zala.

"I'm only destroying the active brain. It has redundant biology." I pointed to several smaller pink masses. "It can grow a new one. But that'll take some time, and the creature should go into a low metabolic rate that'll ease the stress on the ecosystem until I can find a way to fix things more permanently."

I placed the sample in a storage compartment. "My work is done here for now. We should go to our next stop."

"Shouldn't we take a look around?" asked Zala.

"No need. I'm fairly certain we have what we came for."

Zala didn't argue. Nor did she ask any questions, aside from one asked while we trekked our way to the surface.

"Are you still clinging to your inside agent theory?"

"I'm past questioning it right now. I'm only following the trail to see where it goes. One way or another, we'll find our answers at the end."

She chuckled.

"Do you find that amusing?" I asked.

"Yes."

We reached the snowy white surface.

"You aren't going to tell me why?" I asked.

Grinning, Zala snapped shut her softsuit helmet, hiding her face. She trudged off toward the saucer without another word. Snarg chirped and scuttled after her.

I smiled to myself, though I couldn't say why, as I followed.

Other than the coordinates, there was a single image on the disc. A stylized scorpion hieroglyphic. It was just as good as a set of coordinates.

The Everlasting Dynasty was the oldest civilization still active on Terra. Its inventors and strange alchemical science, enabled by a mysterious fountain at its heart, had made it the undisputed master of Africa and much of Asia. But empires crumbled. It was an undisputed truth. Given a long enough time line, even the most powerful nations fall. The nature of their undoing varies, but the end result was always the same. The greatest civilizations are only a few thousand years from being forgotten, as the Dynasty most probably would have been, if not for its peculiar talent to cling to existence as a small dot on a map beside Egypt.

I briefed Zala on what to expect. The Everlasting Dynasty was an insular nation. Though it had none of its former glory, it retained an ability to defend itself. A desperate Axis had invaded in the last days of WW II. Archival newsreels of panzers being melted by solar rays and giant scorpions devouring terrifying platoons had made quite the impression, and as long as the Dynasty kept to itself, the rest of Terra was content to let it alone.

I landed my saucer outside the ancient city and instructed Zala to leave her weapons behind. She insisted on having her sword, and I relented. I had Snarg stay aboard. She didn't tend to get along with the Dynastic scorpions.

A contingent of bare-chested Terra Sapiens greeted us. They said nothing, leading us through the ancient city and into the throne room of their queen. We stood at the foot of a high golden staircase. Servants parted the embroidered curtains at the top, revealing their queen.

Serket had once been Terra Sapien, although the endless millennia and Dynastic science had altered her immortal body in mysterious ways. She was at least as old as her faded kingdom, and probably a few centuries older. She still stood tall, moved with grace, but she wrapped her flesh in the finest blue silk bandages and wore a hood that covered her head. Her only visible features were her eyes, two bloodred pinpoints of light, and the portion of her mouth visible between two folds.

A pair of giant scorpions trailed obediently behind her. The Everlasting Dynasty had mastered the art of genetic manipulation, via its peculiar alchemical sciences, while the rest of Terran civilization was huddling in caves for warmth.

Serket clapped her hands lightly. A servant rushed over and sprayed a light mist down his queen's throat, allowing her to speak.

"Hello, Emperor."

I bowed. "Queen Serket."

Two more servants took her hands, leading her down the golden staircase. She didn't seem to need them, but she had developed her quirks over the centuries.

"So good to see you again," she said. "It's not every day that I receive the Warlord of Terra."

"Former Warlord," I said.

She laughed. It was light and melodious until her voice cracked. She coughed. The throat sprayer dashed over and gave her vocal cords a fresh coat.

"To reign once is to reign forever," she said. "I ruled the known world. The land for as far as the eye could see and all its people and beasts were mine to command." She gazed into the distance. "But time is not always kind. Even to immortals."

More servants threw silk pillows on a golden throne. After their queen was satisfied with their job, she shooed them away and took a seat. The most trying aspect of dealing with Serket was all the long pauses required as she was doted upon.

"So tell me, Emperor, *former* Warlord of Terra. What brings you here?"

"We think someone is stealing water from your fountain," said Zala.

Serket's eyes flashed. A servant offered her a platter of dates. She had another servant pick through the dates until he found one worthy of her. He placed it to her lips. She took a nibble and nodded her approval.

"The fountain is my most precious resource." She paused for another throat moistening. "I assure you no one has stolen a drop of it."

"Perhaps there's been a theft you just haven't noticed yet," said Zala.

Serket chuckled. "I'm not used to seeing you with such foolish company, Emperor."

"My apologies, Queen," I said, "but she has a point. The thieves we suspect are very clever. They managed to abscond with some items of my own."

She narrowed her eyes and studied the long, delicate fingers on her right hand. "Most distressing, I can imagine. But the Everlasting Dynasty has protected our fountain for over five thousand years without a single incident."

"There's always a first time," said Zala.

Serket shifted in her throne then shifted back. Pillow wranglers ensured they were in the proper position each time.

"Three thousand years ago, I would have had your companion ritually disemboweled for that remark. But this is a different age, I suppose. I may be immortal, but I'm not unchanging. I can accept that the world is... more civilized. The rabble rules it now, and while that is disappointing, it is the way of things. Perhaps in another five thousand, the world will return to its proper order."

She clapped. A giant scorpion with a throne mounted to its back scuttled from behind a curtain. Her servants transferred their queen to the new conveyance.

"In the meantime, perhaps it would ease your concerns to see the security for our fountain."

The scorpion lumbered down a hall, and we followed, flanked by guards.

"Not very pleasant, is she?" asked Zala, under her breath.

"You're still alive," I replied. "That's exceedingly polite from her perspective."

"And what about you?"

"I'm Warlord of Terra. That puts us on relatively equal footing. And, yes, I know I'm not officially holding the title, but Serket's old-fashioned. Once you're royalty, you're always royalty."

"Such nonsense."

"If I recall correctly, Venus is ruled by a queen."

"Our queen proves herself by facing the Twelve Divine Trials. All this queen does is drink from a fountain."

"I stand corrected. Yours is a far superior arbitrary system of governance."

We entered a tremendous open space. Red stains, new and old, spattered the stones under our feet. Bones and broken weapons lay scattered across the room. Zala reached for her weapon, but changed her mind when three spears were put to her throat.

A blue spotlight fixed on us. My exoskeleton shut down.

Serket's scorpion throne sprouted dragonfly wings and flew her to a balcony overlooking the chamber.

"You'll forgive the insult," said Serket. "I never would have dreamt of such an offense even a thousand years ago, but even a queen must sometimes put her honor behind other concerns."

"It's a different world," I agreed.

"One rarely to my liking, but I adapt as I must."

"What's going on here?" asked Zala.

"Serket is working with the Brain," I said.

"And just when did you deduce this? Before or after we walked into the trap?"

"On the flight over here."

"And you couldn't bother letting me know?"

"If I told you everything I know, you'd be terribly bored. So I leave out the little details. For your entertainment."

Zala moved in a whirl. I wasn't paying attention to the details, but by the end of it, she had a spear in each hand, and the guards were all on the floor, either dead or close enough not to worry about.

"Thanks for your consideration, Emperor."

A device mounted on the coliseum walls was the source of the spotlight. A single candle, amplified and filtered through a scope containing crystalline prisms, was all that was required to interfere with my exo. The nature of the science eluded me, like most Dynasty technology. I'd have loved to study the device, if only for a glimpse of forgotten science, but Serket wasn't one to share her secrets with the outside world, and I had more than enough secrets of science to explore without pressing the issue, even when I ruled Terra.

Zala hurled a spear. It arced beautifully and pierced Serket in the chest. The queen grunted, leaned back in her throne while a pair of handmaidens wrenched it free.

"How terribly uncouth," said Serket.

Zala shrugged. "Had to try."

"You could try for the spotlight," I said.

She threw another spear. It clanged against the spotlight's cast iron exterior, and the blue light flickered.

Zala prepared to hurl another spear, when a door on the other side of the arena opened and a monstrous arachnid lumbered forth. The purple-and-yellow behemoth, easily thirty tons, with pincers that could snap a full-grown snarglefot in half, plodded sleepily.

"She really loves scorpions," said Zala.

The monster shook itself alert. It focused its many deep black eyes on us.

"Could you take care of this for me," I asked. "I'm a bit indisposed at the moment."

Zala drew her sword. Without any hesitation, she charged the great beast.

I turned my attention to Serket. "How long have you been working for the Brain?"

She spoke, but kept her eyes on the battle. "Always so eager for knowledge. It's one of the things I do so love about you. I was always rather fond of you. Shame that I must kill you now."

The arena rumbled, and the scorpion howled. From the corner of my eye, I caught a glimpse of the unsteadied beast swaying as Zala did something to cause it to fall back a step. Stabbing it in some creative place, I assumed.

"It's been, oh I don't know, a few years now," said Serket. "Time becomes... vague when one's immortal. But it was well before I met you, Emperor. Before you even arrived on Terra. He wasn't just a brain then, of course. But he was mortal and knew he must live on. For the greater good, as he liked to say."

"He can't have been the first to approach you for the secrets of immortality."

"Most certainly not. There have been others. I tell them what I tell all. The secrets of my fountain are not mine to give. Drinking the undying water grants long life, but the effect varies among individuals. Only I have been given true immortality. A quirk perhaps? A gift from the gods? Who can say? This didn't discourage him. He said the waters were all he needed, that he could decipher their secrets on his own. So I let him have a few drops to experiment with."

"I'm surprised you let him have any."

The scorpion growled, and Serket clapped her hands. "Oh my, very good."

I glanced at the fight. Zala was astride the monster's back. She'd speared out half its eyes and sliced off two legs. It was now trying to shake her loose, but she clung to her sword, buried in its back.

"And it worked?" I asked Serket.

A servant offered her another date, but she waved him away. The giant scorpion fell hard to the floor, squirming on its back as Zala dashed around, looking for a fresh vulnerable spot.

"And it worked?" I asked again.

"What worked?"

"The Brain found a way to use the water?"

She sighed, paused for another throat moistening.

"I suppose. In some manner."

"I'm surprised you let him have the water in the first place."

She waved her hand. "He was very persuasive. One so rarely meets interesting individuals. Though I have lived countless lifetimes, such curious brilliance is an infrequent thing."

"You never let me take a look at the water."

Serket ran a delicate finger down her cheek. "You never asked."

It had never occurred to me. I'd just assumed it was out of the question. It was little mistakes like this that both annoyed and amused me. I didn't like slipups, especially obvious ones, but if I were truly infallible there wouldn't have been a point in doing anything. It was only in those small moments of uncertainty that I found the challenges that kept me engaged.

"Could I have a sample now?" I asked.

She leaned forward, clasped her hands.

"No."

I heard the scorpion beast's death rattle. Or thought I did. But the monster wasn't dead, only wounded and frightened. It skittered backward on its six legs, covered its cephalothorax with its claws, and cowered from Zala.

"Interesting," said Serket. "You do keep the most unique company, Emperor."

Zala sheathed her sword.

"Aren't you going to finish it off?" asked Serket.

"There's no glory in killing harmless beasts."

Serket nodded to a servant, who sounded the gong. The arena doors opened again, and packs of merely wolf-sized scorpions charged toward us. But chains around tails restrained them to a dozen feet away.

"She *really* likes scorpions," said Zala, drawing her sword again.

"There's no need for that," said Serket. "Lay down your weapon, and exit the arena peacefully. You have my word that no harm shall come to you."

"You expect us to believe you're letting us go?" asked Zala.

Serket laughed. "Nothing of the sort. I'm only granting you a moment of respite until I can determine an amusing way to get rid of you."

"Lay down your sword," I said.

"Are you mad, Emperor?" asked Zala. "I'm the only thing standing between you and death."

"You're a fine warrior, Zala. But even you can't stand against that. If she wanted us dead, she wouldn't ask you to disarm."

"But you can't ask me to surrender. It goes against everything I've been taught."

"Don't think of it as capitulation. Think of it as a strategic retreat."

"I don't retreat."

Serket made a show of yawning. "I find myself growing bored. Perhaps watching you be ripped apart by my pets would be worthwhile after all."

"You've said you're going to trust me, Zala," I said.

"You walked us into a trap. As a matter of fact, you keep walking us into traps."

"Details."

She leaned in and whispered. "This blade is tempered from the rarest, most sacred Venusian steel. It has been in my family-caste for nine generations. It is my soul. If I lose it, I shall have to seriously consider ritual suicide to atone for that sin. But not before I find you, wherever you might try to hide, and step on you, crushing your cartilaginous body beneath my heel. Very, very slowly."

She put a finger on my dome and smiled with menace.

"Have I made myself clear?"

It was fortunate that Neptunon faces are so innately difficult to read because her threat, while not unexpected, was still a wee bit terrifying. The look in her eyes, the conviction in her voice, proved she meant every word. Getting killed by my own ally was something I had considered, but for the first time, it seemed a genuine possibility. It was another uncertain moment, and I smiled.

"You don't believe me?" she asked.

"Quite the opposite," I replied.

Zala held up her sword. "This blade was tempered from the rarest, most sacred—"

"Yes, I heard you," said Serket. "Very inspiring. Very amusing."

Zala placed the weapon at her feet. Guards rushed from another door and surrounded her. They aimed their spears at her but kept their distance.

"See that she is fed and cared for," ordered the queen. "I trust she won't do anything foolish."

They led Zala away, although the word *led* implied they were in charge when all they were doing was following Zala from a safe distance.

Once they were out of the arena, Serket's scorpion throne flew down and with a slight yellow glint in her glowing eyes, she asked, "Care to join me for lunch, Emperor?"

Serket arranged an elaborate banquet, where all manner of rare and exotic foods were presented to her in grand ceremony in her lavish dining room, decorated with golden statues, fine tapestries, and assorted works of expensive art. The room was made for a huge table, but instead an intimate round table sat in the center. Serket had a chair for herself and a tank of water for me. She'd taken my deactivated exoskeleton and stored it away.

Her minions stoked the heating unit under the tank while another sprinkled rose petals on the surface.

"I trust everything is to your pleasure," said the queen. "Perhaps more salt?"

The salt-dispensing servant hurried forward at the suggestion.

"No, I'm comfortable." I bobbed on the surface. The petals were more irritating than helpful, but I was a gracious guest. "Are the walls covered in platinum?"

"Yes, but it's recently gone down in value so I'm thinking of having it replaced with gold."

She nodded to a servant whose job it was to ring a bell, which he did with speed and efficiency. At the far end of the room, although all the ends of the room were far if you were technical about it, a procession of more servants appeared. Fine young Terran specimens danced in the lead while scattering flower petals. In the middle of the parade, an entire roasted pig was borne aloft on a platter by four muscular servants. A flute player and a juggler brought up the rear.

"It's strange, isn't it?" asked Serket as the food made its way slowly in our direction. "I don't believe I've ever entertained you before. Not even when we were equals."

"An oversight on my part," I said. "Warlording leaves precious little social time."

"Yes, it is a terrible responsibility, being master of all. I sometimes wonder if the peasants know how lucky they have it."

Twenty seconds later, the food finally made its way to our table. Serket nodded approvingly at it. She didn't take a bite. Serket didn't eat much. A date a day would've been more than enough to sustain her along with a small portion of undying water. It wasn't anything I could digest either. The bell ringer rang, and the servants carried it away with equal spectacle. Seven servants fussed over their queen.

"Why did you join the Brain?" I asked.

"I already told you. He is a singular intellect."

"And I don't believe that. We're alone." Servants barely qualified as furniture to Serket. "Why don't you tell me the real reason?"

She shrugged. "I fail to understand why you insist on talking about such things. A distasteful topic, don't you agree?"

"It's money, isn't it?" I asked.

Serket resigned herself. "Yes...money. It turns out that my treasury is not as endless as my life. And the resources of my empire, such as it currently exists, are not up to the task of keeping me in the manner propriety demands."

"I would imagine it's hard to plan a retirement fund for eternity."

"So it would appear, Emperor. I do try to keep my needs simple. I've reduced myself to a banquet a day and feasts only on Sunday. And the royal foundries' production has dribbled to a mere thirty statues a day."

She pointed to a lofty golden reproduction of Serket reclining on a throne. Dozens of these works of art decorated the palace, all of the queen, each of them unique.

"That one has been there for six days," she said. "It bores me. Yet it remains. Can you see now the trials I must endure?"

"You're a tower of strength," I said.

"Thank you. But, of course, this isn't all about me. My people need things too. You would think it would be enough to have the honor to serve me. But they insist on the luxury of feeding and clothing themselves. Shelter. Amusements, I presume, of some sort. And medical coverage. The dental plan alone was driving my kingdom to bankruptcy."

She pointed to the tall man fanning her with a giant feather. "You? How much vacation do you get?"

"Three weeks, Your Gloriousness," he replied.

Serket shook her head. "I never realized how much I took

slaves for granted. My people live to serve me, of course. But that means also that they must live."

"You could always allow them to export their talents," I said. "Your goldsmiths and silk merchants are the finest on Terra."

"Yes, because I must have the finest things. But these things are not meant for the commoners, the upstarts. And my people already have the most sacred trade of all. I couldn't ask them to do anything else." She snapped her fingers. The bell ringer rang his bell. The meal procession started again. This time, with a platter piled high with fruit and cheese. "See how happy they are?" she asked. "Aren't you happy, my people?"

The servants all nodded and murmured their approval. I noticed that they all had very nice teeth.

"But a servant-based economy, as perfect and beautiful as it is, still needs capital from somewhere. These platinum walls don't pay for themselves. I give the Brain a few drops of my precious water on occasion, and he supplements my coffers. And everything continues as it should. In a perfect world, such sacrifices would not be demanded of me, but this is not a perfect world."

She held out her hand, and her team of helpers sprang into action. They moved her to her feet, and she stood without the slightest effort on her part. "The question now, Emperor, is what to do with you?"

"Changed your mind about feeding me to your pets?"

"Oh that was just a moment of whimsy." Her throat sprayer coated her dried vocal cords before she coughed up a titter. "But why kill you when I can ransom you? Someone would surely pay handsomely for you. If not the Brain then the Saturnites, perhaps?" She paced around my tank theatrically. "Or the Venusians? Tell me. How did you end up with a Venusian bodyguard? I thought they despised you."

"I've done my best to accumulate the right kind of enemies. The kind that don't like each other nearly as much as they don't like me."

"A sensible design."

"If it's money you want, Serket," I said, "I could always write you a check."

"Don't be crude," she said. "I couldn't take your money. I have too much respect for you. It's tragic enough that I'm reduced to such low means. I couldn't ask that of you."

"That's very kind of you."

"Without decorum, where would we be?"

The fruit was inspected, approved, and returned to the kitchen. Serket cut the banquet short. "Such unpleasant talk seems to have ruined my appetite. If you'll excuse me..."

She addressed an underling. "See that the Warlord is comfortable while I arrange the details of his transfer. Keep the Venusian well fed and unharmed. Just in case Venus finds her valuable enough to purchase. And if they don't, I can always feed her to my beasts in the arena, which should be worth some amusement."

Serket climbed on her throne, and the scorpion walked from the room.

"And see that the statue is changed. If I have to see it once more, I'll go mad. Good day, Emperor."

"Good day, Serket."

She exited. The heavy doors sealed shut behind her.

"I don't suppose I could write you a check?" I asked of the servants.

They laughed. Serket, for all her shallowness, was truly their goddess queen. It wasn't unfeasible that one or two contemplated the offer, but for the most part, their loyalty to Serket was unswerving. It helped that she was smart enough to take care of them.

A trio of burly, tanned warriors escorted me down a long hallway, pushing the tank before them.

"He doesn't seem very intimidating," said one. "How did he conquer the world?"

"It's not hard," I replied. "All you have to do is think ahead, be prepared. And a certain amount of flexibility is helpful too."

"Did you use an army?"

"No army," I said. "I like to get my tentacles in the mix."

They sneered. Doubtlessly, they found the idea of a leader getting involved in daily affairs to be as repugnant as their queen did.

We turned down another hall, went through a series of chambers until I was wheeled through a garden, a vast sea of lush green and exotic flowers. A crystal window transformed the harsh desert sunlight to gentle warmth.

"This is my last offer," I said. "I won't make it again. Name your price."

"Or you'll do what?" asked the tallest one. "Make your escape by dragging your boneless body across the ground?"

They chuckled.

Something rustled the leaves of a nearby bush.

My escorts drew their swords. Two of the guards pushed the third forward, toward the rustling plants. He stabbed the garden with his weapon then stepped a foot into the waist-high growth and poked about some more.

"There's nothing here," he said. "Must have been a—"

Something yanked him beneath the greenery. He barely had time to yelp before silenced.

"This is not what I wanted," I said. "I accept that it's necessary to harm others sometimes, but it's annoying. Never mind the existential dilemma of whether or not I have the right because I'm comfortable with that when required."

"Inform security," said a guard. "We have a breach."

His companion dashed off. He turned the corner, disappearing behind a topiary sphinx. The sound of his sword clattering to the ground echoed through the garden.

"You're just doing your job," I said to the last guard, "and I can respect that. But there are larger concerns at stake. It might help if you drop your weapon and step away from the tank. She might not view you as a threat then."

Growling, he turned on me and stabbed into the tank. I darted to the side. He swept the blade around in the water, but even in the small tank, I was a slippery target. He tipped the tank over. It shattered, and I lay exposed on the wet stones.

"For my queen!" he shouted.

"Your queen wants me alive," I said.

He stopped the fall of his sword.

Snarg rose up behind him, but I gave her the hold command via the sonic transmitter hidden in my right gill. Nobody ever checks the gills. They just see a fifteen-pound cephalopod outside of my exoskeleton and think I'm harmless.

The guard peered into Snarg's milky white-and-yellow eyes.

"One command from me, and she'll rip you apart," I said. "It's not as if I want her to, but I've never been able to train her to capture or incapacitate. She goes for the kill. It's in her nature. Observe the way the spikes along her back are trembling? That signals unusually high levels of aggression. So at least your death should be quick."

The guard dropped his sword and ran. Snarg instinctively wanted to pursue, but she was well trained. She slinked low to the ground. I petted her with a pair of tentacles, and she cooed.

"Good girl."

A seat opened on her back. She gently wrapped her maxillae around me and dropped me into place. The cockpit dome snapped closed. I fed Snarg a directive, and she obediently skittered on her way.

I used the time to read a scan of the palace. A recon satellite gave me a layout and the location of all life-forms over one hundred pounds. One life-form was marked as a blue dot. That was my first stop.

Snarg was fast and capable of surprising stealth when demanded of her. My bionic chilopoda scuttled through the halls with nary a sound. The guards were easily avoided. The sentry golems, impressive as they might have been five thousand years ago, were ponderous and oblivious to anything short of a crashing ruckus. Only the scorpions proved any real threat of discovery, and Snarg's superior enhanced senses gave her ample warning to stay ahead of them. We reached our destination without incident.

The dungeons were a vast catacomb of empty cells shrouded in torchlight. They were a relic of a time when Serket had been powerful enough to imprison any who offended her. But that was a long time ago, judging by the dust on the cell bars. We found an iron door with a pair of stationed guards. They made a brave show, but Snarg hissed and they bolted down a darkened hallway.

With two snips of her mandibles, she sheared the hinges and the door fell aside. Zala stepped out of the settling dust.

"What kept you?"

"Warlord business," I said. "You wouldn't understand."

We crept on our way. Zala proved nearly as sneaky as Snarg when she put her mind to it, though I could tell it displeased her. But she could be practical when required. We made our way to the fountain room. It lay deep within Serket's palace. There weren't any guards. Though when we entered the room, steel portcullises slammed shut over every possible exit. Serket was less concerned with someone finding the water than with them leaving with it.

The water dribbled down from the top of the golden fountain, along an elaborate path of grooves, to drip into the basin at the bottom. A few ounces of the pristine water were collected in the basin.

"That's it?" asked Zala. "That's what's so important?"

"There used to be more." The portcullises cranked open. Serket and her scorpion throne trundled from a shadowed hallway. "Thousands of years ago, the waters flowed like a river. Now, a few cups of water a day is really all we can expect."

Reinforcements charged in behind the queen. Guards, golems, and scorpions ringed the chamber within moments.

"Without the fountain, there is no Dynasty," said Serket. "So you'll understand how very precious it is to us. I would ask you to step aside." Her eyes flashed. "And I won't ask again."

Zala readied her spear.

Snarg retched, spitting up a small black box. The device pinged.

"Oh, Emperor," said Serket. "Have you really descended to this?"

"I will blow up your fountain," I replied.

"And kill yourself in the process? What could be gained by that?"

"I'm well protected in here." I tapped the dome.

"But what of your companion?"

"Oh, she would die," I admitted, "but, honestly, I'll have to kill her one day anyway, so might as well get it out of the way."

"Foolish mortal," said Serket. "I can't die. What makes you think I fear death? And you can't destroy the fountain. You could, at worst, force us to dig it out again."

The look on her guards' faces said they were less cavalier about the prospect, but they wouldn't back down in front of their queen.

"First of all, this isn't a spear in the chest or a lost limb. There's a difference between being immortal and being immortal in bits and pieces. Secondly, you could dig out the fountain, but why put yourself through that? It might not be the end of the world, but it would be inconvenient."

Serket yawned. She drummed her fingers and had a servant pick a piece of lint off her cape.

"I do so despise inconvenience, Emperor."

THE END

Three months after my victory against the Saturnite peril, I sat in my Swiss chalet, working on a new device for the future of Terra, when Grant, my Terran butler, interrupted.

"Lord Mollusk," he said. "I hate to be rude, but if you don't leave soon, you'll miss the parade."

I didn't look up from my work.

"Is there another one?"

Grant nodded. "Yes, Lord."

"Tell them to start without me."

"As you wish, sir." He turned to leave.

"Grant, can I ask you something?"

"Of course, sir."

I checked the device. Satisfied it passed inspection, I tossed it into a heap of them I'd collected in the corner.

"Don't you think these parades are getting a tad... tiresome?"

"I'm afraid I don't understand, Lord Mollusk."

"How many parades do I really need?" I asked. "This is the third this week and it's only Tuesday."

Grant smiled. "But, sir, you saved Terra from horrible enslavement. You can hardly be surprised that her people want to express their gratitude."

"Yes. Gratitude." I started assembling another device from the various pieces piled on the table. "Would it be ungrateful on my part to just skip this one?"

"Shall I send your regrets then?"

"Do that. Tell everyone I'm busy. A lot of pressing science and stuff."

"Shall I tell them to postpone it to a more convenient time?"

"No, just go ahead and do it without me." I fitted two parts together with a screwdriver. "Lots of science to get to."

Grant nodded. "As you wish, sir."

He left, and I continued assembling.

After an hour, I took a break to check the parade coverage. All across the planet, in this world's greatest cities, throngs of Terra Sapiens celebrated Warlord Mollusk Day. Or maybe it was Emperor Mollusk Is Great Month. I'd lost track of the number of holidays, both official and unofficial, dedicated to my amazing achievements. And while they were amazing, there was a point where it stopped being interesting.

Today was New York City's chance to throw the official official parade. There were always plenty of unofficial parades and a slew of unofficial official parades. But the official official parade was the biggest one. It traveled across the planet, moving from city to city, growing larger and more elaborate each day. What had started as a simple motorcade with me on the back of a convertible had become an industry unto itself.

The floats had become so complex that many colleges now offered degrees in float engineering. There were factories that worked all day, every day to meet the demands for confetti and balloons. And celebration fatigue was a growing international problem.

Yet still the Terrans kept at it with no signs of slowing down, throwing all their resources toward monuments in my honor and praising me in every way their culture could conceive.

There were 106 movies about my life, each more grandiose than the last. And while I was indeed the one who repelled the Saturnite invasion, I hadn't ended WW II by punching out Gorilla Hitler. Nor had I birthed the Industrial Revolution, split Pangea, synthesized the amino acids that led to the development of life in the system, or played with Hendrix at Woodstock '69.

I forced myself to watch the parade broadcast for a few minutes. Not that I needed to worry about missing it. The announcers reminded me that there would be an immediate rebroadcast after the post-parade coverage.

The dark-haired female of the duo smiled brightly while speaking in her perfect-diction announcer voice. "It's a shame that Lord Mollusk couldn't be with us today, but we know he's watching over us."

"Yes, he is, Melanie," said her equally peppy male equivalent. "As long as Terra has Emperor Mollusk, we can always be certain we're safe."

They both laughed.

"Coming up next, Bill," said Melanie, "is the Beautiful Emperor Mollusk Choir."

"Oh, I love these kids," said Bill. "What's the name of that song they're famous for?"

Melanie glanced at the index card in her hand. "According to this, Bill, it's 'Beautiful Emperor Mollusk.'"

"Dopey me," he said. "I should've remembered that."

"Especially considering it's the only song they sing, silly Billy."

They chuckled in perfect harmony.

"We'll be right back after a word from our sponsor," said Bill. "Emperor Mollusk Creates the Universe. *Opening in a theater near you."*

"Oh, and it's a good one," she replied. "I was privileged enough to see an advance screening. In the film, Lord Mollusk goes back in time and—"

He put a finger to his lips. "Now, now, Mel. You don't want to ruin it for everyone, do you?"

I turned off the TV.

Mind control was a delicate science. Obviously, I'd miscalculated somewhere.

So it was that a week later, I sat by my fireplace in my Venezuelan palace and addressed the Terrans one last time.

"Hello. Emperor Mollusk here."

I smiled at the camera.

"First of all, let me just say that I've really enjoyed our time together. You're a terrific species. You really are. And it's been great fun ruling over you, but..."

I paused. This was proving harder than I thought it would be.

"It's not you. It's me. Turns out that now that I've solved most of your problems, I'm not finding merely ruling you to be particularly satisfying. It's been a problem of mine for some time. Even before I came to your world. But that's not important. I'm just here to say that, effective as of this moment, I am no longer Supreme Warlord of Terra. You're free to rule yourselves again."

It was probably only my imagination, but I thought I sensed the collective gasp of a billion souls echoing through the atmosphere.

I held up a spherical device.

"I've distributed these across the planet. They contain a counteragent to the microbes I've seeded in your global water supply. And I've already had the mind twisters deactivated and disassembled.

"Unfortunately, the effects of this conditioning will take several decades to fully disappear. Thirty years, give or take. For the foreseeable future, you'll still experience a reflexive and irresistible urge to adore me. Please refrain from doing so."

I paced to one side of the fireplace and back again.

"I've done things. Things, upon reflection, that I'm not sure I'm happy I've done. I can't undo most of them. But I can give you back your world. You aren't ready for it, of course. But you weren't really ready for it before, and to your credit, you managed not to blow it up just fine without me. Oh, sure, I fixed a few problems here and there. You can keep the improvements. You're welcome.

"Since you'll need a few decades to get back to your old selves, I'll stick around in the meantime. Just to handle any emergencies that might pop up, but treat me as you would any other resident of Terra. If you happen to see me on the street, feel free to say hello. But no more bowing. No more autographs. No more parades and holidays. And enough with the statues already. They're all very nice, but after a point, it just becomes silly."

I sat in my fine leather armchair and interlaced my fingers.

"Right. Not much left to say at this point other than it's been a pleasure being your conqueror. Take care of yourselves."

I made a slashing motion and the camera operator cut the feed.

"How was that?" I asked.

"Excellent, sir," he said.

"I probably should've prerecorded it." I slouched. "Well, no point in worrying about it now. It's done."

I walked to the balcony and looked at Puerto Ayacucho bathed in the glow of sunset. The streets were empty. Everyone was at home, watching my broadcast. I gave them a few minutes to process my message. An order to be themselves was still an order, and they were programmed to follow all my orders without question. Slowly, the Terrans filtered out of their homes. They walked past my home. Most ignored me. One or two waved to me, though they tried to act casual about it.

I did the polite thing and waved back.

I studied the statue, a twenty-foot-high depiction of me built into the square just beyond the tree line. The granite monument seemed ridiculous right then, and I wondered why it hadn't seemed so before.

"Have that destroyed tomorrow," I told a servant.

"Yes, sir."

"Have them all destroyed," I said.

"As you wish, Lord."

I thought about ordering him not to call me Lord, *but they'd eventually figure that out on their own.*

"Except maybe that one in Moscow," I said. "I've always liked that one."

"Yes, sir."

"And the St. Louis statue. It'd be a shame to destroy that one after they took down the Arch to make room for it. On second thought, don't destroy anything just yet. Not until I've had some time to think about it. Can't hurt to keep a few mementos around."

"Very good, sir." He bowed and left.

I stood there on the balcony and thought about things. For all my intelligence, I rarely wasted time contemplating. I was usually too busy researching and building and experimenting, but in that moment of self-analysis, I realized how dissatisfied I was with my accomplishments, grandiose as they might have been.

But then I grew bored, went to the lab, and started designing a better death ray.

We left the Everlasting Dynasty with a few ounces of undying water and the blessing of the queen. As I expected, she had no information on the current location of the Brain or his larger plans.

We stopped at Cairo, where the Terrans were more than happy to allow me access to a state-of-the-art lab for a few hours.

The lab door opened, and Zala entered.

"I thought you were going to get some rest," I said. "You're not much good to me exhausted."

"It's been nine hours, Emperor."

"Has it?" I studied the latest batch of spectroscope readings. "Must have lost track of time. Wonders of scientific exploration and all that. Have a nice nap?"

She stretched. "That couch left a kink in my shoulder."

"You could've used a hotel," I said. "I wouldn't have left without you."

"I'm not leaving you unprotected."

"Very dedicated of you." I glanced up from the readout. "If you'd like, I could set you up with some basic cybernetic augmentations that would reduce your need for rest. Wouldn't take more than a day and some simple surgery. Just think of how much you could accomplish with a built-in chainsaw and eyes able to scan the entire electromagnetic spectrum."

"I'll pass."

"Pity. Though let me know if you do change your mind."

Zala leaned over the table where I had placed all the components we'd gathered on this adventure. The half-assembled catalyzer from the moon incident, the unfathomable extraneous bits from jelligantic. The fluid sample from the Great Gynoecium and the vial of undying water.

"I'm sure you can't wait to tell me what your keen observational mind has gleaned from these odds and ends, Emperor."

"If you insist..." I joined her at the table. "My data suggests that all these parts can be put together in the following manner. Observe."

I took apart the catalyzer, putting aside most of its parts. But with the few left over, I screwed and snapped them with the bits from the jelligantic node. Then I screwed the sample of Gynoecium sap and mixed a few drops of undying water with it. The black sap turned a fresh white color. I handed her the device, just big enough to be held in one hand.

"This is it?" she asked.

"Were you expecting something more?"

She shrugged. "I don't know what I was expecting. What's it do?"

"I don't really know," I replied. "But it's the only configuration that makes the slightest bit of sense."

"How can you not know what it does?"

"Because it's only a component," I said. "It's like looking at a screw and knowing what model of spacecraft it belongs to."

"Surely, you can make one of your educated guesses," she said.

"Surely." I took the device and turned it in my hands. "It depends entirely on the function of the Gynoecium sap. It could be a power source. Or it could be artificially stimulated to generate its own psionic effect. It's really quite fascinating how the sap responds to the undying water. It doesn't merely preserve the sap, but also has a positive energy yield. It's low output, but properly manipulated, it could produce enough energy to power a larger device for a minute or two."

Zala tried and failed to appear interested.

"I don't know why you insist on asking for explanations that will just bore you," I said.

Her scales darkened. "I don't know either."

I opened a slot in my exo and tucked the mystery part away.

"What do we do now?" she asked.

I went back to studying data. "I don't know. The disc has no more information."

"Perhaps you missed something. If this is truly the work of an inside agent, then possibly there's something hidden even more obscurely."

"There's nothing else on the disc, Zala," I said. "I checked. And then I checked again. And then I checked one more time. I ran it through every data recovery method I know as well as several new ones I invented today. If there's one thing I'm sure of, it's that this disc has nothing else on it."

"Then what's your plan?"

"We wait."

Her tail whipped around. "That's not a plan."

"It's a plan," I said. "Just not a very good one. If you have a better one, please share it."

Zala's feathers ruffled. She waved her arms in a sweeping gesture around the lab. "Use this. Do something. Notice some tiny detail. Jump to some ridiculous conclusion. Do what you do, Emperor."

"What I do isn't as easy as I make it look," I said.

"Easy? Since embarking on this mission, we've had one narrow escape after another. You've yet to convince me that the Brain hasn't been five steps ahead of you at every turn. I'm charged with guarding you, but you refuse to tell me everything I need to know to do so. Half the time, you treat the lives of those around you as assets to wager recklessly. And other times, you're willing to risk your own life for the protection of this planet you no longer even rule."

"This is why I prefer robots," I mumbled.

Zala hissed. It was a sound reserved only for the most absolute levels of Venusian disgust and frustration. She was midway through storming from the lab when I stopped her.

"When we were leaving the Gynoecium cave, you asked me if I believed if there was really an inside agent working against the Brain. Do you remember that?"

She leaned against the doorframe and narrowed her eyes. "Yes?"

"When I gave you my answer, you laughed."

She half smiled. "I remember."

"When I asked, you wouldn't tell me why."

Zala chuckled. "And it's been bothering you ever since, hasn't it?"

I paused long enough to hopefully appear disinterested. "I'll admit to some nagging curiosity."

"You can't stand it, can you? Not knowing."

Her eyes flashed with a sinister light.

"Deal with it, Emperor."

She turned to leave when a Terran military officer appeared on the lab's main screen.

He said, "Lord Mollusk—"

I interrupted. "Please, General. It's Emperor."

"Yes, Lord Emperor Mollusk. You requested that we alert you to any unusual activity reports. We have reports of unidentified craft descending on Paris."

"Thank you, General. Order your defense forces not to interfere, evacuate everyone within ten square miles of the Champ de Mars. I will handle this personally."

He saluted. "By your command, Lord Emperor Mollusk."

"Emperor," I said. "Just Emp... Oh, forget it."

Zala and I hurried to my saucer.

"Is it the Brain?" asked Zala.

"I wouldn't be surprised. And it can only mean one thing," I said. "He means to steal the Eiffel Tower."

We arrived in Paris in under twenty minutes. That was still more than enough time for the Brain's ships to have surrounded the tower. Three heavy towcraft employed tractor beams in an effort to uproot the monument.

I took aim and blasted one of the craft. It floundered, struggling to maintain its equilibrium.

The towcraft spit out several dozen fighters. They came roaring toward me. I blasted them out of the sky while engaging in evasive maneuvers.

The Brain appeared on the transmission screen. "Emperor, where do you come from?"

"Didn't see this coming?" I asked. "Even with your antitime radio?"

My craft zipped low over the city. I fired off a volley of rockets. Pursuing fighters exploded.

"I don't need absolute knowledge of the future to defeat

you," said the Brain. "You're only one saucer against fifty fighters."

I came to a sudden stop, and the fighters flew past. They buzzed like a school of hungry piranhas. Beams burned against our shielding. Zala eyed the rapidly draining power levels.

The Brain cackled. "Surrender, and I just might let you live."

The saucer sounded the warning klaxon.

"Shields at thirteen percent," added Zala unnecessarily.

I hovered while the fighters continued their barrage.

"If you have one of your superweapons," she said, "you should use it now."

A backup squad of my own robotic fighters zoomed over the City of Lights. They shot a few of the Brain's ships out of the air. The struggle broke into pitched aerial battles as our forces waged war.

"You don't give up easily," said the Brain. "I can respect that about—"

I hit the comm mute.

While our fleets kept each other busy, I blew a towcraft in two. Its flaming wreckage came crashing down. The other two craft struggled with their cargo beams.

I opened communications. "You aren't getting the tower."

"I'll admit I didn't know you'd interfere," said the Brain, "but that doesn't mean I didn't come prepared."

Something tore its way out of the broken mass of metal of the towcraft I'd shot down. A six-story automaton stepped from the debris, none the worse for the crash. It was a standard Martian combot design. Four legs and four arms mounted on a cylindrical body. There were a few cannons mounted on it, but it was mostly designed to inflict terror on the enemy by stomping its way through their ranks. At the top of the cylinder, a clear dome showcased a huge Terra Sapien brain that glowed a bright emerald.

"Tremble at my most fearsome weapon." The Brain on my screen howled with laughter. "The radioactive mind of Madame Curie!"

Shrieking, the Curie bot smashed nearby buildings with her flailing limbs.

"You can stop me from capturing the Eiffel Tower. Or you can save Paris from her rampage. But even you can't do both."

The Brain's image faded from the screen.

I hesitated.

"You can't be debating this," said Zala. "If he gets that tower...I don't know what will happen. But it can't be good."

Fires burned as fighter craft crashed around me. Paris had always been my favorite Terran city. But I couldn't live here anymore. Whenever I looked across the City of Lights, I remembered the day necessity had forced me to destroy half of it. I'd rebuilt it, but now, seeing pockets of it ablaze with damage and Madame Curie demolishing it beneath her terrible claws, I discovered that I couldn't let it happen again.

I ordered my squadrons to focus their attack on the robot. They broke off and strafed Curie without effect. Her brain radiated a sharp green flare. The superior shielding on my saucer was able to protect us from her disruptive pulse. My fighters weren't so fortunate. Most dropped from the sky. Several zipped around in random flight patterns until colliding with each other or the ground. One or two outright exploded.

Curie demolished a city block in three stomps.

I zipped toward her and shot her with the full assortment of blasters and death rays on my craft. They had no effect. The mutated brain powering and guiding the combot was some kind of energy sponge. Every blast I threw at her was absorbed and channeled back into her.

"They're escaping with the tower," said Zala.

"I'll deal with that later."

I launched an assortment of ballistic weaponry, ranging from missiles and rockets to explosive neutrino spheres. They met with limited success. Most exploded at a distance from Curie when they were disrupted by interference generated by her. Others veered off target, exploding around the city.

An alien force seized control of the saucer. Curie wasn't only giant and radioactive. She was also telekinetic.

My attempts to counter proved pointless after she drained the saucer's power. The engines went dead. As did my exoskeleton. Snarg gurgled as her cybernetic parts shut down. She could function without them, but it did take the zip out of her step.

Curie pulled us into her arms and clamped her claws into the hull.

"Do something, Emperor," said Zala.

"I'm open to suggestions."

"Reverse polarity or reconfigure something. I don't know. Do some of that scientific magic you're so adept at."

What I said then must have shocked her. It certainly shocked me.

"I'm out of ideas."

With a triumphant howl, Curie hurled us away like a Frisbee. We sailed helplessly, bounced around without the inertial dampeners, skipped across the street twice, before grinding to a crashing stop.

There wasn't enough power left for even the emergency lights to work.

I sat in the darkened cockpit, in my own nonfunctional exoskeleton. It couldn't have been long. A few minutes at most. But in the black quiet of the cockpit, I sat and thought about nothing.

"Emperor?" Two pinpoints of light, Zala's eyes, appeared in the dark. "Emperor, are you alive?"

"I'm alive," I said. "But I can't move."

"Hold on." She grunted and groaned as she dealt with her own problems. "Your pet rolled over on me. I'm almost free."

Snarg gurgled.

"Don't get mad at me, you stupid bug." Something clanged against something else. "There!"

Another light illuminated the darkness. Zala had a small flashlight. It wasn't very bright, but a hungry sea slug takes what it can get. The cockpit was steeply tilted. Zala managed to climb her way toward me.

"Are you hurt?" she asked.

She shone the light on my dome. I'd unplugged myself from the exo, and it was now little more than an unwieldy aquarium.

"I'm not dead, but I'm unwilling to commit to anything more at the moment. Are you?"

"I'll live."

Her face was cut and bruised, and it obviously pained her to move. As could be expected. Neptunon physiology, aside from our highly developed brains, was relatively simple and difficult to traumatize.

I didn't comment on her pain. It would have only insulted her.

"We need to get you out of here. You'll have to let me carry you." She ran her fingers along the cracked dome. "Is there an emergency release on this thing? Or do I have to break it open?"

"Perhaps we should wait for help," I said.

"We can't stay in this saucer, helpless and exposed."

She was right, but outside of my exo, I was just a squishy genius exposed to a dangerous world. And Zala was one of my worst enemies.

"Damn it, Emperor. You're just going to have to trust me."

"I've never been very good at trusting," I admitted.

"Maybe this would be a good time to start. Do you feel that?"

Few sounds penetrated the cockpit, but a slight shudder ran through it. One right after another. Each tremor stronger than the last. The advancing footsteps of Madame Curie.

I pushed the release. The dome popped open, spilling water and nearly causing Zala to slip. She reached down, and I wrapped my tentacles around her arm.

"My gods, Emperor. You are slimy."

"I like to maintain a healthy mucous sheen."

I secured myself to her arm. But not before I opened the exo compartment and removed the mystery component.

She grunted. "Not so tight, Emperor."

"Sorry." I pointed toward a lever. "That's the emergency exit."

The tremors intensified. She pulled the lever. A section of cockpit wall fell away, and she jumped out as Snarg dragged herself behind us. We cleared the wreck just as Curie wrapped her metallic hands around it. She lifted it off the ground, studying it like a broken toy.

Curie discarded the saucer, tossing it aside. The combot cast a bright red spotlight on Zala and me.

Zala turned to run, but Curie slammed a leg in our way. The giant robot bent closer. Her monstrous green brain flickered with atomic energy. Loyal Snarg, though barely able to raise her head, growled.

I held the device in my tentacles. It was useless. I might as well have been holding a hunk of scrap metal.

The shadow of the towcraft rolled overhead. Curie trundled away, and the craft tractored her into it. And then the two towcraft and their remaining fighters flew away, along with the tower. The air shimmered as they vanished behind a stealth field, disappearing in their triumph without even bothering to crush me underfoot.

And there wasn't a damn thing I could do to stop it.

My saucer was unsalvageable, but it was a simple matter to bring in a new one. I had hundreds stationed across Terra for my needs. And thousands of spare exos. Snarg was fine once her batteries were recharged. And Zala's injuries were easily treatable with a bit of modern medicine.

A nurse applied a bandage to the cut on Zala's forehead. "The patch should seal the cut. You might have a scar."

Zala was too proud to show weakness. She acknowledged the doctor with a grunt.

"Thank you, Doctor," I said. "That will be all."

"Yes, Lord Mollusk. Just press the button if you need anything else." The doctor left the room.

I stood at the eighth-floor window. My view of Paris was obstructed, but I could see the fires still burning. Sirens filled the night as the Terrans fought the blazes. The damage wasn't catastrophic. Certainly nowhere near as devastating as the beginnings of the Saturnite invasion. Paris would survive.

But the flames hypnotized me, and though the view was facing the wrong way, I didn't have to see the empty space where the Eiffel Tower should have been to be reminded it was missing.

"What's wrong with you, Emperor?" asked Zala.

Snarg, sensing my melancholy, skittered submissively at my feet.

I stroked her between her antennae.

"He beat me."

"It wasn't your finest hour, but I'm sure you'll get over it."

"You don't understand. He won. I lost."

"Oh, I understand. I was there." She stood, tested her arm. It was still tender. "And, yes, you were defeated. Handily."

"You're enjoying this, aren't you?"

She beamed. I'd never seen her so happy.

I turned to her. "I've never been beat before."

With a dry chuckle, she jumped off the table. "Then answer me this. Why aren't you Warlord of Venus?"

"I've failed before. Many times before. That's what comes from taking risks. Even I can't control all the variables."

"It's always a pleasure to hear you admit that," she said. "You should do it more often. So if you know you're fallible then why should you be bothered by this particular defeat? Humiliating as it might have been."

"You're really enjoying this."

She tried to wipe the smile off her face, but the best she could do was to lessen it.

"This is different," I said. "This feels... different."

"Different," she said. "A bit vague, isn't that?"

"The Brain has the anti-time transmission."

Zala drew her scimitar and practiced a few swings to see how her arm responded. "He had that before. It didn't seem to bother you before."

"That's because I assumed I was smarter than him."

"Are you saying you're not so certain now?"

I didn't answer, and she lowered her weapon.

"Emperor, are you telling me you think he might be smarter than you?"

"I don't know," I said softly.

"This can't be the first time you've considered the possibility there might be someone capable of outwitting you. There are billions of intelligent life-forms in the system. I'm no scientist, but I would think it would seem statistically unlikely you could be smarter than all of them all the time."

I stroked Snarg's antennae. "I'm aware of that. Intellectually."

"But now you have indisputable proof. For the first time in your life, you have to admit that someone was smarter than you. No way to deny it, is there?"

I didn't answer, which was an answer in itself.

"I thought you were made of sterner stuff, Emperor."

She pushed the smile from her face and joined me at the window.

"You were beaten. Humiliated. Your defeat was devastating and total. You failed on every level." She stifled a smirk as she smoothed her feathers. "It happens."

"Not to me."

She shook her head. "It happens to everyone. So for once,

just this once, you were not in charge of your destiny. You weren't the one making the decisions. You overconfidently blundered into a fight you couldn't win and learned a hard lesson. No matter how gifted you are, no matter how smart and powerful and capable, you're going to lose sometimes. You can't win every battle. Even you, brilliant as you are"—I appreciated that she refrained from using any sarcasm in the word *brilliant*—"will make mistakes. And, yes, this was a big one.

"But you're still alive. You're still a genius who can build a doomsday device out of wool, coconuts, and cardboard. So maybe the Brain is smarter than you. So what? So what if he handed you a crushing defeat. And I think we can both admit it was crushing."

"You're really enjoying this."

"It was almost worth getting killed to watch," she admitted. "Almost."

She said, "Do you want to know why I laughed at the cave, Emperor?" She clasped me on the shoulder and smiled, without malice. With perhaps a smidgeon of genuine affection.

"You might be an egotistical, megalomaniacal, manipulative criminal. But you don't back down from a challenge. Even against a foe who might very well be ahead of you every step of the way, you're still determined to see this through. You can't walk away. Not from science. Not from mysteries. Not even from this world that you endanger just as often as you save. It's that character flaw that has led you toward every mistake you've ever made. But I realized then that it's also about the only thing I like about you.

"You failed, Emperor, walking into a trap created by your

own hubris. And maybe that overconfidence was warranted, but your devastating defeat was bound to happen sooner or later. If not this time, then the next. Or the next after that. But if there was one life-form in this universe I never expected to lose confidence in himself, it would be you. And if you just hand that defeat to the Brain, then you're not the Neptunon I thought you were.

"Nobody is quite as smart as they think they are. Not even you."

Zala left me to my thoughts. As she exited the room, she chuckled to herself.

"Devastating," she muttered with a chortle.

I couldn't say if Zala's lecture motivated me or if I would've snapped out of my spiritual ennui on my own. It'd be a lie to say my defeat in Paris didn't weaken my normally invulnerable self-confidence, but I'd never been one to drift on the current. Even when I should've known better.

I'd nearly destroyed Terra as many times as I'd saved it. I assumed there was a better than average chance that one day I would. But that wouldn't prevent me from exploring the edges of dangerous science. It was a driving compulsion, and I couldn't pretend to be in control of it.

The Pluvian philosopher kings had suggested that there was no good or bad. There were only order and chaos, and by the laws of physics, entropy was bound to come out on top. But to not fight against chaos was still the ultimate sin because it was a tacit betrayal of the foundations of all sentient life-forms everywhere. And a universe without life was entirely pointless while a universe with life was only mostly pointless. And in a mostly pointless universe, having to decide whether to wallow in defeat or go forward toward certain defeat, there wasn't much choice at all.

Zala had been right. The Brain might be my one unsolvable problem, but one way or another, I had to see it through.

I passed the next twelve hours modifying and planning for our next encounter. Zala left me to it, and after I was confident enough in my powers of science, we were aboard my saucer, flying toward the sacred city of Shambhala.

"How do you know they'll be there?" Zala asked.

"I don't," I replied. "But after acquiring the Eiffel Tower, I can only assume they're planning on transmitting some sort of signal. And that takes power. Given that the tower is the most powerful transmitter array on Terra, I'm assuming the most powerful power generator will be next on their list."

When she didn't pose another question, I wasn't sure how to react.

"It's only a wild guess," I said. "Educated, but with nothing to back it up."

She sat back, folded her arms across her chest, and nodded. "Yes, I can see that."

"Aren't you going to use this moment to point out the very likely possibility that I'm wrong?" I asked.

"Should I?"

"No, you shouldn't, but you usually do. Or at least make some passing reference to my arrogance. Or something like that."

"Would you like me to?"

"Not particularly."

"Then I won't."

She smiled slightly. Her thoughts were obvious. Though it wasn't in my nature to dwell on my defeat, my confidence remained shaken. For the first time since…well…forever, I didn't trust my judgment. I didn't need Zala to question my competence, but there was a certain ritual we'd developed in the last few days.

"You don't have to take it easy on me," I said.

"Oh, I'm not."

Her smile remained. We both knew what she was doing. Her respectful acceptance of my plan, without challenge, was a reminder of my own fragility in the guise of an act of compassion. It was irritating, and that was precisely the point.

She glanced at the snowy caps of the Himalayas passing below the saucer. "Why is the generator in such an out of the way place anyway?"

"The engine taps into a previously unknown form of energy I call molluskotrenic. It's present across the planet, but is strongest and easiest to tap here."

"Doesn't exactly roll off the tongue, does it?"

"I discovered it. I get to name it."

"Fair enough."

"Although I didn't quite discover it," I said. "Some Terra Sapiens had tapped into the field in the past, using it for basic weather manipulation, life extension, and other things. They used it to found a secret city called Shambhala."

"Then shouldn't it be called *shambhalotrenic*?" she asked.

"They didn't really know what they had," I replied. "And they would be dead if I hadn't built the engine and harnessed the power more efficiently. So I think getting to name the thing is a small price to pay. The Shambhalans are a humble people in any case. They don't care what it's named as long as they're free to continue their lives of quiet meditation and philosophy."

"They sound delightful," she said flatly.

"You'll probably like them. They follow a strict warrior monk code. They like to talk about honor. A lot. So that's something you have in common."

Shambhala was a radiant green patch in the snowy mountains. The proper city possessed certain qualities of traditional Asian architecture, a cross-section of the various cultures of the region. There were even Western influences, no doubt brought in by wanderers and truth seekers from across the globe. Everything was stone and wood. I'd offered to update their building materials, but the monks refused. They'd chosen an isolated way of life, and as long as the molluskotrenic supported them, they had no reason to look elsewhere.

The engine stood beside the city.

"That channels unlimited energy to Terra?" Her skepticism was understandable. The engine didn't glow. It didn't shoot bolts of power into the sky. Aside from being a steel construction in a primitive realm of wood and steel, it was unassuming.

"And then some," I said. "The source of the energy remains mostly a mystery, even to me, and it isn't enough in itself. But with it, I was able to build a perpetual-motion machine that generates m-rays that are transmitted across the planet and converted into electricity."

"M-rays?" she said.

"When you discover a new form of radiation, I'll let you name it."

Shambhala had a landing pad just outside the city. We disembarked and were greeted by a bald Terran in an orange robe. He smiled and bowed.

"Emperor Mollusk, you honor us with your presence."

I returned the bow. "Most Illustrious Master of the Ten Sacred Palms, be assured the pleasure is all mine."

I quickly introduced Zala and the Illustrious Master. But I skipped the chitchat.

"I have reason to believe your city is in danger from outside forces," I said.

"Shambhala is a place of peace," he replied. "We offend no one. In a thousand years, no one has set foot in our paradise with violent intent. The gods smile upon Shambhala."

"Let's hope you're right."

The Illustrious Master always smiled, but he smiled a little less. "You have been a great friend to Shambhala. And we would be honored to hear your concerns. Your council has proven a blessing in the past, and I would not easily dismiss them. Apologies if I have offended you in my actions."

"And I apologize if the perception of my own offense has offended you, Illustrious Master."

We bowed.

"No apology is necessary," he replied. "If I have given you the impression that one was required, I sincerely apologize for the error."

"And I apologize if the error seems in need of apology."

We bowed again.

Zala stepped between us. "Didn't you want to take a look around, Emperor? To be sure everything is in order?"

The Master said, "Of course. How inconsiderate of me. I apologize for my inconsideration."

He started to bow, but Zala stopped him with a hand on his shoulder.

"Yes, apologies all around. Apologies for everyone. But we should get on with it."

The Master led us through the city streets. Shambhala was a quiet place. It didn't bustle. The only noise was that of songbirds, children playing, and the unified grunts of dozens of monks practicing martial arts.

He nodded toward Zala. "Your companion speaks her mind. It is admirable."

"Sometimes," I said.

Zala slowed as we passed a monk going through the seventeen righteous sword motions. The peculiar weapon favored by the monks had holes in the blade that whistled as the sword sliced through the air.

"The ancients say enlightenment is found in the song of a blade," said the Illustrious Master.

The ancients also said enlightenment could be seen in the green leaves of a cabbage. And heard between the beats of a hummingbird's wings. And in a thousand and one drops of sweat. And beneath the rock that never moves. And in a thousand other places.

"I must confess, Emperor Mollusk, that your visit doesn't come as a surprise to us."

"No, I didn't think it would."

I'd noticed the monks gathering around us as we walked through the city. It was hardly subtle. Every person we passed joined us, and soon we were surrounded by several hundred citizens. Men, women, and children of all ages. Their gently smiling faces portrayed no threat beyond their growing numbers.

Zala must have noticed too, but she didn't offer comment.

"You understand that we of the sacred city owe you a great debt, and that when the outsiders came to pervert your technology, we almost considered fighting against them. But, of course, it isn't our way to raise our fists in violence. For this, I must apologize most sincerely."

He stopped and bowed.

"If your esteemed companion would surrender her weapons to us, it would make things easier."

Zala laughed. "If you want my weapons, you'll have to take them from—"

A monk's spinning kick nearly took her head off. She was just quick enough to avoid it. He threw several punches at her. She dodged, smashed him in the nose with her elbow. He collapsed. An elderly woman and a child rushed forward and helped him limp away.

"I thought these people were pacifists," said Zala.

"We are," answered the Illustrious Master. "But we have been violated most unfortunately." He bowed and turned his head to show the scar under his right ear. No doubt some sort of implant was at work here. "Now the skills that have aided us in our quest for inner peace have been perverted, and I can only humbly beg your forgiveness for our actions."

Three swordmasters advanced on Zala. She drew the pistol on her hip.

"Don't do that," I said. "You'll be shooting innocent people."

She grunted, put the blaster away, and drew her scimitar.

One of the swordmasters whirled his weapon in a flashing pattern. "I apologize if my blade prematurely ends your own journey toward enlightenment and only hope you can forgive me in your next life. And should you end mine, I apologize for forcing you to spill—"

Zala punched him across the jaw, sending him sprawling. "You're forgiven."

The Shambhalans, every single one aside from the Illustrious Master, rushed Zala. I lost her in the chaos, but her battle cry came from somewhere in the muddle. She couldn't win this fight, but she wasn't going to make it easy on them.

"Your companion is very stubborn," observed the Master. "But as the ancients say, enlightenment can be found in the unwinnable battle."

"It seems you can find it anywhere," I replied.

"Ah, so continues your own journey."

I left Zala to fight her own quest for enlightenment in her own way. The Master led me to the temple at the center of the city. I wasn't surprised to see the Brain, in a seven-foot exo, standing on its steps.

"So good of you to join us, Emperor. Where is the Venusian?"

"I'm afraid her path to enlightenment may involve some bruising," said the Master.

"No matter," said the Brain. "I'll take it from here. After you've subdued the Venusian, bring her along."

The Illustrious Master bowed.

"Where is it?" I asked. "Where's the tower?"

The Brain pointed behind me. The air shimmered as he

deactivated the stealth field that hid the Eiffel Tower standing beside the molluskotrenic engine.

"No doubt you have many questions, Emperor, and we will answer them in good time. But we have a few minutes before everything is in final preparation, and it's about time we get the formal introductions out of the way. We've been waiting to meet you, face-to-face, for far too long."

He led me into the temple. Once an open space where the monks of Shambhala would meditate to the sounds of a sacred gong (there were many sacred things in the sacred city), it was now an audience chamber. Along the walls, hundreds of disembodied Terra Sapien brains sat in their own fluid-filled spheres.

"The Council of Egos welcomes you, Emperor."

And the Council cheered.

It was difficult to distinguish one Terran brain from another. Fortunately, they had metallic nameplates screwed to their spheres. I had a cursory self-education on Terran history, and I recognized many of them. The Marquis de Sade, Countess Elizabeth Báthory, Genghis Khan, Julius Caesar, Florence Nightingale, Pol Pot, Chairman Mao, Soupy Sales, Cleopatra, Susan B. Anthony. Just to name a few.

"Where's Hitler?" I asked. "I don't see Hitler's brain."

"That idiot?" replied P. T. Barnum. "He was too annoying and demanding. There's no place for that in the Council of Egos. We serve a higher purpose, a grand design."

Mussolini snickered. "We flushed him."

"Not everyone is worthy of the Council," said Zu Ding. "For some, the conversion process is too difficult. It doesn't take. Greta Garbo, Confucius, Oscar Wilde, the wondrous preservative elixir distilled from the undying waters failed to work for them."

"Terrible shame," said Buffalo Bill Cody.

"Indeed," said Zu Ding. "And others go mad. They usually fall into a catatonic state. Or worse."

"Jane Austen wouldn't stop screaming," said Archimedes. "And Madame Curie descended into a bestial state. Although as you learned, there were other side effects that proved to be beneficial to keeping her around."

"And, of course," said Zu Ding, "still others insist on clinging to antiquated notions of morality. Einstein called us insane. He claimed the preservation process must have unhinged our minds. Can you imagine the absurdity of that? We have found a way to transform ourselves into demigods of pure intellect, and he thought us delusional megalomaniacs."

The Council burst into cackling. They fed off each other, continuing for some time.

Zala was brought in by a pair of monks. She was battered, but the Shambhalans had retained enough of their restraint that she was still able to walk under her own power. She stood beside me.

"I'm surprised they didn't have to kill you," I whispered beneath the laughter echoing off the walls.

She wiped some blood from the corner of her mouth. "If experience has taught me anything, Emperor, it's that you seem to delight in walking us into traps. I wasn't shocked by this turn of events. But I could hardly be expected to surrender meekly, could I?"

The laughter died down, and for a moment, I thought the Council might be done. But then Tolstoy burst into raucous guffaws, and it triggered a new burst.

"They certainly are a jolly bunch," she said. "Should I be worried?"

"I haven't decided yet," I replied.

The Council's laughter stopped, shut off like someone had thrown a switch.

Zu Ding said, "The Council of Egos share a singular vision of tomorrow. Old rivalries, old ideas, must be set aside if one is to join us. We cannot tolerate those who are unwilling to adapt to the new order. We were very close to voting to remove Davy Crockett and López de Santa Anna at one point. But now look at them? The best of friends."

"We play mahjong on Wednesdays," said Santa Anna.

"I don't even remember why we used to squabble," said Crockett.

"All the bickering and infighting that defined us as a species," said Otani Kozui. "A waste of time, a distraction. The system is waiting for us to bring order to its chaos and instead, we've wasted thousands of years quarreling over borders and nations and other meaningless inanities."

"Until you came along, Emperor," said Barnum, "and showed us that Terran unity is possible. The Council has worked from the shadows for thousands of years, but all our efforts were slow and ineffective. Even as our number grew, we found ourselves unable to overcome stubborn Terran nature. It took an outsider, a true master of science and conquest, to show us the way."

The brains murmured their approval.

"You're their hero," said Zala. "You've been trying to stop them, and all this time, they've been admiring you."

"And why shouldn't we?" asked Zabaia. "Since the dawn of

Terran civilization, haven't we looked to the heavens for guidance and salvation? And hasn't Lord Mollusk come from above to save us from ourselves, as dreamt of by prophet and peasant alike?"

Zala laughed. No one laughed with her, and the sound echoed through the chamber.

"Oh, tell me you aren't serious."

She laughed again.

"You think Emperor is your messiah?"

"It is not an inappropriate word," said Barnum. "He has come to deliver us from ourselves, to show us the way."

I smiled, despite myself.

"You're loving this, aren't you?" she asked.

"It's nice to be adored," I admitted.

"This is absurd. He isn't a god. And this ill-conceived religious nonsense—"

The crowd murmured over her.

"This isn't a religion," said Cleopatra. "Such childish things are beneath the Council."

"Religion offers nothing but empty promises to desperate mortals who know only fear," said Joseph Lyons.

"Some promises are emptier than others," added Torquemada.

"What's that supposed to mean?" asked L. Ron Hubbard.

"Oh . . . nothing," replied Torquemada.

"Fellow consuls," said Martin Luther, "this is not the time for this particular argument."

"Nobody asked you for your opinion," said Hubbard. "Not that they ever had to."

"Consuls, please," said Mussolini. "Don't make us consider flushing you."

"Wouldn't want to look bad in front of the messiah," said Zala with every bit of sarcasm at her disposal.

Barnum said, "You misunderstand us, Venusian. We aren't suckers who place our hopes behind blind faith and irrational wishful thinking. That is the way of the old Terra Sapiens. We've transcended our distracting flesh and blood to become beings of pure intellect. And that intellect tells us that Emperor Mollusk has come to save us from ourselves."

"You're all mad," she said.

"But of course, you couldn't comprehend," said Sigmund Freud. "It's the flesh that surrounds you, that smothers your rationality with all its confusing neurological impulses. Once we've separated you from such confusion, you will see."

The floor opened up before us, and a small steel table and several surgical robots rose into the temple.

Several monks, apologizing over each other, seized her. She fought like a Turillian devil, knocking several to the floor. But there were too many. They dragged her to a table. She struggled with every bit of her strength and training, but it didn't do any good. They strapped her down and still she struggled. A brain containment sphere was wheeled into position by her head while the robots sterilized a buzz saw.

"We'll save her from herself," said Barnum. "Unless you have any objections, Lord Mollusk."

The chamber went quiet.

"You can't let them do this, Emperor," said Zala. "I'm a Venusian warrior! I deserve to die on my feet with a sword in my hand."

I said nothing.

The Brain put an arm around me. "Say the word, and we'll do

whatever you desire. No tricks. No loopholes. You are the leader we've been waiting for, and you have our absolute loyalty."

"What are you waiting for?" said Zala. "Tell them to let me go."

I remained silent, pondering.

"You aren't actually considering this?" shouted Zala. "How many times have I saved your life?"

"How many times have you told me you're going to lock me away?" I asked in turn. "We aren't really friends, are we?"

She sneered. "You could at least do me the honor of killing me rather than turning me into one of these bodiless abominations."

She made a good point.

"Before you make your final decision," said Queen Victoria, "there's something we'd like to show you. Something we know you'll find enlightening."

The room dimmed, and an image projected in the air above the Council. My image.

"Hello, Emperor." My recorded voice crackled with static and the image fizzled. "Good to see you, so to speak. As you've already grasped, I am the one who sent this message from the future. I apologize for the poor quality of the transmission, but as you know, anti-time projection is an imprecise science."

Zala said, "You? You're the one who has been behind this the whole time?"

"Yes, I'm afraid that's true," said Future Self. "Pity you figured it out too late, my dear Zala."

"Is this a live transmission?" she asked.

"No," he replied. "It's not live. I just have memorized this conversation from the last time I had it, and am recalling your end of it. It's merely a simulation, as I can't hear you right now, but I did hear you then and that's close enough."

"How do I know you're me?" I asked.

"Who else could I be?" he said. "I suppose I could be a second renegade Neptunon. We do look alike, and this garbled transmission isn't helping. I have no way of proving who I am. I could have recorded your responses from an outside source, so that isn't conclusive. Or I could be a clone. Perhaps one you didn't even know about. A clone of a clone. And from the vantage point of the future, there is any number of tricks I could use to my advantage."

The image faded into gray static, then slowly clarified.

"And the question you're now asking yourself is what would I have to gain from lying to you? To what grand purpose would this sort of deception work toward."

"He's good," I admitted.

"I'm you," he said. "And, regardless of how impossible this assertion is to prove from your point in the space-time continuum, you know that this is true. Who else would be ingenious enough to manipulate you so expertly, to lead you on a grand chase designed to remind you of who you are? Who else but you could possibly outsmart you?"

"My gods, Mollusk," said Zala. "He is you. No one else could say something so obnoxiously self-satisfied with a straight face."

Future Self laughed, and the Council of Egos laughed with him.

"A being of your talents doesn't belong on this pitiful little world," said Future Self. "You were made to conquer! It is your destiny to lead the universe to glory!"

He raised his fist. The council roared.

Even I felt that was a bit much.

"Perhaps that was a bit much." He smiled wryly. "This is less about destiny than inevitability. You can't stop being who you are, Emperor. This misguided retirement leaves you unsatisfied. Don't bother lying about it."

I didn't.

"And I don't have to ask you how the last few days have left you feeling more alive and stimulated than you have in years."

I did.

"Your retirement was an experiment, but that experiment is over. It's a failure, and you are too intelligent to deny that. I get your reluctance. I know there are unpleasant aspects of this hobby that don't appeal to you. But if you don't do it, someone else will. And we both know that they'll do it with less style and subtlety, with armies and death rays, and all sorts of unimaginative destruction."

"They'll fail," I said. "The system can't be conquered. It's a logistical impossibility."

"Yes, it's impossible," he agreed, "and that's exactly why you'll do it."

"Don't tell me that you've already done it?" I asked.

"No. I'm in the future, but not far enough that I can guarantee results. But guarantees are boring. No, I can't make any promises other than to say that it'll be a hell of a lot of fun trying. And if you fail, at least you can say you gave it your best shot.

"In ten seconds, these fine surgeons will remove Zala's brain. Or they'll release her. The decision is entirely in your hands. I trust you'll make the right one."

The image panned to the right to reveal a brain in a sphere. The purple brain had a distinctive partition down the center of its frontal lobe. It was a Venusian brain.

Zala's voice came from its voice synthesizer.

"Hello, Emperor."

The surgeon's saw whirred as he lowered it toward present, full-bodied Zala.

"It's a trick!" she shouted. "It has to be! That could be any Venusian brain! By the Fifth through Eight Gods, if you let them remove my brain, I swear I'll—"

"Stop," I said.

The surgeon's saw switched off.

Zala exhaled with relief. "I knew you'd come to your senses, Mollusk."

"You could at least anesthetize her," I said.

A nurse placed a mask over her mouth and switched on the gas. Zala cursed my name for the minute or two it took for her to lose consciousness.

The Brain bowed. "The Council of Egos awaits your first order, Lord Mollusk."

"I assume there's a machine somewhere," I said. "A device nearby that is the culmination of our journey."

The Brain bobbed in his fluid in way of a nod. "It is nearly complete."

I inwardly winced at the distinctive sound of a motorized blade cutting into bone. It had to be done, but I doubted Zala would understand the necessity of the decision.

"Well," I said. "Let's get to it then."

The doomsday device occupied a great cavern beneath Shambhala. A square-mile excavation of machinery, science, and conquest. Pipes funneled coolant. Webs of shimmering wires stretched across the four towers. Robotic technicians polished the machine and operated the steam vents to keep it from overheating.

"Is it everything you thought it would be?" asked the Brain upon my first glimpse of it from the viewing platform.

"It's beautiful. I wonder what it does."

"You don't know?"

"I have some idea," I replied. "A few possibilities. But I'll admit its exact function escapes me."

We stepped onto a moving walkway and sped slowly toward the center of the grand device.

"We must admit we aren't certain ourselves," said the Brain. "The science of the device is beyond even our greatest intellects. Tesla thinks it's a device meant to harness the global electromagnetic field to power an even greater machine that we haven't built yet. Archimedes theorizes its purpose is to turn the entire planet into a solar death ray. Lovelace thinks it is nothing less than the computer that will access the software of the universe itself, allowing one to rewrite the very laws of physics with the push of a button." He laughed. "There are, of course, hundreds of theories bouncing around in the Council, but even the most intelligent of us must admit that we simply don't know. I suppose they'll be comforted to hear you don't know either."

I frowned.

"What is it, Lord Mollusk?" asked the Brain.

"I've never been on this side of things before," I said. "Skipping all the research, planning, and construction to arrive at the plan nearly completed. It's interesting, but I'm not sure I like it. That's part of the fun. This just seems too easy."

"That's the burden of your genius."

"I suppose. Who are you anyway?" I asked the Brain. "I'm not an expert on Terran history, but I recognized most of the names in the Council."

"My name is unimportant, and you haven't heard of me. If you had, I wouldn't have been doing my job properly. It was my flawless background in covert operations that led to my recruitment."

"Well, if you're going to be working for me," I said, "I should have something to call you other than the Brain."

"Call me Omega."

"It's a touch melodramatic, isn't it?"

The Brain said, "It doesn't matter."

"Then I'll call you Buddy."

Buddy was silent for a moment.

"I'd rather you didn't."

"Oh, relax, Buddy. What's in a name?"

His brain bobbed in its tank. "I'd prefer something else."

"You'll get used to it, Buddy."

His shoulders sagged. "As you wish, sir."

We stepped onto a lift and were lowered into the control room at the heart of the great machine. Countless levers and switches covered the walls. A bank of monitors offered a steady stream of information. I spent several minutes studying the data being offered.

"Does that help any?" asked Buddy.

"Somewhat. Though it's mostly just status reports on the functionality of the machine. How long did it take you to build this?"

"Five months."

I looked out the window at the vast machine before me. "All this in a mere five months? I'm impressed."

"You flatter me, Lord."

"When will it be ready to activate? No, let me guess. When this red light here turns green, it's time to throw the switch."

"How did you—"

"Future designer," I said.

"Of course..."

A pair of guard drones and an eight-foot exoskeleton lumbered into the room.

"If I could interrupt your studies for a moment," said Buddy, "I thought you'd like to meet your new bodyguard. Or rather your old bodyguard in upgraded condition."

I spared a glance at Zala's Venusian brain floating in the chest of an ape-like exoskeleton.

"Yes, very nice."

I turned back to the data streaming across the screens.

"You son of a pribt." She raised a metal fist as if to smash me, but her arm locked.

"You'll find your new body is counterprogrammed to prevent any harm to our leader," said Buddy.

She lowered the arm reluctantly. Three-foot steel talons popped out of her fingertips, and the blaster mounted on her shoulder whirred and clicked.

"Trust me, Mollusk. I'll find a way."

Buddy said, "You should be honored, Venusian. You stand beside the greatest—"

"So I've heard. Mostly from him. I don't need to hear it from you too."

"Give her the sword," I said.

A drone handed her the scimitar.

"I kept it for you," I explained. "It is a Venusian soldier's soul, isn't it?"

She took the weapon in her hand. "I have no place to put it."

"You'll find a retractable scabbard in your right leg," I said.

The scabbard opened, and she tucked away the weapon. "How did you know?"

"It's how I would've designed it," I said. "Or should I say it's how I will design it at some point in the future?"

The control room went pitch black. Only for a moment. The lights snapped back on. The data scroll continued. A bell sounded. The ready light turned green. And everything vibrated, almost imperceptibly.

Snarg perked up. Her antennae twitched, and she squeaked.

Buddy, his voice barely an awed whisper, spoke.

"It's ready."

"What's it doing?" asked Zala.

"An excellent question," I replied. "I don't think it's doing anything important at the moment. Just idling, waiting for someone to start it."

"Yes, Lord." Buddy gestured to the dramatically large lever built into a console. "All that's left for you to do is turn the machine on. And our new glorious future begins."

Zala stepped between me and the lever. "You can't do this, Emperor."

"I have to do this. Causality demands it."

"So you're doing it because you *have* to do it."

"Step aside," said Buddy.

"No, it's fine." I studied the rows of blinking lights at the heart of the machine. "Space-time is greater than any one of us, Zala. Even I'm not beyond it. This machine, that message from the future, everything we've gone through has led up to this moment. This is how it's meant to be."

"Are you listening to yourself?" She had no face, but I could picture the sneer. "I didn't think anyone told the brilliant Emperor Mollusk what to do. You've never lived by anyone else's rules before. Why start now?"

"Shall I deactivate her?" said Buddy.

"No. She has a point. What would happen if I didn't throw that switch? Can I choose not to become my future self? It's an intriguing possibility."

"If anyone could spit in the eye of destiny," said Zala, "it'd be you."

Buddy remotely powered off her exo.

"That was tiresome. And pointless. You will throw the switch. You know you want to. You need to see what this machine does. Your curiosity doesn't allow you any other choice."

"I suppose you're right," I admitted.

"You know I am, Lord Mollusk."

For a moment, I wasn't so certain. Mysteries of fate and possibility danced at the tips of my tentacles, and while I was confident I knew the answers to them, I also did love a good experiment. But throwing the switch or not throwing the switch, there was no way to know for certain which I was supposed to do. If time was fixed, if the only difference between the present me and the future me was a matter of vantage point, then there really was nothing I could do to prevent myself becoming him. I already was him. I just hadn't arrived there yet.

I couldn't outsmart myself. Especially a version that had the benefit of everything I knew *and* everything I would know. The logic was flawless, unavoidable. Whatever I chose, it would lead to future me. And if that was true, I might as well turn on the machine and see what happened.

I grasped the lever, but hesitated to throw it. I looked at Zala's brain, hovering in the bubbling fluids. "You'll understand." I yanked the lever. "One day."

The machine hummed to life. Flashes danced across the webs of wiring as something deep within the machine rumbled. The machine vented huge clouds of steam while multicolored lights running along the towers crackled to life. But the exact purpose of the great invention remained hidden.

"Thank you, Emperor." Buddy laughed. "Thank you for being every bit as foolish as we knew you would be."

He reactivated Zala's exo, and she stirred to life. "Mollusk, you fool. Your own scientific curiosity has finally undone you."

"It was bound to happen sooner or later," I replied.

The image of my future self appeared on the monitors.

"Yes, Emperor, it was. We both knew this day would come."

The camera zoomed out to show the Council's robotic henchmen had been just out of frame in the previous transmission. The guards held their weapons on me.

"As you've discovered at this moment, the future the Council of Egos has promised you comes with a few provisions. Indeed, they want our science and our genius. Our leadership? They could do without it."

"Did you really think that the greatest minds in Terran history would bow down to an alien overlord?" asked Buddy.

"I had doubts," I said, "but then I thought if you genuinely were the greatest minds in Terran history, then it would be a logical conclusion. But I can't say I'm terribly surprised. Why should Terrans be any brighter than any other race in the system?"

"We were bright enough to trick you," said Buddy.

"On a positive note," said Future Self, "it's not all bad. As the Council's chief scientist, you'll be afforded the luxury of focus and unlimited resources toward research and development of technology for the Council's use."

"*Focus* means I'll be your prisoner, I assume," I said.

"We can't have you running free, causing all sorts of trouble, can we?" said Buddy.

"No, I suppose you can't."

"But you're looking at it all wrong, Emperor. Your new position means you can finally indulge your scientific curiosity and apply it toward practical goals. I know that, for some reason, you're reluctant to inflict harm on others. But the beauty of this is that you won't have to. All we ask is that you design and create the weapons and tools we need to conquer the system. You don't have to get your hands dirty. You can leave that to us. If you like, we'll keep you blissfully unaware of the world outside your lab. You'll never have to deal with the messy consequences of what you discover. You can live in a realm of pure theory and discovery, unfettered by pesky morality."

"That does sound tempting," I admitted.

"You aren't going along with this?" asked Zala. "You can't just absolve yourself of your sins by refusing to hear about them."

"Guilt requires knowledge. You can't feel bad about something you don't know about."

"That's absurd. You can't ignore the harm you could unleash if you give in to these brains."

Buddy switched her off again. "She really is bothersome, isn't she?"

"You get used to it after a while," I replied.

The machine's vibrations grew more intense.

"What does it do?" I asked. "You wouldn't have let me turn it on if you didn't know."

"Of course not." Barnum chuckled. "It's a quantum certainty generator."

"So I actually designed one."

"Yes," said Future Self, "and it works. The machine manipulates the universe at a quantum level. For any action, there are multiple outcomes of varying probability. With access to this device, an operator can reduce the probability of any unwanted event to less than one-thousandth of a percent. Entropy is, of course, always a necessary part of any system. But, for all practical purposes, this machine allows one to know the results of one's actions with near absolute certainty. Its range of effect is only a few days into the future and a few hundred miles at this point, but with time, as the molluskotrenic engine feeds more and more power into the Eiffel Tower, that radius will increase. With each passing moment, more and more of the universe falls under our absolute control."

"Fantastic," I said. "I'll admit I didn't even think such a device was possible. I could never get the math to work."

"You will."

Buddy laughed maniacally. I took advantage of the distraction to remove the strange component from a compartment in my exo. I snapped it into a plug on the console. The component sizzled around the edges as it fused with the machine. Buddy was too busy gloating to notice.

He continued his rant. "So you see, Emperor. With this machine and your genius at our disposal, there's nothing that can stop us. We have harnessed the primeval forces of creation. Tomorrow, next week, and a thousand years. Eventually, the machine will make us unto the gods themselves."

"You don't expect us to just go along with this?" asked Zala.

"I expect you to do exactly what I already know you will do. Guards, take them away."

Snarg rose to my defense. The guards blasted her with their rifles, and she fell limp.

Buddy laughed as the certainty generator's hum rose to an ultrasonic pitch. The flashes dancing across its filament mesh burned brighter. The console smoked and sparked. Green coolant leaked from the banks of monitors.

"Wait. This isn't supposed to be happening."

"The future doesn't always come out exactly how we think," I said.

"What did you do? You sabotaged it somehow? But how—"

Snarg stopped playing dead. The guards blasted her with their useless weapons. She smashed them with brutal efficiency.

Buddy moved toward me. A slash of Zala's mechanical claws severed his right leg at the hip joint. He hopped on his other leg until she kicked it out from under him.

"How is this possible?" he asked.

"It's a bit complicated," I replied. "Perhaps I'll explain it to you some other time."

The second tower caught fire. White-hot flames licked its sides as black smoke billowed forth.

Zala, Snarg, and I ran across the moving walkway as the machine continued to fall into chaos. The wires sizzled. The pipes belched steam. Fluids gushed. It continued to hum, and the hum grew into a fever pitch.

"What's happening?" asked Zala. "And why is that humming so damned loud? It's making my head itch."

"Technically, you don't have a head," I said. "It's your brain. Except your brain doesn't itch. It's a neurological reaction. The bad news is that it will get worse before it gets better. The good news is that your Venusian physiology will keep it from incapacitating you. It'll be unpleasant, but you should be fine."

Something exploded. The section of catwalk we'd just been walking on a few moments ago collapsed. It tumbled into the depths, smashing several other walkways on its way, sending scrambling maintenance bots into seething clouds of oblivion.

Another quake loosened the bolts on our own perch. It listed to one side. We edged our way onward as the walkway swayed.

"This was part of your plan?"

"Could be," I said.

I plunged forward into a plume of black smoke and felt my way back. It was slow going, but even as everything fell apart around us, we managed to avoid getting caught in an explosion or thrown to our deaths. Only after we were back at the base of the steps leading back to the surface did I have to deal with Zala.

"Don't you owe me an explanation, Emperor?" she asked.

"I'm not sure I do."

"You removed my brain."

"I had no choice. It was the only way I could convince the Council of Egos that I had fallen for their trick," I said. "They had to believe they were manipulating me or else they never would have trusted me enough to turn on the machine. If you're worried about your body, I can put you in a new one."

"You can't just promise to return me to normal and undo the profaning of my sacred warrior's code. My body is not optional, to be discarded at your convenience."

"I don't think this is the right time to discuss this."

The smoke and flames forced us upward. But halfway to the

exit, she pushed her way in front of me and wouldn't let me pass.

"You're right," I said. "What I did was unforgivable. But I've done worse things, so you'll excuse me for not being exceptionally troubled by it. If you want to destroy me for it, then we'll work out the details later. Right now, I can only tell you it was necessary for the larger plan."

"That's your explanation? There's a larger plan that you failed to brief me on?"

"I believe I've mentioned I'm not very good at working with others," I said. "I'm inconsiderate that way. It's well established. As for the larger plan, I'll admit that I'm mostly assuming that at this point."

"You didn't sabotage the machine?"

"I think I did," I said, "but I can't be positive at this moment. Although I doubt it would have worked in the first place. Using a quantum certainty generator against the entropic forces of the universe is like paving over the ocean. It's both needlessly difficult and unimaginative."

Snarg pounced on a squad of guard bots.

I sighed. "If we need to do this here, we'll do it here. I'm deactivating your protection protocol, Zala." I pushed a button on my exo's arm. "There. You are now free to harm me. I won't lift a finger to stop you. Kill me if you want to, but you'll never get your body back that way. Or discover the answers to any of your questions. I suggest you do it quickly while the guards are entertaining Snarg."

Zala drew her scimitar. "One stab." She tapped my exo's transparent head dome with the flat of the blade. "With one stab I will avenge my world and myself for all your crimes, Emperor."

"Well, do it or let's go."

She raised the sword, and for a moment, I thought she just might follow through.

Zala returned the weapon to her sheath. "Don't think this means I won't kill you the next chance I get."

"Wouldn't expect it to."

"You didn't disable my protocol, did you?"

"I'm not stupid," I said.

We reached the surface. The Shambhalans stood around us. Zala aimed her weapons at them.

"Stand down," I said. "They're no danger."

The Illustrious Master bowed. "We are in possession of our own wills again, Emperor Mollusk. You truly are the greatest friend Shambhala has ever known. And we must apologize again for our actions, and apologize for the inadequate nature of that apology."

I bowed. "And I apologize for the headache you must be feeling now. That's feedback from the disabled implants. It should fade soon enough."

"You are most gracious, Emperor Mollusk."

"You'll want to get your people out of the city," I said. "This isn't over yet."

"As you wish."

We exchanged bows, and the Shambhalans went one way while we went another. Toward the center of the city.

"The machine disabled the implants?" asked Zala. "Is that what it was made for?"

"Among other things."

We made our way to the central temple. Security clones tried to stop us, but Zala and Snarg made short work of them.

The stone beneath our feet trembled and quaked. But Shambhala endured as it had for centuries before.

We reached the temple, and I threw open the doors. The Council of Egos bobbed silently in their globes.

"They're catatonic," said Zala.

"Incapacitated," I said. "The machine is using the Great Gynoecium's sap to generate a psionic wave. They're lost in their own private fantasies, I assume. On their way to ruling the universe, if only in their own minds."

"So that's why I have a splitting headache."

"Sorry about that. Can't be helped."

"You've beaten them?"

I nodded.

"You've beaten them with their own machine?" she asked.

"In point of fact, it's my machine. They only built it for me."

The steady hum faded, but the effect on the Council of Egos would persist for another week or two.

"Then that's it?" asked Zala.

"Not quite. If I'm right, there's one final thing we'll have to do."

A roar shook Shambhala. Just across the courtyard, a combot smashed its way out of the building it'd been stored in. The enraged robot lumbered toward the molluskotrenic engine. And she was in no mood to go around anything that stood in her way.

I activated the beacon in my exo. My saucer drifted overhead, and cargo beamed us upward.

"We have to destroy the radioactive brain of Madame Curie."

Once in the cockpit, I double-checked systems. My last encounter with Curie had been a disaster, and I wanted to avoid a replay of it.

Curie stomped her way toward the Eiffel Tower, drawn by the m-rays it emitted.

"If your machine incapacitated the Council, shouldn't it have stopped her?"

"Madame Curie is a unique case. The radioactivity and preservative elixir must have changed her on a biochemical level. It hasn't had the same effect. Instead, it seems to have triggered some hyperaggression coupled with a ravenous appetite."

The torches in any building she passed flared out as she absorbed their heat.

Curie's massive exoskeleton wasn't built for speed. Her movements were slow and clumsy. But what she lacked in grace she made up for in sheer size and power.

The fifteen-ton glowing brain flashed as she unleashed a blast, disintegrating a wooden tower in her path. I hoped the Shambhalans had already activated that section of their city.

I flew overhead, and fired a few shots at her. She absorbed the power, growing stronger from it.

"I thought you were prepared for this fight," said Zala.

"Preparations only go so far. I'll need to do a few more calibrations."

Curie telekinetically seized the saucer. The craft wobbled as its lights blinked on and off.

"She's draining our power," said Zala. "Again."

I flicked a switch. A control panel sparked, but the saucer slipped free.

Curie growled curiously. Her brain glowed brighter as she increased the telekinetic pressure, but the saucer's countermeasures kept us out of her grasp.

I tried several more volleys of various artillery and beam weaponry with no result, and her own blasts were easily skirted by the automated guidance systems. Bored, Curie turned her attentions back to the tower.

"Should I even ask what horrible thing happens if she reaches that?" asked Zala.

"What makes you think something horrible has to happen?"

"You really expect me not to?"

"The tower is an extremely efficient transmitter for the near limitless energy being generated by the molluskotrenic engine. I can only reason her absorptive appetites are drawing her to it. And while she seems capable of absorbing vast amounts of energy, I have to assume that she has limits. Eventually, she'll reach critical mass."

"She'll explode."

"Inevitably."

"And let me guess. It could unleash enough to knock Terra out of orbit and send it hurtling into the sun. But not before it careens through the system, destabilizing the orbit of every other planet, sending them all drifting into deep space."

"Do you have any idea how much force it would take to knock Terra out of orbit? Where do you get these ideas?

"No, the worst that would happen would be a fifty- or sixty-megaton blast. And Curie's atomized brain fragments would pollute the atmosphere. But the real danger is if she damages the engine keeping the molluskotrenic field under control. There's no telling how it might react once uncapped. I can only concentrate on so many simulations at a time.

"So in any outcome, it's a global catastrophe. I'm just not sure if it's merely millions or an extinction-level event."

"Just turn off the engine."

"I can't turn it off."

"What do you mean you can't turn it off? Didn't you give it an off switch? An override? Something?"

"Molluskotrenic energy doesn't operate that way. I could show you the math, but you wouldn't understand it."

Curie roared as she stomped on dozens of smaller homes in her way.

I skimmed the saucer forward and landed in the streets of Shambhala, between Curie and the tower. The landing gear extended, locking into place as three sturdy legs. The sides separated and transformed into jointed limbs ending in mechanical hands.

"This is your plan? You're going to engage this monster in hand-to-hand combat?"

"No, I'll be too busy trying to find a way past her defenses. I'll need you to pilot."

"But I don't know how."

"It's just a jumbo exoskeleton. Now plug in."

"How—"

An interface jack extended from her right arm. I pointed to the slot in the controls.

"Are you even certain it's compatible?" she asked.

"I designed it in the future. Remember? It'll work."

The tower before us toppled. Curie stepped from the dust kicked up in its destruction.

"Zala, I can't be responsible for the deaths of millions. Not again. I know you'd like nothing more than to see me suffer another humiliating defeat. But is it worth millions, possibly billions, of Terran lives?"

Curie crushed a tower, and the dust kicked up swallowed her.

"Damn it, Emperor," she said. "And damn you for your manipulative ways."

The interface locked with a click. She was adjusting to the new sensory input, so she could be excused for not attempting to dodge the flare of radiation Curie hurled at us. The saucer's shields held.

"Don't let me down," I said.

Zala banged her massive fists together. Curie stomped her legs like a sumo wrestler. She charged forward with unstoppable fury. Zala was too slow. Curie plowed into us, hoisted us up in the air, and hurled us aside. The cockpit stabilizer kept us from being tossed around, even as our battle robot came crashing down upon a Shambhalan granary.

Curie turned away from us and moved toward the tower.

I offered no comment as Zala struggled to right us.

"It would have been nice if I'd been given a chance to practice this," she said.

"The saucer knows what it's doing," I said. "You just have to give it your warrior instincts."

I could've pushed a button and had the saucer right itself. But she needed the practice.

"You don't have to win the fight," I added. "You just have to keep her busy until I find a way to stop her."

She got the saucer to its feet. "And how long is that?"

"When I know, you'll know."

Zala ran at Curie. The two robots grappled, fighting for the advantage. They stumbled and weaved through the sacred city. A sacred meditation chamber and an ancient kung fu school were demolished.

My computer beeped.

"Hmmm. Interesting."

"Tell me you've got your answer." Zala grunted as she struggled with Curie.

"Just concentrate on your end," I said. "I'm working on it."

Curie's brain flashed an intense green. The flash overwhelmed the saucer sensors, and in Zala's moment of blindness, Curie knocked us off our feet again. As our sensors cleared, Curie stood over us, holding a crumbling edifice of stone over her head.

"Oh, glipft," said Zala.

Curie smashed it down on us like an eighty-ton hammer. The damage was minimal, but while Zala struggled to free us from the rubble, Curie grabbed another Shambhalan tower and repeated the maneuver. She did it three more times, until the saucer was half under the rubble.

I pushed a button. The saucer powered down, playing deactivated.

Curie howled triumphantly and returned to her journey toward the tower. She'd reach it in seconds.

I reactivated the saucer. Zala struggled to free us. "She's too powerful, Emperor."

I glanced at the warnings of various damaged systems. The saucer was no match for Curie. If I'd had another week or two to study the data, another week to redesign, more time for Zala to train, we might have been able to overpower her. But we didn't have that time.

Zala pulled us out of the rubble, but it was too late.

Curie had reached the tower. Just being near it drew bolts of crackling electricity to her. Her brain flared with the absorbed power. The saucer sensors started beeping.

Zala ran forward, but I took control. The saucer stopped moving.

"New plan," I said.

Curie drew more power. The molluskotrenic engine pumped more into her, like a raging river pouring through a shattered dam. The warning readout on the saucer shattered, and a klaxon blared.

"Emperor..."

"I'll need you to be quiet, Zala. If my calculations are off, this could go very wrong, very fast."

The Eiffel Tower and Curie burned bright red. The engine poured out enough energy to power Terra for a thousand years, and still, Curie drank it in with no signs of satisfying her endless thirst. Her giant brain became a beacon of emerald doom.

"Now."

I gave back Zala control, and with fearless Venusian abandon, she plowed into Curie. Curie put up a mild defense, but she had absorbed too much. She was dizzy with it, confused, disoriented. The atomic-brain version of drunk.

Her robotic body wasn't quite as resilient as her brain. The seething amounts of raw power had damaged it. With one punch, Zala smashed in the cylindrical torso. She yanked off an arm and bashed Curie across the dome with it. The dome cracked.

Several dozen strikes later, the robot was in pieces. Curie's immense brain slid out like an exposed prize, and Zala moved to step on it.

"I wouldn't do that," I said. "She's primed for a seventy-megaton pop."

Curie still drew power from the tower. There was no way to stop the process at this point. Curie's brain continued to glow brighter as it popped and bubbled.

"What now?" asked Zala.

"Now we let nature run its course," I replied as I took control of the saucer.

I picked up Curie's brain. The reaction was so potent now, the saucer's countermeasures were failing. She would drain our power within a minute. I soared up in the atmosphere, into space, as far as my dwindling reserves would allow. Then I hurled Curie away into orbit. Shrieking, she spun off into the distance.

I pushed a button, and the Eiffel Tower fired off a blast of all its excess power. The bright blue bolt met up with Curie, and the blackness of space lit up with a hell of an explosion. It was only too bad there was no sound to accompany it.

The blast wave washed over the saucer. We tumbled in the void, with the barest sparks left in our exoskeletons. With my last bit of energy, I activated the emergency beacon.

Zala's voice crackled from her barely functional speaker. "What now?"

"Someone will find us. Eventually. Or our orbit will decay, and we'll get back to Terra the old-fashioned way."

"Given the number of enemies you've gathered over the years," she said, "I think I'd be more concerned over who might find us here. If the wrong ship comes along—"

"It's irrelevant," I said.

"How can you say that, Emperor?"

"Because it is."

I studied the small blue planet below. It was safe once again. For how long, I couldn't say. But for now, it wasn't at risk of blowing up or being conquered. And I found that was more than enough.

A supervisor handed me the delivery notice. "Here's the last of them, sir. Just sign there, if you don't mind."

"Thank you. Just put them with the others."

They unloaded the crates while I made some adjustments to a machine.

Snarg chirped as a shadow fell over me.

"Hello, Zala," I said.

"Hello, Emperor. How did you know it was me?"

"Snarg only chirps like that for you. She really likes you."

The ultrapede pushed against Zala, nearly knocking her over.

"You are a disgusting beast, you do know that?" asked Zala of Snarg.

Snarg squealed and licked Zala's hand. She sighed, stroking Snarg's antennae while attempting to wipe away the congealing mucus off the other.

"Emperor, would you mind?"

I paused to spray solvent. Then commanded Snarg to give Zala some space. Snarg skittered in a submissive posture and cooed.

"Don't take it personally," I said. "I like to keep her around because she's useful."

"Yes, well, I suppose she is at that," said Zala.

"I wasn't talking to you." I chuckled. "I would've thought you'd have left for Venus by now to file your report. Is your new body giving you any problems? I've never cloned Venusian biology before."

"No, it's working fine." She looked at her hands, wiggling her fingers. "Although it does feel a bit weird sometimes. There are some old aches and pains I'm missing."

"I can clone you a new body with those included."

"Not necessary." She sniffed her arm. "Though I am enjoying that scent of newborn."

"That'll go away in a few weeks," I said.

"Pity. Although I guess I can't expect to be taken seriously as a warrior if I smell like a youngling. And I can't complain. I think this body is a little younger than my old one."

"Consider us even."

"Even? You removed my brain."

"Yes, and then I put it in a new body. That makes us even."

"That's not..." She smiled. "Forget it, Emperor. I knew you were a criminal when I agreed to protect you."

"That's a touch rude, isn't it?" I said. "Especially since I had them leave out the obedience implant in your new body."

Zala's face went blank.

"I'm joking," I said. "The implant is there. It's just inactive."

She remained unamused.

"If I wanted your obedience, I would've left you in the exo."

She studied my face, wondering at that slight trace of a smile and its meaning.

"You can't expect me to trust you, Emperor."

"No, I don't suppose I can."

She nodded to the crates. "What's in the boxes?"

I opened one to allow her a look at the contents: transparent globes containing the disembodied brains of the Council of Egos.

"What are you going to do with them?" she asked.

"I'm storing them here."

"Isn't that unnecessarily cruel? I didn't think you were the vindictive type, Emperor."

I pointed to the machine in the middle of the warehouse. "It's a modified version of the telepathic ecstasy field generator. They're still in a blissfully unaware state. Right now, they're all living out their shared fantasy of galactic conquest."

She closed the lid. "I don't know if I find that cruel or generous."

I replied, "They're happy and no longer a threat. I leave the morality of their punishment and/or reward for others to decide."

"Very pragmatic of you."

I made some final adjustments to the machine while Zala watched.

"So if I understand this little adventure, you were the mastermind behind it all. The Atlantese assassins. The fiasco on Dinosaur Island. Your disastrous defeat in Paris."

"All me," I said.

"But how? And why?"

"After researching the potential of the anti-time radio, I knew that, if it fell into the wrong hands, someone might try to use it against me. So I planned a fail-safe, should the need arise. I would simply broadcast a message from the future myself, designing it in such a way that my opponents would think they had the advantage."

"But you didn't build the radio."

"No, I didn't. But the plan didn't require me to. It only required me to build a transmitter at some point in the future and send the proper message to the past. Of course, the problem with this is that the party who built the radio in the past would be the only one to receive the message. This required that they believe the message to be genuinely from themselves in the future. So I couldn't issue a direct message. I had to convince them that they were in charge and that the message was intended to lead them toward their ultimate goal while actually working toward my own."

"But the assassins. And the dinosaurs. Those things could've killed you."

"Seemingly. But, of course, plotting the outcome of all those events renders the threat meaningless. The Council of Egos understood this as well. That was why it was necessary to convince them that their goal wasn't my death, but capture and enslavement. They needed to believe that they were manipulating me."

"And the machine you had them build?"

"Busywork, a decoy. Needlessly complex and incomprehensible, and little else. Aside from the brain-jamming pulse components hidden in its design and fully activated by the components I left myself scattered as unnecessary bits I'd planted in their weapon designs."

"But why did it explode?"

"They probably put it together wrong. Or maybe I designed it that way. Or I will design it that way. Haven't gotten around to it yet. It's on my to-do list."

Zala chuckled. "This plan of yours seems needlessly complicated. There must have been a simpler way than to put yourself through all that."

"If it were too simple, the Council would never have believed it. It had to be ridiculous, even unnecessary, in order to fool the Council. The heart of the plan was basically to have the Council build the machine that would destroy them, reveal themselves to me, and then allow me to activate it. But in order for that to happen, I had to convince the Council that they were manipulating and tricking me while the exact opposite was occurring."

"You were tricking them into thinking they were tricking you into thinking you were tricking them into tricking you?"

"I think there's one too many tricks in there," I said. "The Council thought all my manipulations were intentional misdirections to stoke foolish overconfidence on my part. But in fact, all my manipulations of myself were really manipulations of them. And myself too. Except that they never bothered to question whether or not they were being manipulated. They just assumed they were ahead of the game and didn't seriously ponder the possibility they weren't."

Zala shook her head. "Nope. It's still confusing."

"Look at this way. In my battle of wits against the Council of Egos, only the person who triumphed in the future gets to broadcast the message to the past. And I won."

"You won because you won. That's a meaningless tautology."

"Under normal circumstances."

"And if the Council had won..."

"But it didn't win," I said.

"But if it had..."

"We wouldn't be having this conversation," I replied. "But we are. That's all you need to know."

"So you knew all along what was happening?" asked Zala.

"The nature of the plan meant that I couldn't be certain that my future self sent that message. It wasn't inconceivable that all my careful obfuscating was the calculated machinations of another. That's the nature of space-time. You really don't know what the future holds until you get there."

"But in Paris, you seemed so distraught."

"I was distraught. It was necessary to design the plan so that even I would doubt it. If I could fool myself, then my odds of fooling the Council were all the better. Of course, now that we're here, I realize my doubts were a manipulation of my own genius. And I find the contradiction very satisfying."

She sighed. "Yes. You're brilliant. I can't even deny it anymore."

"Curious. That's even more satisfying."

"Although I'm not sure how comfortable I am with the paradox of you inventing a scheme from the future after seeing it unfold in the past. It seems like you're violating some law of physics."

"Thermodynamics," I said.

"Yes. That."

"There's a slight possibility that the use of the anti-time

radio could have triggered an impending total quantum collapse. My data has been inconclusive. It will probably correct itself."

"And if it doesn't, I assume the universe will explode," she said.

"I'm keeping an eye on it."

"I'm sure you are." Zala laughed. "You could have told me at some point that you were behind this."

"I told you I had an idea who the agent was. I just didn't tell you it was most probably me."

Zala glared. "Might have been nice to know."

"Why? What would've been different? If you'd known, you might not have taken the situation as seriously as required. And if I'd been wrong, you would've just used it as an excuse to ridicule me."

"You sacrificed my battleguard," she said.

I raised a hand. "First, I warned you about bringing them along. Second, I protected them as best as I could, despite your insistence."

She sighed. "Yes, you did. But you also allowed a monster to rampage in Atlantis. You nearly got us killed numerous times. You let them remove my brain."

"Yes, and I've rectified that."

She held up her hands. "Let's not start that discussion again. One last question: How did you get me involved in this? How did Venusian intelligence discover this plot?"

"I have no idea. I suppose some mysteries are just best left unsolved."

"Surprising to hear you say that."

"I have more important things to worry about. I still have to build my anti-time transmitter and broadcast the message to the past. Or is that rebroadcast? No matter. After that, I'll see about saving the Great Gynoecium. Then I'll have to check on the rebuilding of Shambahla, Paris, Atlantis. There's a lot of cleanup to be done. And the Terrans still are going to need me around. To keep things from falling apart."

"Are you certain of that, Emperor?" asked Zala. "It seems to me that you're a danger to this world. Without you, the Saturnites wouldn't have invaded. And the Council was only a threat because of technology stolen from you. Your efforts on Terra's behalf seem to revolve around cleaning up your own messes."

"Only seventy-four percent of the time," I replied. "I ran an analysis."

"Statistically, it seems like a losing argument."

"Would it be preferable to let the planet blow up?"

She laughed. "I can't argue with that."

I closed the machine's panel. We exited the warehouse, and I locked the door behind us, leaving the Council of Egos to their blissful delusion. I envied them for just a moment.

We walked toward my saucer, parked in the street. "Can I give you a lift somewhere?"

"No, thank you. I've arranged my own transport to Venus," she said.

"Regardless of the source of the danger, Zala, the Terrans are still in no position to defend themselves. If these are my messes to clean up, then you'll admit that I'm the best Neptunon for the job."

"And then there's the fact that this is the last planet left in the system that doesn't want to execute you."

"That too."

"But for how long?" she asked. "If you're telling the truth and reversing the mind alterations you've done to them, then one day, won't they wake up and realize that they only needed you because of what you did to them in the first place? I imagine they'll be upset about that."

"Most probably," I agreed.

"What will you do then?"

"I haven't given it much thought," I said. "Perhaps by then the other civilizations of the system will have forgotten my crimes."

She smirked.

"It's conceivable," I said.

A bolt from the sky blasted my saucer into so much scrap. Zala and I were just out of the range of the rain of falling debris. The shadow of a Venusian transport craft fell across us. It landed, kicking up dirt and wind, and only moments after setting down, three full battleguards, armed to the scales, disembarked and fanned out in a semicircle. They leveled omega-level proton cannons in my direction. A trio of powered war armors, each a heavy battalion in its own right, brought up the rear.

Zala half smiled. "Venus never forgets."

Snarg curled around me protectively.

"The mission is over. Your life is no longer in danger. It's time to answer for your crimes." Zala drew her sword. "You must have seen this coming, Emperor."

I gave Snarg the stand down command.

I grinned. "Yes, I must have."

My exo began to beep.

"Self-destruct device?" Zala raised an eyebrow.

"Would I really be that unimaginative?" I replied.

The beeping grew louder, more insistent.

"You could be bluffing," she said.

"I could be," I agreed.

The beeping turned shrill. Snarg perked up, squeaking in time with the beat. Several of the less disciplined soldiers winced and covered their ears.

"Fall back," said Zala.

A soldier protested, but she silenced him with a glance.

"I said, fall back."

The soldiers saluted and marched into their craft.

Zala sheathed her weapon, gave Snarg's antennae an affectionate stroke.

"One day, when you've run out of tricks and places to hide, you'll answer for your crimes." She put away her sword. "And I will be there on that day."

"I'd be disappointed if you weren't."

"I'll be seeing you, Emperor," she said as the hatch closed.

The ship zipped away, disappearing in moments.

Snarg chirped longingly.

"I wouldn't worry. She'll be back."

I pushed a button and a new saucer hovered to land beside the ruined one.

"How does dinner in Paris sound?"

My loyal ultrapede shrieked. She did love French food, and the nutrient paste always tasted all the sweeter in the City of Lights.